WHEN DARKNESS KILLED HER

D.A. REED

When Darkness Killed Her
by D. A. Reed

Cover design by Phillip Lowe.
Page layout by M. A. Reed and E. L. Reid.

ISBN 978-1-387-86754-7

In honor of my friends
and their characters who were of my imagination.

D. A. Reed

When Darkness Killed Her

Chapter 1

Heart thudding in his chest, Troy Daniels stopped walking and stood silently. Darkness swirled around the glow of the flashlight, licking at the light, trying to smother it. Maybe it should.

Troy wasn't sure why, but he clicked off the light and let darkness surround him. He could hear other searchers inching away, some calling out, some simply walking, their own lights cutting through the murky night in an effort to find something. Anything.

Night sounds swept over the young man and still he waited silently, ears straining to hear past crickets chirping and toads croaking. He stood for so long he found himself alone in the forest, and his fingers began to feel the chill of the spring air as they shifted on the handle of the flashlight.

Studying. That's what he should be doing. Getting ready to finish his Master's degree in forensic science, not out in the middle of mist-shrouded woods harboring ideas of finding lost girls and bringing them home.

They were probably already dead.

What had he heard that made him halt his search? Why was his gut twisted with foreboding and his pulse racing as if he had run five miles? Why was sweat soaking through the thin t-shirt under his jacket even while he stood statue still?

In the distance, muted sounds whispered across his ears. Troy cocked his head, listening intently. Were those voices? Branches breaking? He instinctively crouched, though the moon was only a sliver on that dark night and offered no light. He was virtually invisible.

The sounds came from in front of him and slightly to his left. There were no searchers in that area. They had a grid, and that area of forest was not yet trampled by the community determined to bring the young girls home. Despite their outward resolve, there was an underlying current of understanding that their search was more of a recovery mission than anything else. Recovery...of their bodies.

The sudden crack of a gunshot startled Troy to the point he fell over from his crouched position, hands skidding through the leaves and pine cones littering the forest floor as he tried to avoid smashing his face into the ground. The reality of what he just heard barely registered before the screaming began.

Terror shot through the scientist's chest, but the screams were like a jolt of electricity, and Troy was up and running before realizing what he was doing. He had no weapon, and he was alone. Hardly the makings of a hero who could save the world; but he kept running anyway.

A second gunshot had Troy skidding to a stop, his breaths coming in gasps, his chest heaving as anguish ripped through him. There was no way to know what those shots meant, yet somehow...*he knew.*

Forcing air into lungs constricted to the point of permanently closing, Troy once again began to run, though the desire to continue was no longer there. He didn't want to find what was at the end of his frantic journey through the woods because – as he listened past the guttural sounds of his own breathing – he realized...

The screaming had stopped.

Chapter 2

Seventeen Years Later

Caitlin O'Reilly instinctively hunched forward as a bullet thudded into the wood at her back. Sawdust choked her, and she felt slivers of wood slicing through her police uniform shirt as she slid down the boards another inch, trying to make herself invisible. She had been there five minutes and she was already drenched in sweat. Taking a deep breath, Caitlin adjusted her grip on the department-issue 9mm that seemed embedded in her palms.

"You shouldn't be here, Caitlin," Donovan O'Reilly yelled as he spun around his own pallet of protective wood. He fired two shots toward their assailants, then dove back into hiding.

"You *called* me, Dad!" Caitlin yelled, daring to peek around the wood. Another shot from across the warehouse splintered the wood inches from her face, pelting her with sharp fragments. Wincing, she ducked back behind the pallet, tearing one hand from the stranglehold on her gun to lightly touch her cheek. A bright red smear of blood covered her fingers when she pulled them away. Irritation tightened her features, and Caitlin glared at her father across the aisle.

"Come on," Caitlin muttered under her breath as her father shot up above his wood pallet to fire off another shot. "*Where are you?*" She had called for backup before entering the warehouse. As soon as she heard the first shot, Caitlin knew she couldn't keep her word to her father about coming alone.

So where were the other officers?

Two bullets slammed into the wood her father crouched behind, and Caitlin thrust her arm around the side of her protective pallet and fired blindly in the direction the shots came from. "How many are there?" Caitlin yelled to her father as another volley of bullets rained down in their direction.

Donovan ejected the magazine from his weapon. "I'm out," he called, waving the empty gun at his daughter.

Caitlin fumbled at the side of the leather belt strapped around her waist. Tearing open the Velcro on the fabric case, she took out a magazine and slid it across the aisle where her father waited with an outstretched hand. Snatching the magazine, Donovan slammed it home and leaned back against the wood.

"Two, I think," Donovan said, wiping sweat from his forehead.

"That's it?" Caitlin asked in disbelief, fighting a hysterical urge to laugh. They were pinned down by only two gunmen? It seemed like they were under attack by an entire army.

"They're trained, Caitlin," Donovan said, running a hand over his silver hair. "You've got to get out of here. I never would have called you if I had known…"

Known what? Caitlin wanted to ask, but another round of fire stopped her from speaking.

When the warehouse fell silent again, Caitlin peered around her pallet, then at her father. "I'll go, but you have to go first."

Donovan shook his head rapidly. "I need to cover you or you'll never make it out alive."

"We're leaving together or we're dying together," Caitlin yelled as Donovan spun out to fire off another three shots. Her words were tough, but terror lodged in her throat. Her stubbornness came from her father. Unaltered genetic code. She knew him well enough to know he would never leave until she was on her way out the door in front of him.

Waiting until the answering volley of bullets died down, Donovan looked across the aisle at his daughter. "What did you get into, Dad?" Caitlin rasped harshly as she locked eyes with her father.

Donovan's face remained stoic, and he stared at her without blinking. It was hot in the warehouse. Unbearably hot, and sweat rolled down his temples and soaked his shirt. He stayed silent.

"Dad, I left Derek standing in a gas station convenience store with a bag of chips and a Mountain Dew dangling from his fingertips," Caitlin spat, anger coating her words. She fought for control over her emotions, but lost the battle quickly. "My *partner*. Answer. My. Question." The last three words were driven across the aisle in a succinct, no nonsense manner. *What the hell is going on?*

Donovan O'Reilly's gaze shifted away from his daughter casually, and Caitlin felt a scream building in the back of her throat. The man was insufferable.

"On three," Donovan said quietly, his eyes peering around the wood before coming back to rest on his daughter.

Caitlin immediately shifted her position, her combat boots scraping across the concrete. Every instinct told her not to follow his directions; her *pride* told her to ignore them. But she didn't have a choice. She had seen that look on her father's face her entire life. Donovan was following his own orders, no one else's, and she could obey or fall behind.

"One…"

Donovan edged his shoulder closer to the edge of the pallet. Caitlin wiped sweat from her brow.

"Two…"

Where were the other police officers? Why weren't they barging in, guns blazing?

"Three!" Donovan yelled, and Caitlin launched herself forward, toward the door she knew lay behind rows of wood and heavy machinery, yet couldn't see.

Caitlin heard her father begin firing, ducked her head down when their attackers began returning fire. Then she heard a sound she knew would haunt her for life.

The dull thud was a different sound than that of a bullet hitting wood. The grunt that followed sent icy fear down her spine, and Caitlin pivoted in mid-stride, having taken only a few steps. Everything seemed to move in slow motion as Caitlin's gaze landed on the prone figure of her father, blood pumping onto the concrete from a wound directly over Donovan O'Reilly's heart.

"Dad!" Caitlin screamed. She lunged back toward her father, stumbled, fell to her hands and knees as her gun clattered across the hard floor and out of reach. Caitlin scrambled the few feet to her father's body on her hands and knees, unaware that the warehouse had fallen eerily silent.

"Dad. Dad, please," Caitlin sobbed, tears blinding her as the words fell from her lips. Her hands shook uncontrollably as she cradled her father's face in her hands, then moved them to his neck to find a pulse. Her anger was instantly erased, fear riding hard in its wake.

"You can't do this," Caitlin whispered as her fingers found nothing but warm flesh. "You can't do this!" she screamed, the primal cry ripping from her lungs as she pressed her palms flat against the wound in her father's chest.

Blood. There was so much blood. Her knees slipped as she fought to find purchase in the widening crimson pool flowing across the concrete. "You can't die on me," Caitlin whispered as she leaned down and placed her cheek against Donovan's. "You can't die on me."

The sound was like a cannon going off, and fiery pain ripped through Caitlin's shoulder. She collapsed over her father's body, her eyes wide in shock as agony permeated every cell of her body.

Her mind ordered her to get her gun, her father's gun, *any* weapon. But her body wouldn't obey her commands, and her mind felt dull. Her eyes were closing of their own volition, and she fought it because she knew that meant the end.

Caitlin heard them coming. Boots slid across concrete, the sound a death toll to her ears. *Stay awake,* Caitlin ordered herself, even as her eyes slid closed. The footsteps stopped, halting at the edge of where her blood mixed with her father's.

Then there was nothing.

Chapter 3

The full skirt of her knee-length black dress brushed lightly against Caitlin's legs as she emerged from her car, wincing slightly. Taking a moment to adjust the strap of the sling cradling her arm, she then began walking toward the back door of her father's firm.

Emblazoned in white letters across the metal door leading into the alley were the words *Nightwatch Investigations. Except you won't be watching anymore, will you, Dad?* Caitlin thought to herself as she fitted the key into the lock.

Of course, if all of the people at the funeral could be believed, Donovan O'Reilly would be watching over his daughter from heaven, every moment of every day. Well-intentioned family and friends, wanting to make things better. Caitlin wished she believed her father was keeping an eye on her from above, but she couldn't partake in that particular sentiment.

The problem rose from the fact that Caitlin herself had died. She didn't remember any bright lights, and she definitely didn't remember any ability to look down on those she loved. There had simply been an all-encompassing darkness.

The darkness that, at least, had been better than the pain.

Though metal, the door opened soundlessly on well-oiled hinges. Caitlin didn't expect anything less. There wasn't any detail about this building or Donovan O'Reilly's work that would escape his notice or fall into disrepair. Conscientious to a fault. About everything but his daughter.

Once inside, Caitlin paused, breathing deeply. She didn't smell anything of her father here, nothing that would trigger memories from her teenage years, or through to the present. It smelled like new carpet. Caitlin vaguely remembered her father mentioning a local company had installed new carpet the week before.

The heels of her black pumps sank into the plush flooring as she followed the hallway toward the front of the building. The emergency lights stayed on throughout the night and shed enough light for her to avoid feeling as if she was drowning, but she still felt the prickle across her shoulders, still felt sweat forming under her hair at the nape of her neck.

She hated darkness.

Mid-way to the front, a soft glow made Caitlin pull up short. She let her small handbag slide from her good shoulder and soundlessly fall to the ground. Bending at the waist, she reached inside the soft leather and extracted her personal weapon of choice, a Px4 Storm Beretta. It slid into her palm, a perfect fit, and Caitlin continued down the hall, the gun extended and ready.

It was a testament to her shaken mental state that Caitlin didn't bother sneaking up on whoever was in the foyer of *Nightwatch Investigations*. She simply walked into the light. Relief was instant at being in a well-lit room, but her eyes stayed narrow as she swept the Beretta in an arc, covering the room in seconds until it came to rest on a large black woman sitting at the lobby counter, her own gun trained between Caitlin's eyes.

They both lowered their weapons at the same time.

"You beat me here," Caitlin said tonelessly, not really surprised to see her father's office manager sitting at the desk she had occupied for seventeen years.

Loretta Lewis – "Mama Lewis" to those who could get away with calling her that – placed her Heckler and Koch HK45 handgun on her desk and stood to her feet. "I needed to feel him for a few more minutes before going home, Aednat. He was never more alive than when he was on a job."

Caitlin allowed her petite five foot five inch frame to be swallowed by the woman who had been like a second mother to her for almost twenty years. People often misjudged the short, heavyset woman with black hair, billowing skirts and peasant tops, assuming the older woman with gray streaks running through her hair was simply a grandmotherly type hired to push paperwork.

Those who tried getting around the granite counter without permission, however, met the full wrath of Mama Lewis, and some even met Mr. Heckler and Mr. Koch, as Loretta liked to call the "baby" she kept hidden in the drawer near her leg. No one spoke to Donovan O'Reilly unless Mama Lewis deemed him or her worthy of her boss' time.

Caitlin felt Loretta's hand slide down her thick chestnut hair, the same as she used to do when Caitlin was a child. "What do you need, Aednat?" Mama Lewis crooned in her ear.

That voice and the nickname her father christened her with as an infant almost broke through Caitlin's wall. Almost. Aednat, pronounced "ay-nit," meant *little fire* to the Irish. There were only a select few allowed to call Caitlin by that name.

Between the "incident" seventeen years prior and her father's death several days ago, Caitlin felt that what little fire remained was building, roiling inside, fanning into an inferno. She didn't feel many emotions right now. There was emptiness, confusion…and rage. Lots and lots of rage.

"I think I just want to sit at his desk for a while," Caitlin said dully as she pulled back from Mama Lewis.

The large woman nodded firmly. "Go be near your Daddy. I'll make sure you aren't bothered. Unless there is someone you want me to allow through…?"

"Troy," Caitlin said quietly as she turned to walk back down the hall. "Just Troy."

After retrieving her handbag, Caitlin turned into the last office on the right, flipping on every light in the room as she walked across the vast space. Loretta had always griped that Donovan should have the very first office off the foyer, but Caitlin knew why her father chose this one. It was quiet, no distractions as people came and went from the foyer. He could be in his own little world back in his office.

Tossing her handbag on the burgundy leather chair in front of her father's desk, Caitlin gently laid her gun on the desk and sank down into the plush leather of the high-backed office chair, immediately kicking off her shoes. Running a hand down her face, Caitlin leaned her head back and simply went still.

There were so many questions, so much anger.

Who had killed her father? Why was he even at that warehouse? *Why had his killers let her live?* Why was she allowed to walk away with just a bullet in her shoulder instead of one between the eyes?

Caitlin didn't understand why she was still breathing, sitting in her dead father's office, smothered by questions and a suffocating, unshakable wrath. Then there was the emptiness. She was alone now; truly alone.

Emelia O'Reilly had been the light of Caitlin's life for five glorious years. Then a sixty-year-old man had a heart attack while driving down the expressway, jumped the median, and embedded his car in the front of her mother's Honda. Mercifully, if such a word could be used about such a tragedy, Emelia was killed instantly. Caitlin had been home with her father; Emelia was alone in the car.

Donovan's world had been shattered with the death of his beloved. Caitlin believed her parents shared the love of storybooks and movies. The kind of love that only came once in a lifetime. The fact her father never remarried – never even came close to choosing another wife – confirmed that belief for Caitlin.

Father and daughter forged a connection few parents ever experienced with their offspring. The death of the woman they both loved more than any other welded them together, creating a steadfast and precious bond. They became each other's best friend, and Caitlin often chose activities with her father over those with her school friends.

Then she turned thirteen, was kidnapped, and died.

There isn't any kind of relationship that can survive death, Caitlin thought as she slowly turned her eyes toward the ceiling.

Chapter 4

Caitlin could hear the slightest of sounds. Those who didn't understand tried saying she had hyperacute hearing. Caitlin knew it actually resulted from fear. From being in darkness, of never knowing what was going to come at her. She learned to listen, to *hear*, minute sounds so she could prepare herself for what was coming. It was a survival technique, pure and simple.

So she wasn't surprised in the least when Troy Daniels rounded the corner and stepped into Donovan's office, his shoes nearly soundless on the new carpet. Troy leaned his shoulder against the doorframe, crossing his legs at the ankles, hands shoved deep into the pockets of his dress pants. He silently watched Caitlin for a full minute before speaking.

"I wasn't sure Mama Lewis was going to let me in," Troy finally said ruefully.

The corner of Caitlin's mouth turned up in a small smile. "You were the one name on *The List*."

Troy pushed off from the doorframe and walked into the room, taking the burgundy chair in front of the desk not occupied by Caitlin's handbag. "Well, don't I feel special," he deadpanned.

Caitlin wasn't fooled. He knew as well as she did that she needed him right then. She quietly regarded the man on the other side of the desk, digging her toes into the soft carpet and gently twisting the desk chair back and forth, ever so slightly.

Troy Daniels. Eleven years her senior, blond hair cropped close, average height, lean build, and one of the smartest people Caitlin ever met. He also saved her life seventeen years ago.

The most important people in Caitlin's life all arrived seventeen years ago. Bundled and delivered, a packaged deal. Troy was first, a quiet young man just out of college and suddenly wrapped into Donovan O'Reilly's payroll as lead forensic scientist for *Nightwatch Investigations*.

"What was he working on, Troy?" Caitlin asked softly, her words quiet, but her eyes hard.

Troy stared back. "Your father was the best private investigator in Healey, Michigan. He was working on a lot of things."

Caitlin blew her breath out hard, ruffling the strands that had come forward to frame her face. "Come on, don't be like that. I've been in the hospital and haven't had a chance to look at his journals. The police won't tell me anything. I need to know, Troy." *I need to know who killed my father,* hung silently in the air between them.

Troy's eyebrows rose. "No one in your precinct is giving up information? What happened to the 'wall of blue'?"

Caitlin shook her head, struggling not to feel defeated as she leaned her head back on the chair once again. "I think I'm on the chopping block. Derek isn't telling me anything. And I don't think it's because I ditched him, either."

Derek Sands, Caitlin's partner. The partner she left stranded in a gas station convenience store when her father called, saying he needed her help, that he needed her to come right away. That she had to come *alone.*

For anyone else, Caitlin never would have broken protocol. She knew better than to ever leave her partner, much less leave her partner without any form of transportation. It was the fact that her father actually asked for *help* that brought forth a fear so deep Caitlin willingly put her career on the line.

She couldn't call Derek to explain why she left him there – his phone was sitting in the cup holder in the center console next to her elbow. Caitlin knew his radio was on his shoulder, knew he could call for a ride, that another patrol car would swing by to pick him up. She also knew it would bring a serious mark on her record if Derek chose to make her abandonment of him known.

Troy steepled his fingers, tapping them together lightly. "I think you need to take a little longer to heal, to regroup, before you worry about his cases. Or what to do with this place," he added, taking in the large office with a sweeping glance.

Caitlin squinted her eyes in confusion. "What do you mean?"

Troy looked back in her direction and shrugged. "You could take this place over, you know."

Caitlin looked at him in disbelief. "You mean, leave law enforcement? I can't just walk away from the Healey PD."

Troy shrugged again. "Why not? Your father did."

That brought Caitlin up short. Her father had done exactly that.

Her gaze jerked back to Troy as he stood suddenly. Leaning his palms on the wide desk, Caitlin's closest friend looked her dead in the eye, then lightly rapped on the wood twice with his knuckle. Caitlin looked from his hand and back up to his eyes, confusion marking her brow. She knew him well, better than most. She could swear that gesture had been more than just an absentminded motion.

"Now isn't the time to worry about work, Caitlin. Not here, not at the precinct." Troy looked deeply into Caitlin's eyes and once again rapped on the desk with his knuckle. "You need time to heal. Physically and mentally."

Standing upright, Troy used the index finger of his left hand and flicked a loose pencil from beside a notepad, hard enough to land it on the floor next to Caitlin's feet. Her eyes narrowing, Caitlin bent to retrieve it, but stopped suddenly when Troy shook his head ever so slightly.

"Come over tomorrow. It's Sunday, a day of rest, and something you desperately need." Caitlin watched as Troy casually put his hands back in his pants pockets. "Britt really wants to see you – has been asking about you multiple times a day. You need to show her you're in one piece. The girls would love to see you again too."

Troy turned and headed toward the door as Caitlin stared after him in consternation. "I'll grill. Don't bring anything. I know your favorite beer."

"I'm not supposed to drink while on painkillers," Caitlin said slowly, still working through Troy's behavior in her mind.

Her friend shrugged, an impish grin splitting his face. "I don't think one will hurt. We have an extra bedroom if you've suddenly turned into a lightweight."

Caitlin glared at him.

"Come over. It'll be good for you," Troy said, his look abruptly turning serious.

Caitlin hesitated, then nodded once. Troy let his gaze drop to the pencil on the floor, then back to her eyes. An instant later he was gone.

Caitlin stared at the pencil resting near her bare foot for a total of two full minutes. Motionless, her hands clasped in her lap, Caitlin ran through the conversation with Troy several times in her mind. Finally, she tucked her dark hair behind her ear and bent at the waist to retrieve the writing utensil.

Donovan O'Reilly taught his daughter many things, but Caitlin had also learned by adopting the adage "Children should be seen, not heard." While no one in the *Nightwatch* family believed that to be true, Caitlin learned quickly and at a young age that if she was simply quiet and still, people would forget she was in the room and talk about things that shouldn't be discussed in front of a child.

She also came to understand that men like Troy didn't make idle gestures. The light tapping on the desk, the pencil on the floor…he was trying to tell her something. As she bent down, Caitlin's eyes darted around the area near her feet and the desk. It took her two seconds to find the disk.

About the size of a quarter, the black disk was adhered to the underside of the desk. If Caitlin hadn't been looking for something out of the ordinary, she never would have noticed it. Her hand automatically reached out to pry it loose before reason kicked in and she stopped short.

Caitlin straightened, placing the pencil on the desk with a precise movement, then adjusting the sling encasing her injured arm to buy herself some time to think. She wasn't naïve. The disk was a listening device.

Her father's office had been bugged.

Chapter 5

Her first instinct was to yell for Mama Lewis, to ask what the heck was going on at *Nightwatch*. Caitlin immediately negated that thought before her lips even parted to speak. Her father's office was bugged, and she didn't know who had adhered the disk to the bottom of Donovan's desk. As much as her mind rebelled at the thought, it could have been someone in the firm.

On the heels of that realization came the desire to tear the building apart. Was this the only bug? Or did every office have a black disk lying in wait? If every office had a listening device, it would mean that someone from the outside had planted the bugs. Caitlin's mind immediately flew to the new carpet. *What was the name of the company that installed it?*

Caitlin's eyes tracked around the room nervously. Were there cameras as well? Or just audio? Suddenly feeling extremely self-conscious, Caitlin stood, her good hand shaking as she smoothed out the skirt of her dress. Shoving her feet into her heels, Caitlin walked around the desk and slung her purse over her shoulder as she walked by the burgundy chairs.

She had wanted to search her father's notes and files while she was there, but now she didn't dare. *Was there video?* The question continued to pound against Caitlin's brain as she stood at the door and surveyed the room one last time.

Donovan's office was tastefully decorated, but completely impersonal. There wasn't a single photograph of Caitlin or the two of them together, nothing to indicate he had a family.

"Why won't you put it on your desk?" Caitlin asked when, at fourteen years old, she brought in her favorite picture of the two of them after realizing his office was bare of personal effects. Donovan had smiled, thanked her, and promptly stuck it in his desk drawer.

Donovan looked at his daughter, his gaze gentle but firm. "If people look around and see that I have a family, it instantly makes you a target. I won't put you in danger, Aednat."

After what happened the year before, Caitlin immediately fell silent, no longer interested in having her picture displayed.

Caitlin turned from the doorway and looked down the hall. The foyer was dark. Mama Lewis had gone quietly, not wanting to bother Caitlin. The young police officer was grateful. She wasn't sure she would be able to hide her anxiety right then.

Moving quickly, Caitlin walked out of the building, making sure the door locked securely behind her. Troy knew about the bug, Caitlin thought to herself as she started her car. She had to go talk to him. She needed answers.

Putting the car in gear, however, Caitlin paused before taking her foot off the brake. Troy had instructed her to come over tomorrow. She knew her friend well, and Troy wouldn't talk to her about what was happening if she showed up unannounced. He would send her home and tell her to come back the next day.

Can I trust Troy?

The thought raced unbidden through Caitlin's mind. She immediately squelched the traitorous question before it could take her down a road she couldn't bear. Her foot landed harder on the accelerator than she intended, and the car shot forward, out of the alley and into the street.

Of course she could trust Troy. He was the one who clued her in to her father's office being bugged, after all. The real question was…

Could she trust anyone else at Nightwatch Investigations?

* * * * *

Caitlin unlocked the door to her small house, immediately flipping on the overhead hall light even though the small lamp on the hall table shone brightly. She quickly punched in the code for the alarm system, cutting off the beeping sound that irritated as much as comforted her. Making sure the door was double-locked behind her, she placed her purse on the hall table, withdrawing her Beretta and carrying it with her into the kitchen.

A soft scraping sound met her ears, and Caitlin turned to see her red-footed tortoise slowly making his way toward her across the linoleum. Setting the gun on the counter, Caitlin met the large reptile halfway and bent to scratch under his chin.

"Hi, Tut," she said softly, watching as the tortoise's eyes closed slowly, then opened again just as deliberately as he enjoyed the ministrations of his owner. Caitlin gave King Turtle – King Tut for short, simply Tut if she was tired enough – one final scratch and then rose to find him a nighttime snack.

Caitlin pulled open the refrigerator and drew out some lettuce. Pulling it apart into smaller pieces, she tossed it into a bowl, listening as Tut's toenails clicked along the linoleum until he drew himself next to the counter. Everything took longer with one arm in a sling, but Tut was patient. Caitlin put the bowl down in front of him and the tortoise began eating enthusiastically.

Pulling out a bar stool, Caitlin perched on the edge and watched Tut silently, her chin resting in her hand. People laughed when she told them her pet was a tortoise – until they realized she wasn't joking. Then they tried turning the laugh into a cough in an effort not to appear rude, which Caitlin always found rather amusing.

Caitlin didn't ever apologize for her choice of pet. Caitlin O'Reilly rarely apologized for anything since she wasn't often concerned with what other people thought of her or her actions. She most definitely wasn't going to be apologetic about her choice of household companion.

She loved King Tut. He was perfect for her. Quiet, slow-moving and low-maintenance, and – the quality she loved the most – steady. Slow and steady may win the race, but it also calmed Caitlin's heart. When her thoughts ran wild, when she felt frantic with fear over darkness or memories, when the rage threatened to consume her…Caitlin simply sat and watched Tut.

She envied him, really. Nothing really shook up his world. If he kept at it, slow…steady, he eventually got to what he needed. It was a much-needed reminder to Caitlin that she needed to take a step back. She needed to breathe.

A much-needed reminder that would serve her well at the moment.

Forcing herself to slow her emotions down, Caitlin watched Tut attack the lettuce with exuberance and quieted her thought processes. There were so many questions needing to be answered, and hopefully Troy would help with that later. Caitlin needed to accept the fact she wouldn't get answers that night.

Caitlin blinked slowly, imitating Tut as he ate. The disk. That was what really bugged her at the moment. The more she thought about it, the more Caitlin began to think there wasn't video surveillance at the firm. While Troy's little maneuver with the pencil might seem only slightly odd to her, it would have been a flashing beacon to anyone watching video of the exchange. Especially if they had audio as well. No one purposely flicked a pencil off a desk. It would have sent up one heck of a red flag.

Next on her list was the fact that her father's notebooks and computer had disappeared from his home. Stopping over after she left *Nightwatch*, Caitlin looked for the leather bound notebooks she had watched her father scribble in his whole life. He used them while on the police force, and continued the habit as a private investigator.

Being mindful of the fact that her father's house might be bugged as well, Caitlin did her search quickly, but thoroughly. Coming up empty didn't sit well with her. She had a flash of temper before remembering that her father's death was a murder and the police were launching a full-scale investigation. Any computer or journal found in Donovan O'Reilly's house was sure to be confiscated, at least temporarily. They would probably search the firm as well, if they hadn't already.

Caitlin rubbed a hand down her face as Tut finished his lettuce and clicked slowly away. Her injured shoulder began to throb. Reaching into the small blue ceramic bowl resting on the counter, she curled her fingers around a handful of dried fruit and chocolate chips, her favorite snack. It was habit, and it took Caitlin raising her hand to her mouth for her to realize she wasn't hungry. At all. Lowering her hand, Caitlin let the fruit and chocolate chips trickle back into the bowl, then pushed to her feet.

Grabbing the Beretta off the counter, Caitlin made sure Tut had plenty of water in his indoor shelter, and that the desk lamp and UV light were both turned on for him. Another reason she and Tut were a perfect fit – they both slept with the lights on. Though Caitlin didn't need hers to keep warm.

Flipping the kitchen light off, Caitlin turned on the hall light as she walked, then the light to her bedroom. Mindful of her shoulder, she slipped out of her dress, donned a tank top and shorts, and made short work of brushing her teeth. Sliding beneath the covers, Caitlin lifted her pillow enough to place her gun beneath it. Settling onto her uninjured side, Caitlin pulled the comforter up to her shoulders and lay staring at the door.

The hall light shone brightly, as did the overhead light in her bedroom. There were three people who truly knew the extent of her fear of darkness, and her unusual sleeping arrangement with the lights. One was now dead. Troy and Loretta knew and understood. Anyone else would have thought she was crazy; which was why no one else knew.

There wasn't a man in her life who shared her bed, so it wasn't an issue. When she did manage to hold on to a short relationship, there was never an overnight stay involved. Never. Which was part of the reason the relationships were so short.

Caitlin kept her eyes on the doorway. In the darkness she couldn't see what was coming. At least with the lights on and facing the door she had a chance.

Chapter 6

Caitlin stumbled over the uneven ground and gasped, struggling to stay upright. Her shoulders ached. How long had her arms been tied? First behind her back, now in front...had it been hours? Days? Time was running together in the darkness. So much darkness...

Tears ran down her cheeks, escaping the blindfold defiantly. Marci whimpered from some place next to Caitlin, her own fumbling footsteps loud as she crunched through leaves and dry grass.

"It's okay," Caitlin whispered, wishing she could reach out to her friend. But she couldn't even see Marci, much less touch her. "It's okay," she repeated. Maybe if she said it enough she would believe it was true.

"Stop here," the gruff voice behind them ordered.

The stumbling stopped abruptly. Caitlin shivered, the wind having picked up as they walked. Her thin shirt clung to her small frame, sweat having soaked through it long ago.

"Turn around."

Caitlin shifted her feet, little by little, until she thought she was facing the opposite direction.

"Get on your knees."

Marci gasped, a harsh, guttural sound that threatened to rip apart what little control Caitlin managed to hold over her emotions.

Caitlin herself stalled, partly from shock, partly from fear. She had seen movies. She wasn't stupid.

"Get on your knees!"

Caitlin heard Marci begin sobbing as leaves rustled under her weight. Caitlin tried to lower herself without tipping over. She had learned quickly that everything was harder with your arms tied behind your back. Her mind raced, trying to think of something she could do. But without her sight and without her arms and hands…Caitlin began to shake even harder.

"Please," Marci gasped, and Caitlin could hear the fear, could tell Marci's nose had begun to run because of the crying. The gurgling sound in her throat made the whimper that much more pitiful.

"Keep me," Caitlin said suddenly, not registering that the words had come from her own throat until Marci gasped, and the sounds of the men in front of them went silent. She took a deep breath. She was only thirteen. She couldn't do a lot, but she could do this. "Keep me." Her voice shook uncontrollably, but she pressed on. "Let her go and keep me."

Silence from the men. Marci sobbed uncontrollably. Whispers from the men. Then the most horrible sound Caitlin had ever heard. Laughter.

"Sorry, sweetheart. It doesn't work that way."

A loud boom shook the air and Caitlin's body jerked instinctively at the sound. A sickening thump came from next to her, a startled gasp from Marci, and then leaves crumpled in the direction Marci had been kneeling.

Caitlin didn't need to be able to see to know her best friend now lay dead beside her. She began screaming, the sound ripping from her lungs, burning them with the ferocity of the shrieks. Tears ran down her cheeks uncontrollably, and her body shook so hard she felt she might join Marci on the ground. Not being able to see made the terror so much worse. She had no idea what was about to happen, if a bullet was about to take her own life. The all-consuming darkness left her with no way to brace herself for what might happen next.

She didn't know how long she screamed, but Caitlin's voice finally gave out, and there was nothing left but wheezing gasps as she *tried begging for her own life. Caitlin heard the shifting of the leaves and grass a split second before another boom rent the air.*

It felt like a sledgehammer hit her in the chest, sucking all air, all life-giving force from her body. Caitlin felt her body fall, but was powerless to stop the descent. Pain exploded everywhere, and Caitlin tried to breathe through the pain, but her body was clenched in an invisible vise, her mind slowing down, pain overpowering every sense.

Then the darkness became complete.

———————

Caitlin's hand gripped the gun and ripped it out from beneath her pillow before she came fully awake. It wasn't until she blinked rapidly several times that reality sank in and Caitlin realized she had risen up onto her elbow and was pointing the gun at an empty doorway, her injured shoulder screaming in protest.

Flopping back onto her pillow, Caitlin rested the gun against her abdomen as she stared at the ceiling and tried to get her heaving breaths and pain under control. The harsh breathing turned to sobs, and she fought them back, her jaw clenching tightly as she pressed the heel of her free hand against the area between her eyes, determined to keep the tears at bay.

It was a full two minutes before the tears stopped threatening, a full five before she stopped trembling. The lights, the open door, the gun…all her efforts to be able to see what was coming…it never worked.

The nightmares brought her down every time.

Chapter 7

Troy's eyebrows rose as he opened the door and took in Caitlin's haggard appearance. "Rough night?" he asked, but didn't expect an answer. Caitlin wasn't one for acknowledging the obvious. He opened the door wider. "The girls are in back."

Caitlin didn't need further invitation. Pushing past the man in front of her, she strode quickly through the living room and kitchen, exiting out the patio doors leading to the spacious backyard. A cacophony of noise hit her as soon as she stepped out of the house and onto the grass.

Thunder, the Daniels' Rottweiler, came running at Caitlin full-tilt, jaws wide as he barked a greeting. Caitlin allowed herself to be mauled by the friendly dog, then looked to the right and saw Britt, Troy's wife, kneeling at a flowerbed bordering their property line. Britt turned at the ruckus and smiled when she saw Caitlin, but kept her place when she got a good look at her guest's face and merely waved.

Caitlin breathed a silent sigh of relief. She loved Britt, but what she really needed was time with the two screaming children farther down the slope of grass. She was thankful her friends could read her well enough to give her that time.

With Thunder running ahead, Caitlin jogged down the slope, breaking into her first real smile in days as five-year-old Ranae and seven-year-old Rebekah shouted and hollered from several yards away.

Ranae jumped off a swing, landed with a solid thump on the grass, then took off at a run for Caitlin.

"Auntie Caitlin!" she squealed, and Caitlin ignored the pain in her shoulder and held out her arms to catch the flying child as Ranae launched herself in the air while still three feet away.

Laughing, Caitlin felt her balance take the brunt of the hit, and they both fell to the ground with Thunder pouncing on top of them, his tongue tracing sloppy paths along their cheeks. As Ranae's little arms circled Caitlin's neck and hung on tightly, the police officer felt the pain and rage in her chest ease for the first time in days.

Caitlin had no idea why the girls had the effect on her that they did, but she was thankful for it nonetheless. When she was with them, playing, soaking in their innocence, it felt as if she was transported to another place. A place where evil didn't exist, where nightmares couldn't gain access to weary minds.

As Caitlin pushed herself to her feet, Ranae still firmly ensconced in her arms, Rebekah began jumping up and down from within the confines of a hula hoop. "Look, Aunt Caitlin! I got a hula hoop with my chore money yesterday! Wanna try it?"

Giving Ranae another squeeze, Caitlin set the little girl on her feet and reached for the circular object being held out to her. "I haven't done this in years, so no laughing, got it?" she asked, shooting a mock glare at the seven-year-old who peered at her from under white-blond bangs.

Flipping the hoop over her head and shoulders, Caitlin tightened her jaw against the tugs in her injured shoulder and vowed not to let the girls see her discomfort. They didn't need to know about the evil that lurked in the world just yet. She desperately wanted to shield their innocence for as long as she could. One day it would be gone, and the girlish light dancing in their eyes would fade. Caitlin dreaded that day.

As she gave the hoop a toss to the side and began rotating her hips in an effort to keep the hula hoop around her waist, Caitlin grinned at Rebekah's crooked smile. She had lost a front tooth recently, and Caitlin thought her smile was adorable.

Her thoughts moved back in time to when she held Rebekah for the first time. It had been minutes after her delivery when Troy walked into the waiting room and pulled Caitlin away from her frantic pacing and into the hospital room where Britt was resting, Rebekah cradled on her chest.

Caitlin had stopped short, something inside her threatening to crack open at the sight of the newborn baby blinking lazily in the bright lights of the room. "Come hold her," Britt whispered, and Troy took the baby and gently placed her in Caitlin's arms.

Her life changed that day. Even more so when Ranae was born. She had good friends. The best, really, given all she had been through, all that she struggled with on a daily basis. But these two…Caitlin felt the hoop tilt to the side and begin sliding down over her hip. Rebekah cheered something about Caitlin not beating her record of rotations while Ranae groaned at the lost opportunity for her Auntie to gain the championship. These two brought life to the parts of Caitlin she thought had died seventeen years ago.

Ruffling their blond mops, Caitlin sighed in resignation and turned back toward the house, promising to return for more play after she talked with their dad.

Thunder tried to follow Caitlin back to the house, but she shooed him back toward the girls. Her eyes turned up toward the deck where Troy had started the grill and was laying out hamburger patties and foil-wrapped packages of potatoes. Britt had disappeared, which meant she was getting the rest of the meal prepared inside.

Caitlin's feet hit the first step on the deck, and Troy pointed with his spatula. "Beer. There's more when that one is gone."

She snagged the beer off the side tray of the grill and popped the cap off using the edge of the deck railing. Troy gestured to a deck chair while she put the bottle to her lips, but Caitlin shook her head. She could feel the tension returning, felt the need for answers to questions burning inside.

"What was my dad working on?"

Troy flipped a burger. "A lead on your kidnapping."

Caitlin almost dropped her beer. "What?" she finally whispered, a shaft of ice snaking down her spine.

Purposely not looking at her, Troy shook some seasoning over the burgers and then closed the lid on the grill. Caitlin knew this topic would be almost as hard for him as it was for her, but she needed him to look at her; she needed to see his eyes. When he finally did lock eyes with her, it was a shuttered gaze.

Caitlin shivered, a soft breeze chilling her body and raising the hairs on her arms despite the warmth of the sun. She felt her mind try to shut down, her vision blurring as the memories rushed forward. It was like she was living it all over again, each scene as real as if no time had passed...

———————

Caitlin scooped out a spoonful of chocolate ice cream and watched the fudge drip down from the spoon in a long arc. Shoving the mound of sugar into her mouth, she cut her eyes to the left as Marci frantically licked around the edge of her ice cream cone, the abnormally hot fall day making the consumption of her treat more of a challenge than a pleasure.

Laughing, Caitlin handed her friend an extra napkin, then shifted the strap of her backpack so it settled more comfortably on her shoulder. "If Ben could see you now..." she teased, watching as a stream of strawberry ice cream ran down her friend's hand.

Marci glared at her friend. "Not funny," she growled as she took a huge bite out of the ice cream, forgoing licking the concoction due to pure necessity.

Caitlin twirled in a circle, fluttering her eyelashes as she clutched her spoon and affected a breathy tone. "Oh, Ben, don't I look ravishing with strawberry ice cream coating my face? Don't you want to hold me in your arms and-"

"Stop now, before you end up wearing more of this than I am," Marci threatened, shoving her dripping cone under Caitlin's nose.

Knowing her friend would definitely follow through on her threat, Caitlin stopped twirling, but the twinkle never left her eyes. "So when is he going to ask you to the Fall Fest dance?" she asked instead, taking another large bite of ice cream.

Marci groaned, finally giving up on her cone and tossing it into the nearest trash bin. "I don't know," she complained, scrubbing at her chin with the napkin. "It's like he's trying to drive me crazy by making me wait until the last minute."

Scraping her spoon around the edge of the plastic bowl to eradicate the last remnants of fudge sauce, Caitlin squinted at her friend. "I bet he's just planning-"

Squealing tires cut through Caitlin's words and made her gasp, her hold on the ice cream cup becoming slack as a large black van with tinted windows shrieked to a halt at the curb beside them.

Everything seemed to skid into slow motion as Caitlin and Marci stood still in confusion. Nothing seemed to make sense. Not the now-empty bowl that slowly slid from Caitlin's fingertips, or the masked men who jumped out of the side panel door of the van, or the suddenly terrified look Marci shot Caitlin as her mouth opened in a scream that was lost in the ether of Caitlin's bewilderment.

"RUN!"

Marci's fingernails dug painfully into Caitlin's arm as she turned, already moving back the way they had come. But Caitlin felt as if she was in a dream, a nightmare where she was trying to run as fast as she could, but really wasn't going anywhere.

Caitlin felt her head snap back hard as a man grabbed her backpack and yanked her backward. She screamed, her shoulders jerking painfully in their sockets as she was hauled down the sidewalk. As another man grabbed Marci's pack, Caitlin began fighting, determined to get to her friend.

Suddenly everything went black and hot and suffocating as a hood was thrown over her head. Caitlin was so surprised she stopped dead, which was the biggest mistake of her life. Given the very opportunity he needed, her captor gave one last yank backward, spun her around, and landed a fist in her stomach, sending the teenager to the ground, gasping for breath.

Pain was everywhere, and Caitlin barely felt her attacker lift her off the hard concrete of the sidewalk and carry her to the van. She didn't comprehend the new pain of being thrown into the van, sliding along the rough floor until she hit the panel door on the other side. She just tried to breathe, tried to live to the next moment.

As Caitlin felt Marci's body slam into hers, a hand closed around her neck, pinning the hood even tighter against Caitlin's mouth and nose. She wanted to struggle but couldn't get her mind to work, to comprehend the signals she was trying to send it. Then words whispered next to the hood covering her ear, and Caitlin went completely still, tears soaking the rough fabric over her face, wondering when her life had become a horror movie. Because she had never heard words like that spoken off the movie screen.

One of her captors roughly drew Caitlin's hands together and then looped something hard and with sharp edges around her wrists, drawing it tight. A zip-tie, Caitlin thought dully. Then the phrase was repeated, and both Caitlin and Marci slumped unmoving against the hard wall of the van, the words ringing in their ears.

"If one of you moves, both of you die."

Chapter 8

They never had a chance.

Caitlin would later find out that they were blindfolded for five days. Five days of terror and torture that ended with bullets in both girls' chests. If Troy hadn't found Caitlin when he had, she would be dead.

Donovan O'Reilly did everything he could, pulled out every resource he had in an effort to find his daughter. On day two it became obvious Caitlin was simply collateral damage and it had been Marci the men were after. It was Grant VanMaar, Marci's father, who received the "ransom" call – if you could call it that. They demanded money, but not just any money. The police were intrigued by the kidnappers' phrasing. They wanted "*the* money." And also the "other item that belonged to them."

Seventeen years later, Grant still claimed he had no idea what the men were talking about. When Caitlin got older and began doing her own investigation into her kidnapping, she went to her best friend's father with her own questions. It was obvious to her that he blamed himself for what happened to his daughter, but that he really had no idea what the men were after.

Grant VanMaar owned the most prestigious private military security firm in the country, *Shadow Guards*. It could have been any one of his clients calling, or any disgruntled person who had been on the receiving end of one of the more violent contracts Grant's men fulfilled. The firm had operations going in several different countries, and it took the FBI years to sort through all the firm's data and clients, searching for that one link triggering Marci's kidnapping and then death.

They found nothing. The kidnappers were still free, and Caitlin knew that was part of the reason she continued to feel the deep-seated fear and rage that plagued every moment of every day. How could she move on when the men who shot her could do the same to her again, or to someone else?

Caitlin did her best to shake off the memories clouding her mind, but as she turned her eyes toward Troy, she could tell by the pained look on his face they still looked haunted.

"What did he find?"

Troy sighed heavily and ran a hand down his face. "I don't know."

Her hopes crashed before they could fully form, and Caitlin sagged back against the railing of the deck.

Looking off across the yard to where his daughters chased a frog amid the taller grass, Troy's jaw tightened briefly. "He asked me to meet him under The Bridge two weeks ago," Troy said, naming the meeting place Caitlin's father frequently used when he wanted to conduct a conversation he could guarantee would be private.

The Bridge was actually the base of an abandoned highway overpass on the outskirts of Healey. The highway had been closed off for years, but the government didn't want to fork over the money to have it torn down. Donovan O'Reilly dubbed the abandoned highway "The Bridge" years ago, and that's what it had been referred to by the firm ever since.

"What did he say?" Caitlin asked, her voice barely above a whisper.

Troy sighed and looked back at his friend. "He said to prepare for evidence he would need processed at *Nightwatch* lab. On the down low. That he didn't have it yet, but it would be coming soon." His blue eyes bored into Caitlin's green ones. "That it was related to your kidnapping and it needed to be kept between us. He was excited, like he finally found a break."

Caitlin realized the hand holding her beer was shaking, and she set it down on the flat top of the railing. "But…" she said quietly, already knowing what Troy would say next.

"But he was killed before he could give me the 'evidence'."

Looking down at her feet, Caitlin fought an internal war, anger and depression fighting for a foothold she knew would derail her thought process. She took a deep breath, straightened, and pushed them both aside.

"So we need to find out if he actually obtained the evidence before he died," Caitlin said, the words tight as she forced them out of her throat. She reached for her beer and downed the rest of it in three long pulls.

"Which could be easier said than done," Troy said as he reached into a cooler next to the grill and extracted another beer. He tossed it to Caitlin who immediately turned and used the railing to pop off the top. "Your father was the best at hiding what he never wanted found."

In more ways than one, Caitlin thought, her mind running back over the years to the countless times her father shut her out of his emotions and thoughts.

Shoving self-pity aside, she bore down and forced her brain into full police mode. "So we start at the office." Caitlin brought her gaze back up to Troy. "Who bugged *Nightwatch*?"

Troy lifted the lid of the grill as Britt walked out of the sliding glass door and onto the deck, her hands balancing a tray loaded with condiments. Caitlin and Troy remained silent as Britt slid the tray onto the patio table and then crossed over to where Caitlin leaned on the railing.

Caitlin accepted the hug readily, her nose twitching as Britt's naturally curly hair tickled her face. As quickly as Troy's wife came, she left, calling over her shoulder. "Let me know when we're ready."

"I don't know who bugged *Nightwatch*," Troy said quietly, his eyes moving to his daughters again, making sure they were still out of earshot. "But I know it began years ago."

Caitlin began to feel numb. "Years ago? What does that mean?"

"It means that your father and I may have found the bugs a month ago, but they were there long before we knew about them."

"But Dad swept for bugs regularly-"

"Which is why we know it was an inside job," Troy interrupted grimly. The muscles in his jaw began jumping the way they did when he fought to stay calm. "Whoever bugged the place knew when Donovan was sweeping and would remove them, then replace them after the fact."

Caitlin's nails tapped on the glass bottle in her hand as she thought quickly. "Then how do you know they've been there for that long?"

Troy looked hard at the woman across from him. "Because they are all a model that was discontinued sixteen years ago."

Caitlin felt her mind try to shut down, but she rotated her injured shoulder instead, knowing the pain of the movement would sharpen her senses. Wincing, she latched onto the words that escaped her until just that moment. "They? You said 'They are all a model that was discontinued'. How many are there?"

Troy opened the lid of the grill and flipped the burgers, looking back at Caitlin over his shoulder as he answered. "Every room. All audio, no video."

Caitlin felt her heart pick up speed. "The perp wouldn't bug his own office."

Troy began sliding the burgers onto a plate. "He would if he wanted to avoid suspicion."

Falling silent, trying to process what it all meant, Caitlin watched as Troy walked the burgers over to the patio table and signaled his wife through the kitchen window. Then he walked over until he was standing directly in front of Caitlin.

"Your job with the Healey PD is over," he said, his sandaled feet almost touching Caitlin's flip-flops.

Opening her mouth to object, Caitlin felt the words die in her throat as she looked deep into her best friend's eyes. She could see the truth there, felt it down in her gut. The department would have been in more contact over the last couple weeks if her job was still intact.

"You need to decide if you want to run your dad's business and continue what your father started, or-" Troy hesitated briefly. "Or if you're going to walk away. Ignore it all and start a new chapter of your life and put it behind you."

Caitlin felt heat rise in her cheeks. She knew what *it* was – the kidnapping and everything that went with it. Including the men who still walked free.

"I will stand behind you whatever you choose," Troy said quietly, his eyes searching Caitlin's face. "You know that."

Some semblance of calm returned with Troy's words. He knew her so well. So well that he knew what she was going to do before she did.

"Who can I trust?" Caitlin whispered as Britt carried a pitcher of lemonade out to the deck.

Troy held out a small, folded piece of paper. "He's former military."

Caitlin's eyebrows rose as her fingers curled around the piece of paper. Without looking at it, she shoved it into her jeans pocket. "Was? What does he do now?"

Shrugging, Troy didn't look bothered. "No one really knows. He's worked with my dad before, and my father trusts him with his life."

That made an impact. Troy's father was an Army Lieutenant General. He had seen his fair share of combat, and his opinion of the man whose name was written on the piece of paper in Caitlin's pocket carried a lot of weight.

"I've got your back, Aednat," Troy said softly, his words like a caress to Caitlin's mind.

Her eyes closed, and she nodded once as Britt pulled on the cord attached to a bronze bell. It clanged loudly, and Ranae and Rebekah shrieked gleefully as they began running for the house.

Plastering a smile to her face, Caitlin reached out and scooped up Ranae as she flew by. She would forget about the past, she would forget about the uncertain future, at least for a few hours. Caitlin clutched little Ranae to her chest, craving the comfort the little girl gave.

She would forget...at least until the nightmares came for her later that night.

Chapter 9

Troy felt his wife's hand slide over his shoulder from behind and down to his chest seconds before Britt brought her other arm around to reveal a cold bottle of beer in her hand.

"You are a good woman."

"I know," she whispered seductively in his ear, then stood and circled the couch after he took the bottle of amber liquid from her hand. Settling onto the couch next to her husband, Britt leaned her shoulder against his and tapped the open book in his lap. "You've been on the same page for fifteen minutes."

Sighing, Troy closed the book and placed it on the small table next to the couch. "My mind is other places, I guess."

Britt shifted so she could reach behind him. Her long fingers began kneading the back of his neck, and Troy felt his eyes close as the tension started fading.

"Something happened with Caitlin." Britt wasn't asking a question, but she didn't need to. Troy had learned long ago that not much got past his wife. "Is it the PD? Did they come back with a decision?"

Troy shook his head. "No. Still waiting on that. It has to do with her kidnapping." He opened his eyes and looked at his wife, hoping she would understand. "I can't tell you more than that right now."

Britt's blue eyes darkened slightly, but her features remained smooth as she nodded. "Will she be okay tonight?" Her tone conveyed honest concern.

Worry threatened to creep back in as an image of Caitlin's face filled Troy's mind. She had smiled when she hugged the girls good-bye earlier, but the fear and tension was evident in her eyes.

"The nightmares will be bad tonight," he said finally.

Britt's fingers moved up into his hair. "Caitlin knows where we are. She'll call or come over if she needs us," she said soothingly.

Troy nodded, trying to force the anxiety away. The fingers of his wife's other hand trailed up and down his arm.

"The girls are asleep," Britt whispered.

Troy turned to look at his wife. Her blue eyes contained a heat he knew well. Troy's hand came up to rest on her cheek, his thumb tracing the contour of her cheekbone. Once again, he marveled that she had chosen him over all the other men who tried to gain her attention.

Britt's eyes closed briefly as she leaned into his hand. Then she turned those eyes back on his, keeping them locked there as she leaned forward. Slender fingers reached to take the beer from his other hand, and Britt's lips grazed his ear as she leaned to slide the bottle onto the table.

"Race you upstairs."

Then she was gone, already moving toward the stairs. Grinning, Troy forgot about the beer, his book, and everything but his wife as he hurried up the steps after her.

* * * * *

Caitlin's key turned in the lock on her front door, thoughts already moving from the relaxing afternoon and evening with Troy's family to the name scrawled on the paper in her pocket. She needed to sit down and think about her next move.

Caught up in her thoughts, Caitlin simultaneously reached for the light switch on the wall while pushing the door open. Between one second and the next, Caitlin's mind realized the light scraping sound she heard wasn't King Tut's nails on the linoleum floor, it was the slide of a boot. In one fluid move, the gun in the holster at her shoulder was in her hand and the switch flipped, flooding the living room with light even as the door continued its inward arc.

The man sitting on her couch had his hands raised in submission, not looking the least bit surprised or perturbed by the fact that he was staring down a gun barrel. Caitlin's mind flashed with recognition and she jerked her finger off the trigger she had already begun to depress. The air in her lungs exhaled in a huff, and Caitlin lowered her weapon while glaring at Rick Bannan.

"What," Caitlin began, forcing herself to speak slowly and calmly despite her irritation, "are you doing?"

Rick lowered his hands and leaned forward, resting his forearms on his knees. Light glinted off the short-cropped silver hair clinging to his head. A military cut, the same haircut her father's partner had had since she could remember.

"Your father gave me a key years ago in case anything ever happened to him. We didn't tell you because we knew you wouldn't approve."

Caitlin grabbed the door and swung it closed. "You were right. I don't," she said, her words clipped. She didn't replace her gun in the holster at her back. Rick noticed.

"Aednat," Rick's voice gentled as he used the nickname he knew would soften Caitlin. "You haven't been returning my calls."

Caitlin sighed, forced the tension in her shoulders to dissipate. She walked the few steps to the couch and sank down next to him, placing the gun on the coffee table in front of them. "I haven't been returning anyone's calls," she said, leaning back against the cushions.

Rick shifted his back to the corner so they could talk without craning to see each other. "You've returned Troy's calls." It was said evenly, without a hint of malice or irritation.

She didn't bother to respond. Her relationship with Troy was one most people didn't understand. Britt didn't even understand completely, but she accepted it without judgment.

"So what's up, Uncle Ricky?" Caitlin asked, reverting to the nickname and smart aleck tone she used as a kid.

"There are whispers in the PD," Rick said, getting right to the point. He knew how much Caitlin hated beating around the bush. "Desk duty for the indeterminate future."

Caitlin kept her features blank, focusing on a point just to the right of Rick's shoulder where King Tut slowly made his way into the room. At least she wasn't getting fired from the Healey PD. That was something.

"I see your contacts are still in place after all these years," Caitlin said, purposely ignoring the content of his statement.

Rick rubbed a hand over his short hair and then rested his arm across the back of the couch. "I made some good friends there," he said simply. "Your dad was obviously one of them."

Caitlin didn't bother to respond to that. "Why did you leave the PD so much earlier than Dad did?" Caitlin shifted, pulling one leg up under her as she looked over at the man who had been her father's best friend and partner for as long as she could remember. "I know my dad left because of what happened to me, but I never asked why you left."

Rick sighed and tilted his head back to look at the ceiling before answering. "I don't have a great answer to that," he admitted after a moment of silence. "Your father felt too constricted by red tape to investigate your kidnapping the way he wanted to. I just felt…constricted." He shrugged, his t-shirt tugging across his torso. He may have been in his early sixties, but the man visited the gym regularly, and it showed.

"Bucking authority…gee, that doesn't sound like you at all, Rick," Caitlin teased, feeling a small smile pull at her lips.

Smiling back, Rick seemed relieved to see her mood lighten. "Yeah, well…" he shrugged again.

"So you went to work for Marci's dad, Grant."

"The private security world had the best of both worlds," Rick said, his smile a bit cocky. "Military and police, with the chance to travel, and I was the boss. Of my own team anyway," he amended. "How could I say no?"

"But you did," Caitlin said quietly. "When Dad began *Nightwatch*."

Rick hesitated. "Your dad was the brother I never had. You were the daughter I never had. Family first," he said, his voice turning gruff as emotion moved in.

Caitlin kicked off her sandal and used her toe to scratch under Tut's chin as he finally made it to the couch. "I joined the police force because of the stories Dad told me when I was a kid."

Rick nodded. "He loved the Healey PD and what he could do for the community while in law enforcement."

"Was it hard for him to walk away?"

"In a way, yes. In a way, no. You were the most important thing in the world to him. Needing to find out who hurt you made the decision clear for him." Rick looked closely at Caitlin. "He still loved his work, Aednat. He was still able to help others."

Caitlin nodded, silent for a moment while her mind churned through various thoughts. "Why the wall of silence? Why isn't anyone telling me what's going on in the investigation?" Caitlin asked finally, pulling the conversation away from the personal and back to what she really wanted to know.

Sighing, Rick shook his head. "They had to figure out what to do with you first."

Caitlin felt her jaw clench in irritation. Holding up a hand, Rick staved off her angry words by giving her a stern look. "You can't blame them, Caitlin. You broke the rules, they had to figure out what to do about that. Then they can be more open about what's going on."

"Have you heard anything?" Caitlin asked, watching as Tut slowly turned and began wandering back toward the kitchen. He was probably wondering why she hadn't put out his dinner yet.

Rick shook his head, now looking faintly annoyed himself. "No, they've been silent with me too. Probably because they know I'll turn around and tell you."

Caitlin nodded without speaking. It sounded harsh, but if Rick didn't have any new information, as far as she was concerned the conversation was over. She wanted to be alone.

Sensing her shift in mood again, Rick leaned forward, putting his elbows on his knees. "Any thought as to what you're going to do with *Nightwatch?*"

Glancing at him, Caitlin waited a beat, then shook her head. She didn't feel like sharing the talk she had with Troy earlier about the firm. Giving a sly smile, Caitlin said, "You're the right hand man around that place. Are you thinking you want it for your own?"

Rick barked a short laugh. "I like leaving the admin side of things to the head honcho. I can't do that if I'm leading the place." He looked closely at her. "You're thinking about taking it over, aren't you?"

Caitlin sighed and got to her feet, wanting to officially put an end to the conversation. "I don't know. It's not the way I saw my life going."

None of what's happened in my life is the way I imagined it as a kid. I never knew there was so much evil…

Knowing her well enough to know he wasn't going to get more from her, Rick stood as well. "Let me know what you decide. I'll help in whatever way I can."

Caitlin nodded. "Thanks, Rick," she said softly. She returned his hug, then closed the door firmly behind him. Turning, she headed for the kitchen to get the king his dinner.

Chapter 10

She didn't sleep that night. On the one hand, it was nice not to have nightmares yanking her awake, gun in hand. On the other, exhaustion seemed permanently etched into her mind and body.

Caitlin sat on the couch for hours, the day's events and conversations running through her head in a loop. It wasn't until one in the morning that she realized what was setting her on edge. She stared at the front door, at the lock she now knew wouldn't hold everyone back. She trusted Rick Bannan with her life, but she didn't want him to have a key to her home. She didn't want *anyone* to have a key to her home. Not even Troy.

Her stiff muscles protesting, Caitlin peeled her body from its dormant position and found a hardware store that was open twenty-four hours. Two hours later, she had new locks and deadbolts on the front and back doors.

She resumed her position on the couch.

When the sun rose enough to sprinkle golden rays through her living room blinds, Caitlin got up from the couch to take a shower. Fifteen minutes later she was in her Dodge Challenger.

It wasn't until she walked through the doors of the Healey PD that Caitlin began to shake. This wasn't in the carefully constructed plan for her life. *Neither was your father's death,* a small voice in the back of her head whispered.

Squaring her shoulders, Caitlin nodded at Angie behind the bulletproof lobby barrier and used her security card to enter into the back room. Angie turned from her desk, gaze questioning, rosebud mouth open, but Caitlin shook her head and kept walking.

Not allowing herself to hesitate, Caitlin didn't bother knocking on the office door in front of her. Chief of Police Alan Landstra looked up in surprise, as did the two men sitting in front of his desk. Landstra's mouth hung open, obviously having been interrupted mid-sentence.

Caitlin swung the door closed. "Good, I'm glad you're all here," she said, glancing at the Deputy Chief and the Captain of her squad. Deputy Chief Bruce Kemper and Captain Owen Halstead looked just as surprised to see her as Chief Landstra. She didn't care.

"This will make things a little faster." Pulling her department issue 9mm handgun and her gold shield from her jacket pocket, Caitlin held them up, then placed them on the table immediately to her right that Landstra used to conduct more formal meetings.

"I resign."

The three men simply looked at her, and Caitlin maintained her casual stance, feet shoulder width apart, hands now clasped behind her back. It felt odd not to stand at attention as she had been taught to do while speaking with her superiors, but she was resigning. She figured she didn't need to stand on ceremony.

Gaining his composure, Landstra caught the eyes of Kemper and Halstead and jerked his chin toward the door. Caitlin held her ground as they moved quietly past her and exited the room.

Once they were alone, Landstra gestured toward the now vacant chairs. "Caitlin, why don't you sit down."

"I'd rather not."

Landstra took a deep breath and leaned back in his chair. "You don't need to do this."

Caitlin kept her eyes on a point just over the Chief's head. "I know."

"You were our rising star in the department. Being put on desk duty for a while doesn't mean you can't still make the top tier."

His words made Caitlin falter, but only for a heartbeat of time. "Thank you, sir, but I'm not doing this because of desk duty."

Sighing, Landstra rose from his chair and came to stand in front of her. "I wondered if this might happen. Caitlin, look at me."

Caitlin forced her gaze to that of the Chief, immediately regretting the action.

"We're going to find who did this. You aren't being shut out. We just had to get our ducks in a row, so to speak."

Caitlin's shoulders relaxed slightly. "I appreciate that, sir. Any information you can give me as you proceed with your investigation would be appreciated."

Landstra's eyes darkened. "Don't make the mistake of trying to launch your own investigation, O'Reilly. Leave that to us now. The last thing I want to have to do is identify you in a body bag because you were reckless."

Shifting her eyes away, Caitlin repeated, "Any information you can give me as you proceed will be appreciated."

Silence fell over the room. Then, "I'll be in touch when we know something."

"Thank you, sir."

Stepping into the hallway, Caitlin was surprised to see her partner, Derek Klein, leaning against the wall. *Former partner,* she reminded herself silently. She was going to miss him. They had become friends over the last couple of years, after her first partner moved out of Healey due to a failed marriage.

"I'm sorry," was all she could bring herself to say.

Derek shrugged. "I will say it was the first time I've ever been abandoned by a girl."

Eyeing his surfer blond good looks, Caitlin could believe it. She felt her chest tighten. "Thanks for coming to the funeral."

"They told me it could jeopardize my job if I talked with you before…" he trailed off, his attempt at an apology for not doing more to stay in touch weak at best.

She wasn't going to judge him; she'd left him stranded in a gas station convenience store, after all. Caitlin offered a small smile.

Derek suddenly stepped forward and wrapped her in a hug. Caitlin stiffened, wanting to push him away, but her arms were pinned to her sides. He knew how much she hated to be touched without warning. It took her a moment to realize it wasn't just a goodbye hug.

"The bullet that killed your father was from a Ruger SR9," Derek whispered near her ear. "No matches to anything else in the system and not registered. They haven't found much else in the way of evidence. Whoever those guys were…this was a professional hit."

Derek released her and stepped back. Caitlin realized two things at once. She was definitely making the right choice, and Chief Landstra wasn't planning to be as forthcoming with information as he claimed. Otherwise she would have learned this information in his office.

Nodding once to Derek, Caitlin left the PD for the last time as an officer, slapping her security clearance badge on the counter of Angie's desk as she walked out. Pulling her phone from her pocket, Caitlin scrolled to a new name in her contacts list.

"Hi, this is Caitlin O'Reilly. Troy gave me your number." She listened briefly. "I can be there in ten minutes."

Chapter 11

Caitlin tapped her short nails on the coffee mug in front of her, strangely soothed by the repetitive clicking sound. Her eyes roamed the coffee house, her back to the far wall. Bright colored fabric on the booths and chairs contrasted with the dark chocolate wood, creating a calming effect – for most people anyway. It wasn't working for Caitlin.

Forcing herself to inhale deeply through her nose, Caitlin held the air in her lungs for a moment before releasing it slowly through her mouth. Derek's words kept running through her mind. *"It was a professional hit…"*

She ignored the coffee in front of her as she continued to tap the side of the mug, her eyes seeking the person she was supposed to meet. Anger rolled beneath the surface, but Caitlin fought to stay calm. A professional hit? Fine. Caitlin would take over *Nightwatch Investigations* and she would eradicate the poison responsible for taking her father's life. Then she could move on.

Her roaming eyes landed on a tall man just entering the coffee house. His head was shaved, his chin sported a dark brown goatee, and he looked to be ten years Caitlin's senior. Broad shoulders were covered by a long-sleeved, plaid button-down shirt. The tails of the shirt hung down over his jeans, and brown work boots clunked loudly on the tile floor as he headed straight for her. She could tell by the way he walked that he was carrying a concealed weapon, probably at the small of his back.

Sliding into the seat across from Caitlin, the man stared at her without saying a word. Caitlin stared back. So this was James Walker. The man Troy said she could trust with her life. The man who could help her flush out a killer.

He looked like a construction worker.

"I do have other things to do," the man finally said, his deep voice startling Caitlin out of her perusal. Though pointed, the words were as staid as his countenance.

"What did Troy tell-"

"He gave me the run down. You're looking for whoever bugged your father's firm, who also possibly killed him."

Caitlin nodded, feeling slightly off-kilter. Something about this man intimidated her. She hesitated.

"Did he tell you-"

"About your background? Yes."

Caitlin's eyes narrowed. "Everything?"

"Enough."

She fell silent, studying the man once more. His eyes were dark, and held the wisdom of things seen that would most likely rival her own experiences.

"Can you be loyal-"

"To someone I don't know?"

"Okay, that has to stop!" Caitlin said, her voice rising sufficiently to attract the attention of those seated nearby. Hunkering a little lower into her chair, Caitlin let go of the coffee mug with one hand and slapped it down on the table. "I can finish my own sentences, thanks."

James Walker stared at her silently, then one corner of his mouth tipped up in a lazy grin. "There you are," he said slowly.

Caitlin leaned back, suddenly wondering if Troy had sent her someone a few fries short of a happy meal. "Excuse me?"

"The firecracker Troy told me about. For a minute there I was beginning to think I sat down at the wrong table."

Her eyes narrowed to slits, her temper flared. "You were intentionally annoying me?"

James gave a short nod, the lazy smile still adhered to his face. "There are three types of people in the world." He lifted a hand, index finger extended. "The kind who will run and hide when things get tough." A second finger. "The kind who talk a lot of crap but never do anything." A third finger. "The kind who are motivated and don't let anything stop them."

"So which kind am I?" Caitlin asked, her eyes flashing green fire.

James gave her a full-blown grin, making Caitlin sit back in surprise. "You are Aednat. You are fire, and everyone had best get out of your way."

Caitlin slowly sat forward. To cover her angst, she picked up her coffee and took a large sip, wincing as the scalding liquid burned a path down her throat.

"Fire for fire," James said quietly.

Caitlin glared across the table. "I know you are loyal to Troy. How do I know that *I* can trust you? That you will do what I need even if it's not something you might agree with?"

Crossing his arms, the smile disappeared off James' face. "Because I am loyal to Troy."

To most people, that statement wouldn't have meant much. But to people like Caitlin, that one sentence was a pledge. Caitlin pushed her mug aside.

"One thing."

"Yeah?"

Caitlin looked calmly over the table at the large man. "If you call me Aednat again, that gun at your back won't be able to save you."

* * * * *

"I wanted to thank all of you for being here," Caitlin began, her stomach churning slightly as she looked around the small conference room at her father's staff.

Standing at the head of the table, she was flanked by several large television screens mounted to the walls behind her. The oval table was just large enough to seat Troy, London Hatcher, Bryce Walcott, Mara Dunn, Rick Bannan, and Loretta. Caitlin wanted to let her eyes roam the room where her father's team met to go over cases the firm was working on, but she knew it would portray weakness.

"I really appreciate all of you coming in on your own to help wrap up the cases *Nightwatch* had in progress before my father's death." Her voice threatened to crack on the word *death*, but she managed to keep it under control. "I want you to keep all current cases open. I will be heading up *Nightwatch*, beginning today."

Caitlin took a moment to look at each member of the team in turn, knowing their reactions would tell her most everything she needed to know. London Hatcher, head of the financial division, was grinning and nodding his blond head, Loretta fairly beamed with pride, but the look on Bryce Walcott's face, Donovan's head of security, was one of ill-concealed skepticism. She would come back to him later.

Mara Dunn blinked slowly, her expression blank. Caitlin's eyes narrowed slightly, unnerved by the fact she couldn't read the computer tech's true thoughts. Rick sat, one ankle crossed over his knee, leaning as far back as the chair would allow, fingers interlaced across his stomach. He winked when Caitlin's gaze briefly landed on him, though he didn't smile. Caitlin made it a point not to look at Troy. She already knew what he was thinking.

"I am adding a member to our team," Caitlin continued, wanting to get this part over with. There would be a few on the team not happy with having someone new added without discussion among the group. "This is James Walker," she said, gesturing for James to step forward from where he had been waiting in the shadows by the door. "He will be helping with a lot of the legwork we'll be needing over the next few months."

James walked to the front of the room and stood beside Caitlin, still clad in the flannel shirt and work boots, his hands loosely clasped behind his back. Caitlin, Troy, and James had agreed they wouldn't mention the link between the two men. It would be hard for anyone to find, even if they searched for it, and Caitlin didn't want anyone on the team feeling like the three of them had suddenly formed their own clique.

"What will we be working on, boss?" London called out from the far end of the table.

Caitlin winced at the term *boss*, but chose not to say anything. She *was* the boss, though she found it hard to comprehend that the people she used to visit in the firm when she was a kid were now working for *her*.

"We," she said slowly, meeting the gaze of everyone in the room in turn, "will be investigating the death of Donovan O'Reilly."

Chapter 12

"What the hell was that?" Rick Bannan roared, barely waiting for the door to her father's – to *her* – office to close before expressing his feelings about the new hire at *Nightwatch*.

Caitlin forced herself to walk calmly around the desk before answering the man who had been like family her entire life. She had seen the shock cross his face when James Walker stepped forward, and knew there would be hell to pay for not letting Rick in on her decision beforehand. She probably would have – there just hadn't been time.

Sitting in the chair behind the desk, she gestured for Rick to take a chair. "Sit, Rick."

"I don't think so," Rick growled, the veins in his neck standing out as his hands clenched and unclenched at his sides.

Caitlin's eyes narrowed, and she slowly rose to her feet. Making an exaggerated motion with her hand, she pointed to the chairs in front of the desk one more time. "Sit," she said, her tone closely matching that of the man before her.

Rick glared at the new owner of *Nightwatch*. "You should have told me," he said, ignoring Caitlin's directive.

Trying to keep her own temper in check, Caitlin took a deep breath. "I knew that trying to find out who was behind Dad's murder would take more manpower than we have." A load of crap, but Caitlin couldn't reveal the real reason James was there, not even to Rick.

Rick stepped forward, jabbing a finger at her chest. "You should have told me," he repeated angrily. "I know men, men who I've vetted and trust. Instead, you brought in someone new who none of us know! That wasn't a smart move, Caitlin."

Caitlin's hold on her temper took a nosedive. "Whether you like it or not, James Walker is now a part of this team," she snapped, glaring right back at the angry man on the other side of the desk.

"You have no idea what you're doing. Where did you find this guy? How do we know we can trust him?" Rick said, shaking his head.

"That's not your concern," Caitlin said, anger drowning out the confusion she felt over Rick's unfounded statements.

"Caitlin, you should let me-"

"Let's get one thing straight right now," Caitlin spat, slamming her hand down on the desk so hard she felt the sting all the way up her arm. "*I* am running *Nightwatch*. Not you. If you wanted this job you should have said something last night."

Rick's face began turning an alarming shade of red, and Caitlin wondered what was really behind his accusations. Donovan O'Reilly had been his closest friend. Did he regret not taking over the company so he could run the investigation the way he saw fit?

Caitlin put both palms on the desk and leaned forward. She was young enough to be his daughter, and the lines needed to be drawn now. Rick Bannan and everyone else at the firm needed to know who really ran *Nightwatch*, or her job would become impossible very quickly.

Lowering her voice until it came out with deadly calm, she met Rick's gaze head on. "You will accept James as part of the team and continue under my direction, or you can walk out that door right now. Don't let it hit you on the way out."

She stood to her full height, sliding her hands into her pants pockets in an effort to appear calm. In truth, she felt bile working its way up her throat. She had expected opposition, sure. But not from the man she looked at as family, like an uncle. Caitlin pressed her hands against her thighs to keep them from shaking.

Rick stared at Caitlin for a full minute, the office falling quiet with the exception of their erratic breaths. Caitlin began to fear that Rick *would* walk out the door, and that scared her. He was the one person who knew her father better than she had. She needed his help.

Finally Rick shook his head, and the corner of his mouth curled up slightly. "He wasn't wrong to name you Aednat," he said, straightening to a more relaxed posture.

Caitlin felt her own body sag in relief. He was going to stay.

"I'll wait for your orders…boss," Rick said, and turned to walk out the door.

"Rick," Caitlin said quietly. She waited until he looked over his shoulder. "Thank you."

Giving a short nod, Rick Bannan closed the door behind him just as Caitlin's phone pinged with a text message.

Practically falling into the office chair, Caitlin picked her phone up off the desk and swiped the screen, pulling up a message from Troy.

Meet me at The Bridge. Bring J.W.

Without hesitation, Caitlin made sure her shoulder harness and gun were strapped on tight, threw a light jacket on, and walked to the door just as James opened it, knocking lightly with his knuckles as he did so.

"Let's go," Caitlin said crisply, pushing past him and into the hall, not bothering to ask why he had come to her office. "You're with me."

Chapter 13

James braced himself with a hand against the door as the Challenger roared down a ramp and merged with traffic, barely missing a rattletrap white truck that honked weakly in protest. "Do you always drive like this?" he asked, his voice gruff as Caitlin abruptly swerved into the left lane to pass a vehicle traveling the actual speed limit.

Glancing quickly over at her passenger, Caitlin shrugged, one wrist flung casually over the top of the wheel while the other hand rested loosely on the bottom of the wheel. "Typically. Helps me burn off tension, relax a little." The corner of her mouth tugged upward slightly. "Does my driving bother you?"

"Slightly," James hissed as Caitlin careened back into the right lane after passing all slower moving vehicles. He pried his hand from the door and straightened his shirt, visibly trying to appear more nonchalant than he felt.

"Come on now, Walker. Don't tell me you drive like your grandmother."

"My grandmother's driving was the stuff of nightmares," James said, glaring at his new employer. "I was in three accidents with her as a kid, and I am not excited about the prospect of repeating that with you."

Caitlin felt a gurgle of laughter come up her throat, but she quickly tamped it down before it could erupt. "So sorry for your, ah, childhood traumas, Walker, but if you're going to whine you'll have to start driving yourself."

"I think I can handle it," James growled, then slammed his hand down on the door handle as Caitlin swept the car to the left, pushing the accelerator to the max as she shot past a long semi, then cut sharply in front of the mammoth vehicle to swerve onto the off ramp on the right at a clip that would have made a Nascar driver proud.

The rest of the short car ride was made in silence as James suffered the high speed and jerky turns, and Caitlin's mind wandered to what Troy might want to talk to them about. As a rule, she wasn't a patient person, and she wanted to know what he found.

A cloud of dust swirled around the car as she jammed on the brakes at the base of a pylon holding up the abandoned bridge. A wide arc of bone-dry sand and dirt made it easy for several people to park and meet if needed. The closest five buildings were all abandoned as well, the road leading to the area around the pylon cracked and dotted with clumps of weeds from disuse.

Caitlin stepped out of the car, the dust settling around her riding boots as she let the door fall closed behind her. Troy looked up from where he leaned against the pylon, a laptop in one hand. He eyed James as the large man closed the passenger door with more force than necessary. Caitlin's friend gave her a pointed look.

"Caitlin, you've got to stop doing that."

Shrugging innocently, Caitlin strode toward Troy, her eyes on the computer. "I'm sure I don't know what you're talking about."

Troy shook his head. "Sorry, man," he said, glancing at James. "It's kind of an initiation of sorts."

James's features immediately relaxed. "So, she doesn't normally drive like that," he said, making it more of a statement than a question.

"Oh, she does," Troy said while cutting his gaze to the woman who now stood before him impatiently. "She just ramps it up a tad for first-timers."

"Great," James muttered, yanking on the front of his shirt while rolling his neck.

"So what have you got?" Caitlin asked, obviously done with the banter.

Troy's hand tightened visibly on the laptop in his hands. "I'm not sure if I told you the police have already gone through all the computers at *Nightwatch*."

Caitlin shook her head. "I kind of figured they had, but I forgot to ask."

"You were in a lot of pain from your gunshot wound, and pretty out of it while you were at the hospital recovering. I probably forgot to mention it."

Nodding, Caitlin eyed Troy carefully. There was something lurking in the depths of his eyes, but she couldn't quite define what it was.

"I got to the computers before they did. The night your father was killed, actually."

Caitlin kept quiet, knowing there was more. James' boot scraped across the dirt and stones as he shifted his weight.

"I took what we needed off the office computer and erased what they didn't need to see." Troy's eyes darkened further, and Caitlin finally knew what was hiding behind the calm she usually saw there.

Anger.

Troy was very, *very* angry. She could see it clearly now as her eyes caught the tight line of his jaw.

"If they ever find out…" Caitlin's voice trailed off as fear nudged her. What would she do if Troy wasn't there to catch her every time she fell?

"They won't find out." Troy sounded so confident that Caitlin forced herself to believe him. It was either that or fall apart.

A thought flashed through her mind, and the fear receded. "Why do they still have Dad's laptop and journals?" Caitlin remembered looking for them and realizing they were missing. She assumed the police had them.

Troy's thumb rubbed the edge of the laptop. "I couldn't find Donovan's journals."

Caitlin's mind went dark. *Then where were they?*

"But his laptop is right here."

Her eyes flew to the computer Troy cradled in his arms.

"And I found something interesting," he continued. Troy's voice was flat, a contradiction to the words he just spoke. Caitlin felt her shoulders tense even more. Her friend only sounded like that when he was about to deliver bad news.

"Both Donovan's office computer and his laptop have been hacked."

Caitlin's breath sucked in past her teeth on a sharp inhale, though she didn't know why she was surprised. If the people who killed her father were willing to plant bugs in his office, they would want access to his files and communications as well.

"Have the police found-"

"The police don't know," Troy interrupted as he looked over his shoulder. Caitlin followed his gaze but didn't see anything. Nevertheless, her skin crawled as if they were being watched. They *were* being watched, in a sense. The listening devices at the firm were proof of that.

"You covered the hacker's software," James said, but there was no awe or surprise in his voice. Caitlin glanced at him. It was obvious this wasn't the first time he had been up against something like this.

"I cloaked it," Troy confirmed, his thumb once again rubbing against the edge of the laptop. "I didn't want to remove it. I'm not even sure my skill set would let me," he admitted. "But I didn't want the hackers to know I found it. If they did, they might remove themselves from the laptop-"

"-and we might not be able to trace the software back to the hacker," Caitlin and James said in unison.

Caitlin glared at Troy's friend. The new guy's habit of knowing what she was about to say was annoying.

Troy seemed oblivious to the exchange. "We need someone to look at this. I barely knew enough to find the backdoor and to cloak the software. I can't trace it or find out what files might be affected."

"I know someone," James said, reaching out a large hand toward the computer.

Troy handed it over without hesitation, and Caitlin felt her stomach twist. She knew Troy trusted James, but it still didn't sit well to hand over the one thing that could lead them to her father's killer to a man she barely knew.

"Keys," James said as he began walking toward Troy's truck, laptop tucked securely under his arm.

Troy tossed his keys in a smooth arc, and James effortlessly snagged them out of the air. Caitlin rounded on the forensic scientist as Troy's truck roared to life.

"Are you sure about this?" she asked, referring to the laptop now exiting the lot via spinning tires and flying gravel. He complained about *her* driving?

Troy nodded. "He'll get what we need."

Taking a deep breath, Caitlin rolled her shoulders. "What else was there? Anything to indicate what might have gotten Dad killed? Anything specific he was working on?"

"I've been going through the files. That's why I haven't said anything until now. I knew you weren't in the frame of mind to get that done."

Caitlin wanted to argue, but knew he was right. "And?" she asked instead, wanting to keep some sort of momentum going. She felt at loose ends, as if she should be doing something instead of standing in the middle of a deserted highway with rainclouds gathering overhead.

As if reading her mind, Troy looked up at the darkening sky, his brow furrowed slightly. "Even his encrypted files didn't reveal anything that seemed to have merit." Troy rubbed the back of his neck. "You know your Dad, Caitlin. He knew he was being watched. He wouldn't keep anything about your kidnapping on those computers."

Caitlin frowned. "Do you think he had another one?"

Troy shoved his hands into his pockets and rocked back on his heels, his gaze distant as a raindrop landed on his forehead and traced a path down his temple. "No, I think he'd go old-school." He turned his gaze down to where Caitlin was standing, her face tilted up toward his. "We need to find his journals."

Another raindrop landed on Troy's upper lip, and Caitlin watched as it trailed down across the corner of his mouth.

"Last I knew, you didn't like to get wet all that much," Troy said, and Caitlin focused back on his amused expression as the rain suddenly decided that sprinkling was for babies.

They dashed toward her car, slamming the doors just as the heavens opened to let rain pour out in thick waves. Caitlin leaned her head back on the seat and rolled it to the side until she could see Troy. "So what now?" she asked, her frustration evident.

Troy used his hand to wipe the moisture from his face. "I think we need to go back to Donovan's house." He looked over at Caitlin. "Even if the evidence itself isn't there, I think there will be clues where to find it."

Caitlin felt her emotions shrink down, contracting until she could wad them into a ball and shove them into the far recesses of her mind. She had only been to her father's house one time since his death. She wasn't sure she was ready to do it again.

"Aednat," Troy said softly.

Caitlin tore her eyes away from his and turned the key in the ignition. "I know." She slammed the car into gear and looked at Troy out of the corner of her eye. "You're going to want to buckle up."

Chapter 14

They stood just inside the front door, the small foyer dim despite the new bulb in the overhead light fixture. Caitlin had changed it herself the last time she was there. Thunder shook the modest dwelling and Caitlin hunched her shoulders slightly. She wasn't a fan of thunder. Sounded too much like a gunshot.

Caitlin felt Troy's hand on her shoulder. She didn't flinch away like she did with most people. The heat from his hand sent warmth throughout her body, and Caitlin felt her shoulders relax. Troy was different. He would always be different.

"I'll take the kitchen and living room," Troy said firmly, knowing she didn't need emotion right then. "You take the bedroom and bathroom."

They separated without another word, their searches quiet but thorough. It was a small house, with only one level. The living room, kitchen, bedroom, and bathroom were pretty much the extent of the dwelling, and Caitlin knew it wouldn't take long to search it all. The problem was that her father was really good at hiding what he didn't want found.

———————

"Where is it, Daddy, where is it?"

Six-year-old Caitlin bounced up and down on her toes, frustration stretching her features into a frown.

Chuckling, Donovan O'Reilly knelt next to his daughter and turned her small body toward the nightstand standing sentinel by her bed.

"In plain sight, Aednat. Where most secrets lie."

Caitlin shook her head from side to side, her ponytail whipping at the air next to Donovan's face, her patience gone.

"I don't see it, Daddy. There's nothing there but my jewelry box."

"Exactly," Donovan replied softly.

Caitlin glared at her father. *"There's nothing there,"* she whined, jabbing a finger at the nightstand.

Donovan reached his hand out and picked up the small box engraved with flowers. *"Are you sure?"* he asked, shaking it gently.

Caitlin rolled her eyes. *"Yes, Daddy,"* she grumbled. *"I've checked there twice already."*

"Where is the best place to hide a secret, Caitlin?"

That got her attention, and Caitlin's small body stilled as her eyes followed the box her father again shook with gentle movements.

"Where?" she breathed, somehow knowing – even at that young age – that she was about to be given the answer to something great.

"The best place to hide a secret, my dear Aednat," Donovan said as he slid his finger along the edge of the engraved box, *"is in plain sight."*

With a soft press of his finger, the side of the box sprang outward, revealing a hollow compartment Caitlin never knew was there. She gasped in delight, her eyes round with wonder.

Donovan reached inside with two fingers, drawing them out slowly, his eyes locked on his daughter's face. The light flashed off a gold bracelet that had been hidden in the jewelry box since she was born.

"It was your mother's," Donovan said softly, carefully setting down the box and taking Caitlin's hand in his own. He gently slid the bracelet over her hand until it rested on her wrist, still a little too big, but not by much.

"But why hide it away, Daddy?" Caitlin asked, her eyes glued to the bright circle of gold encircling her wrist as she turned it back and forth.

"Because, Aednat," Donovan replied, his face suddenly serious, "sometimes things need to be hidden until just the right time. And then," he continued as he rubbed his thumb along the shiny band, "it can come to light."

———————

Caitlin swallowed hard as she shoved the dresser drawer back in place. She swiped at the tears on her cheeks with an aggravated motion, not wanting to feel anything. Not then. Not there.

Why had that scene suddenly invaded her memories? Why now?

Caitlin's eyes landed on the nightstand, then widened in disbelief. Slowly, she walked forward, then sank down on the edge of the bed. Her hand shaking, she reached out and picked up the small wood jewelry box engraved with flowers. *When had he taken it?* Caitlin had never noticed it missing from her dresser at home.

Her fingers traced each flower, stroking each with a touch so light she barely felt anything against her skin. Taking a deep breath, Caitlin outlined the edge of the box with her index finger, then pressed inward. The side popped out, and Caitlin began to feel light-headed. Tipping the box to the side, she held her free hand beneath the box and watched as a silver thumb drive slid out of the small compartment and into her palm.

Breathing was suddenly difficult, and Caitlin closed her hand around the small object as she felt the jewelry box slide from her fingers to land on the dark blue comforter. "Troy," she called, but it came out as a whisper. Clearing her throat, she tried again. "Troy!" she yelled, her voice sounding odd to her ears.

His shoes pounded on the laminate flooring. "What's going on?" Troy asked as he burst into the room, his eyes slightly wild as he scanned the room frantically.

It was then that Caitlin realized how panicked she must have sounded. She held up the flash drive between her thumb and forefinger. "I need you to get my laptop out of the car. It's in the backseat."

Troy took in the small object held up to the light and turned without another word. It took him less than a minute. Caitlin was waiting at the kitchen table when he came in, shaking water from his short hair and t-shirt.

Wordlessly, he handed her the computer, and Caitlin quickly set it on the table and shoved the drive into the USB port. A few keystrokes later, and they were looking at the frozen image of Donovan O'Reilly, the video paused until the viewer decided to hit play.

Caitlin felt a hitch in her breathing as she looked at the image of her father, the first time she had allowed herself to do so since the murder. Suddenly she wasn't sure if she could do this.

"I can watch first if you want," Troy said, his chest barely grazing her back as he stood behind her, his gaze also fixated on the screen.

Giving herself a mental shake, Caitlin ground her teeth together and leaned forward, hitting the space bar. The video began to play instantly, and Caitlin felt tears flood her eyes as she heard her father's voice for the first time in several days.

"If you're watching this, then…" Donovan's eyes shifted, then focused back on the camera. *"Well, we both know what's happened."*

Caitlin passed a hand over her face, mentally scolding herself to keep it together. She could feel Troy behind her, but he knew better than to touch her or try to console her, and he kept still.

"I'm sorry, Aednat. I'm sorry it's come to this. I had hoped we could solve this together, that we could live the rest of our lives free of this ghost…" Donovan shrugged.

Shaken by the sound of her father's voice, his image, Caitlin felt her heart break all over again as she really looked at the man in the video. His features were haggard, dark circles cloaking his eyes as if painted there with a brush. What had her father been through the last few days of his life? The last few weeks?

"I'm sorry I wasn't the father you needed." Donovan looked down at his hands, then back up, his eyes hardening with resolve. *"I know I let you down, and that is the one thing I will always regret. Please know how much I truly love you."*

Caitlin winced, the words like a balm and a lance to her soul at the same time. His words and his face were hard, but she knew him. She knew he had to be that way so he didn't break apart – like she so desperately wanted to do right then.

"I never did end up loving mayonnaise like you did, even after you forced me to eat all those sandwiches." Donovan winked at the camera, a small smile finally flickering across his lips.

"I'm sorry I never got around to fixing the pantry door. I know how much it irritated you every time you came over to make me dinner."

Caitlin's breath caught on a sob, remembering clearly how she fought with that door, complaining to her father about it every time.

"I wasn't good at housekeeping, either," Donovan confessed. *"I never told you how much I appreciated each time you cleaned the bathroom and vacuumed the floor."*

She could feel Troy's breath on the top of her head, and she tried to will his strength into her own body before her father's words tore her apart.

"Aednat," Donovan said, hesitating slightly as his eyes bored into the camera. *"You were – you truly were – the light of my life. My little fire."*

The video froze, and Caitlin's eyes moved frantically over the screen before realizing it was over; her father's last words to her were done. She felt a loss almost worse than when she realized he was dead, his blood pooling under her own body.

"No," she whispered, the words catching in her throat. "No. That can't be it. I don't understand."

Caitlin turned to Troy, her eyes searching his face. "I don't understand," she said, feeling incredibly lost. "Why would he hide this? There has to be something else here."

Troy's gaze was also distant as he stared over her shoulder at the frozen image of his former employer. "Maybe there's a hidden message," he said, his tone making it more of a question. "In the code of the video? Or the words?"

They both turned to stare at the laptop, feeling more confused than when they began watching the video.

Caitlin's phone ringing brought them both back to reality with a jarring thud. She snatched it off the table when she recognized James Walker's number.

"What?" she snapped, then realized how rude she sounded. But she didn't really care; her nerves were shot.

James either wasn't bothered or didn't notice her tone. "I'm with Charlie, Caitlin. You need to come here. There's something I think you should see."

Chapter 15

It took forty-five minutes to reach the address James gave her. Troy had told Caitlin to drop him off at *Nightwatch* on the way. Said he had something he wanted to check on. His eyes were distant, and Caitlin knew there was something he wasn't telling her, but she also knew it was pointless to push. He would tell her when he was ready.

So she battled the rain and traffic on her own. Though even with the numbers and letters in plain sight and right in front of her, Caitlin wasn't sure she was in the right place. She peered through the rain-slicked windshield at the brick building, her eyes narrowing as she took in the structure that looked as if it might collapse under the force of the now timid rainfall.

She tossed the paper with the address onto the seat next to her. Caitlin felt the weight of her gun pressing against her shoulder, and she made sure her jacket fully covered the weapon. "Yeah, all right," she muttered to herself as she grabbed the door handle.

Caitlin shoved her door open and ran toward the apartment building, praying her car would still be there when she returned. As Caitlin pulled open the door, the glass and metal rectangle wobbled precariously as if it might rip out of the frame just by being subjected to her light touch. Once in the small lobby with the door closed somewhat securely behind her, Caitlin focused on her surroundings, immediately wishing she hadn't. The smell hit her first.

"What the-" she hissed as her eyes began to water. She pressed the back of her hand to her nose in an effort to block the stench of urine and rotting garbage.

"Is there a dead body stashed around here or something?" Caitlin grunted to herself, even though a quick glance around showed there wouldn't have been a place to hide a rotting corpse. Although she wouldn't have been surprised to see one propped up against the dirt streaked wall, or shoved in the corner. It was that kind of place.

This guy is a top-notch hacker and he can't find a better place to live? Caitlin thought to herself as she tried to lift her foot off the tile floor and found it lodged there by an unknown sticky mess.

We are definitely meeting in a public place next time, Caitlin thought, scowling as she pried her foot from the floor and shoved it onto a step filled with garbage. Something crunched, and she shuddered.

The third floor? Really? Caitlin took a deep breath and instantly regretted the action. Coughing, she began climbing, being sure not to touch the railing. *I'm burning these shoes once I get out of here,* Caitlin vowed as she slogged through the trash. Her eyes began to burn from the aroma wafting around her.

When James opened the door to apartment 318 a few minutes later, his eyebrows rose at the sight of his new employer, red-eyed and breathing heavily through her mouth.

"Something wrong?" James asked as he swung the door wide to let her enter.

"This guy better have found my father's killer and wrapped him in a bow," she grated through clenched teeth.

James closed the door with a solid thud and turned into the apartment. "Thought you were tougher than that, boss," he tossed over his shoulder as he walked away.

Caitlin forced herself to keep her hands at her sides, though she dearly wanted to wrap them around James' throat. Taking a deep breath, Caitlin realized two things at once. The stench was gone, and the apartment was only marginally messy compared to the lobby and stairwell. The solid thud of the door closing suddenly registered, and she turned to find a sturdy piece of wood separating the apartment from the rest of the building. It was adorned with almost as many locks as she had on her own doors at home.

"Charlie, she's here," James called out, and Caitlin turned back to the apartment.

It was small, with a main living area stretched out in front of them, a modest kitchen to the right, and a narrow hallway leading back to what Caitlin assumed were the bedroom and bathroom. The furnishings were mismatched and threadbare, strewn with clothing. Pizza boxes and beer bottles littered the counter of the kitchen. It was not a neat place, by any means, but it was light years better than what she just walked through to get there.

Caitlin's eyes landed on a long table set up with all manner of keyboards and other gadgets that she had no hope of naming, then marched up to take in the four state-of-the-art, latest model HD monitors mounted side-by-side on the wall above the table.

All of this barely had time to register before a stunningly beautiful woman walked into the room from the hallway. Her wavy blond hair was pulled into a messy bun at the back of her head, and a small silver arc pierced one nostril. It matched several other silver piercings adorning the one ear Caitlin could see. A navy blue tank top hung off athletic shoulders, and jeans hugged her lithe frame and disappeared into brown ankle boots.

"Help yourself to a beer," the woman said, barely glancing at Caitlin as she headed straight for the table with the computers and assorted paraphernalia. "I don't serve people."

Caitlin was so surprised, it took her until the screens flashed to life to lean over to James. "I thought you said *Charlie* had something for us," she hissed barely above a whisper.

"I did," James replied, his eyes glued to the screens as code began rolling in frenetic lines.

"Then who is *this*?"

The woman sighed heavily and leaned back in her chair, flinging an arm over the back as she looked over her shoulder in exasperation.

"The name's Charlotte. I go by Charlie, if that's all right with you, *boss*," she tacked on with disdain. "Now, if we're done with this little…" she twirled a slender finger in the air to indicate the conversation that was obviously a waste of her time, then turned back to her computers.

"Come on, baby, let's get to work," Charlie crooned, and it took Caitlin a moment to realize the woman was talking to the screen in front of her as more indecipherable – at least to Caitlin – lines shot by with lightening speed. Charlie's left hand reached out to the side even as her right continued typing. Her fingers slid into an open bag of Cheetos and extracted two, which she popped into her mouth and chewed with a distracted air.

Two minutes and five more Cheetos later, Charlie spun in her chair and crossed her arms as she took in the two people lined up and waiting.

"Jimmy here tells me you know the laptop was hacked."

Caitlin felt a laugh threaten to escape as James' whole body stiffened indignantly at the nickname he'd just been saddled with. She cleared her throat instead.

"What you need to know is that the person who hacked this computer is very good." Charlie's blue eyes flashed with what seemed to be equal amounts annoyance and admiration.

"What does that mean?" Caitlin asked, trying to keep her voice and facial expressions on an even keel. She didn't want to frustrate the woman any more than she already had. She needed the answers Charlie had yet to divulge.

"Any self-respecting hacker will make his own tailor-made attacks," Charlie said, reaching a hand back to blindly search for her bag of Cheetos.

"We write our own software," Charlie continued, and the term *we* didn't escape Caitlin's notice. "Now, anyone in the profession your Daddy was in – if he was smart – would write *his own* software to counteract any attempt there might be to hack his baby."

"His *what* – never mind," Caitlin said, waving her hand in the air as she realized Charlie was referring to the laptop.

"There are several things you can do. Once you have the software ready to roll, you can buy," she snickered – Caitlin assumed – at the thought of buying software instead of creating it, "security encryption and tie it into specific folders. This allows you to see if anyone is trying to hack into that specific information."

Caitlin nodded. She wasn't tech-savvy, but she could at least follow that.

Another Cheeto was extracted from the bag. "Now, you can write APIs to piggyback security encryption-"

And now Charlie had lost her. Caitlin held up her hand. "I get it. There are lots of things you can do to see if someone has hacked your computer. Can you trace the hacker's software, or whatever, back to him once he's accessed files?"

Charlie rolled her eyes in affront. "I'm not an amateur, darling."

Caitlin's forehead creased as she fought for patience. "Which means what, exactly?" she snapped, losing the battle for patience. To be fair, she hadn't really tried.

Two fingers reached slowly for the Cheetos as Charlie's eyebrows pulled down slightly. Silence fell over the small apartment as her startling blue eyes probed Caitlin's face. Finally, she leaned forward in her chair.

"Yes, I traced it. But before I tell you who it is, there is something else you should know."

Caitlin felt the muscles in her shoulders tighten even more.

"Your father's computer wasn't the only thing hacked."

It was Caitlin's turn to frown, her eyebrows pulling together in a sharp 'V'. "What do you mean?"

Charlie leaned back, her fingers invading the Cheetos bag. "I mean, you're going to need a new phone."

Thoroughly confused now, Caitlin's hand involuntarily went to the back pocket of her jeans, feeling the outline of her cell phone. "I don't get it."

Sighing, Charlie leaned forward again. "I cloned your cell phone while you were standing here."

"You *what*-"

James pulled Caitlin back by the arm as Charlie held up her hand in a 'halt' gesture. Charlie's eyes bored into Caitlin's gaze, waiting until the former police officer let go of her anger long enough to focus on what she was saying.

"When I found who had been watching your father, I realized that Daddy may not be the only one being watched." Charlie reached for the bag of Cheetos, then stopped herself, her eyes shifting as if distracted. "The person who hacked your father's computer also piggy-backed bugs onto some of the apps on *your* phone."

Caitlin pulled away from James's grip. He let her, both of them stunned by what Charlie's revelation. "What does that mean?"

"It means, darlin', that anytime you're in a mobile hotspot like a coffee shop, they can use that app to find you and track everything you're doing. They can even use the microphone on your cell to listen in on what you're saying – and I don't mean phone calls."

A shiver slithered down Caitlin's spine. "Can they hear me now?" she whispered, her eyes darting around as if someone might be peering in through the window.

Charlie rolled her eyes. "I have security measures in place preventing anyone from hacking into anything in this apartment. Again, I am not an amateur. Anyway, I assume they did the same to your father's phone, but since we don't have it…" Charlie shrugged.

Caitlin glanced over at James, then back to the woman who was yet again crunching on Cheetos. "Why are they watching me?" she asked, though it was more of a rhetorical question. Neither of the other people in that room would know the answer.

After another moment of thought, Caitlin looked at Charlie. "Were any files deleted? Can you get them back?"

Nodding, Charlie took a swallow of beer. "Yes, and yes."

Caitlin shivered. This was unreal. The feeling of violation she felt was one she hoped to never experience again. "If I get a new phone, they'll know I'm aware of being bugged."

"Yes."

Caitlin nodded slowly. "So I keep the phone for now." Her eyes hardened. "Who is the hacker?"

Charlie used the toe of her boot to slowly move the chair from side to side in a small arc. "Let's just say that someone in your firm has been very, very naughty."

Chapter 16

Troy entered *Nightwatch* through the back door and then paused. He wasn't sure where to go from there. The forensic scientist scanned the hallway thoughtfully.

His lab covered the entire basement floor, but Troy didn't turn toward the hallway that would lead him to the stairs. He knew what he was looking for wasn't in his office or lab.

In truth, he wasn't sure *what* he was looking for. An odd feeling had passed over him while at Donovan O'Reilly's house. A feeling that something there wasn't right. Something Troy had seen, but that didn't belong. Something he had also seen…at *Nightwatch*.

Troy began walking down the wide hallway housing the offices of the firm's employees. His eyes discreetly swept the windows of each office, noting who was at their desk, and which offices were empty. Caution was key. There was a mole within *Nightwatch*, he was sure of it. He couldn't appear as if he suspected anything.

Mara Dunn looked up from her desk as he walked by and gave a small wave. The forensic scientist smiled back and kept walking. Nothing on her desk or in her office set off any alarms in his head.

Troy passed Rick's office, noting that the windows were dark. He paused in front of the open door, then stepped through, pausing to let his eyes adjust to the dim light.

"Hey, Daniels! If you're looking for Rick, he stepped out to get something to eat."

The sound of London Hatcher's voice near his shoulder almost sent Troy through the roof. Forcing his breathing to remain calm, he turned and gave his co-worker what he hoped was a normal smile.

"Thanks," he said, noting the sheets of paper the financial investigator clutched in his fist. "You look busy," he noted, trying to draw attention away from the fact that he had been standing in Rick's office.

London snorted. "Yeah, Brad Thomas is still convinced his wife is somehow getting into his business accounts and filching money. He's making me triple check everything. I also wanted to start going through the firm's financials from the last year to see what I can dig up for Caitlin." His features suddenly sobered. "To see if anything Donovan had been doing might lead to his killer."

Troy nodded. "She would appreciate that. Donovan was a careful man when he didn't want something found out, but everyone has habits. There might be a trail he inadvertently left behind that will bring us a lead."

London gave an affirmative nod. "My thoughts exactly." He turned toward his office, but then swung back. "Hey, did you need something?"

Sweat started to roll down his back, but Troy shrugged nonchalantly. "Nothing that can't wait," he said, and grinned.

"All right, man. I'll see you around."

London ducked into his office across the hall, and Troy felt his chest release some tension. He wasn't used to the cloak and dagger routine. Usually he could do his part in the lab and leave the skulking around and investigating to…well, the investigators.

The next office belonged to Bryce, and Troy could see light from the windows spilling onto the carpet even though the door was closed. Troy approached the door and gave it a hard knuckle rap before cracking it open and sticking his head inside. Bryce looked up from a report he was filling out on his desk.

"Hey, Troy. What do you need?"

If there was one person Troy hoped to never get on the bad side of, it was Bryce Walcott. Only about five feet, nine inches tall, the man was nevertheless built like a tank. Muscles pulled at his shirt and rippled down his arms with the slightest movements. His face bore several scars from the fights he got into while living on the street as a teenager. One of the scars was directly between his eyes, puckering the skin and giving the man a permanent scowl. In charge of the security aspects of *Nightwatch*, he was intimidating even when he was in a good mood.

Troy let his eyes quickly rove over the contents of Bryce's office. Nothing stood out to him as being out of place, or sent a warning through his brain. But he needed a reason to be there.

"That new?" he asked, nodding toward a framed eight by ten glossy photograph mounted on the wall. Bryce stood next to a beautiful, buxom redhead whose perfect white teeth flashed brightly as she smiled. Troy instantly recognized her as Evie Langton, the pop singer who recently performed a concert in Detroit.

Evie's concert sold out within fifteen minutes of the tickets going on sale, and when approached about doing a second concert a week later, she graciously agreed. Her agent, Elton Toering, suggested Evie stay in Detroit until the next concert, and arranged several outings for the young star to keep her busy.

The first day, Evie complained of feeling like someone was watching her. Toering beefed up her security detail. The second day, a grainy photograph of her in her hotel room, clad in nothing but her underwear, showed up in a tabloid. That was bad enough, but it was immediately obvious that the picture had been taken from *inside her hotel room.*

Knowing she hadn't had any *planned* company that evening, Toering immediately went to the police. But Evie wanted more. Toering found out about *Nightwatch Investigations* and approached Donovan O'Reilly about finding Evie's stalker. Donovan agreed, and also sent Bryce Walcott as an addition to her security detail, knowing not many people could get past Bryce.

Between Donovan and Bryce, it took less than fifteen hours to flush out the new hire to Evie's security detail who had a dangerous infatuation for the pop star. Using his status as security, he was able to follow her even when off duty, and enter her room when it was vacant, hiding in an unused closet where he took pictures through the slats of the door.

Evie Langton was effusive in her praise of *Nightwatch Investigations*, especially of her "protector and savior, Bryce Walcott." At least, that's how she described him to the reporter who took the picture. She had her arm around an uncomfortable looking Bryce Walcott, hugging him to her side in a much more intimate way than was called for.

Troy had never seen Bryce Walcott scared, but the look in the eyes of the man in that picture was the closest the forensic scientist had ever been to seeing his co-worker panicked.

Bryce glared at Troy, and the scientist decided maybe he should drop the subject of the picture.

"Did you *need* something, Troy?" Bryce ground out while tightening his grip on his pen.

"Right," Troy said, his mind scrambling. Then he realized he could use the excuse Landon unknowingly provided. "Have you seen Rick anywhere?"

Bryce shook his head. "Nope. Been in here doing paperwork all day." His eyebrows lowered.

It wasn't a secret around the office that Bryce wasn't fond of paperwork. At all. It put him in a nasty mood and people tended to shy away from Bryce Walcott in a bad mood. Troy stepped back out into the hall.

"Okay, thanks then." He closed the door hastily behind him. Turning, Troy locked gazes with Landon in his office. With a sinking feeling in his stomach, the scientist realized Landon heard the entire conversation with Bryce – including the question of where Rick might be. Which Landon had already answered.

Troy gave a swift nod and quickly walked back the way he had come before Landon could question him. Maybe he needed to take a step back for a moment. Take a breather and really concentrate on what he might have seen at Donovan's house that caused the uneasiness he was feeling.

Turning into the short hallway housing the break room, restroom, and the stairs to his lab, Troy stepped into the break room. Troy didn't need to go down to his lab just yet. Even though he didn't know what he was looking for, he knew whatever it was, it wasn't in *his* office.

Troy sank down into one of the gray plastic chairs and tossed his phone on the table in front of him. Running his hands down his face, he leaned back and then crossed his arms across his chest. Staring blankly at the cupboards across the room, Troy mentally went back to the moment when he walked with Caitlin through the front door of Donovan's house. He would think through every step he took, and everything he saw while going through the house. *Something* had to give.

Deep in thought, Troy barely glanced up when Mara walked in.

"Hey, Troy. What are you up to today?"

Troy glanced up quickly as Mara walked over to the refrigerator, then shifted his gaze back to the cupboards over the sink. "Just trying to work through something," he said absently. *He had gone through the living room and was back in the kitchen. He rifled through all of the kitchen drawers and cupboards and then began walking toward the refrigerator…*

"You want something to drink?"

Troy shook his head. "No thanks." *Something on the counter caught his eye…*

"Troy, are you sure you're okay?"

The pop and hiss of a soda can being opened finally drew Troy's eyes away from the cupboards. Warning flares cascaded through his brain, but he couldn't put his finger on what was wrong.

As if in slow motion, Troy watched as Mara twisted the aluminum tab at the top of the Mountain Dew can until it popped off, a habit she had since she began working at *Nightwatch.*

"If you need anything, you know you can just ask right? I mean…"

Mara's words warped and slowed in Troy's brain as Mara turned to toss the tab into the trashcan next to the door. It was as if time itself had slowed, each second disjointed from the next.

Abruptly, Troy's mind broke free and scenes flashed with stunning clarity across his vision. The Mountain Dew can on the counter in Donovan O'Reilly's kitchen, the tab broken off and sitting on top of the garbage in the trash. *On top* of the garbage, not underneath as if it had been from a visit before Donovan died. No, that tab, the tab to a drink Donovan never personally drank, was resting *on top* of the trash in the garbage can. It had been placed there *after* Donovan's death.

Suddenly Troy's phone buzzed, lighting up with a text message. Two sets of eyes darted to the phone, and the forensic scientist felt the breath leave his lungs as he read the words on the screen.

It's Mara Dunn.

Chapter 17

"He's not picking up," Caitlin said, tossing her phone onto the console. She gripped the wheel and rammed her foot harder onto the accelerator.

"Troy knows how to take care of himself," James hissed as he grabbed for the door to anchor himself as Caitlin took a corner on two wheels.

But he doesn't have a gun, Caitlin wanted to scream, her mind shying away from what might happen if Mara found out he knew. Troy owned a gun. Several, in fact. However, he never carried one on him, even though Caitlin begged him to countless times.

"How completely obvious," Caitlin muttered under her breath. "The tech guy is the one who hacked Dad's computer."

"I know, right?" James' breath sucked in sharply through his teeth as Caitlin blew through a stop sign. "It would have been much more interesting if it had been Loretta."

The thought of Loretta spying on her father was so ludicrous, Caitlin couldn't help but smile. She looked at her newest employee out of the corner of her eye and watched as James' mouth twitched.

Shaking her head, Caitlin yanked the wheel to the right a little harder than necessary. She wanted to see how much big, burly James could take before he squealed like a girl. So far he was holding up disappointingly well.

Caitlin picked up her phone and speed dialed Troy again. As she listened to it ring, she mentally begged him to hold on.

Almost there, she whispered in her mind. *Almost…*

* * * * *

Troy's eyes flew upward, his gaze connecting with Mara's as she also looked up from the words blaring from the screen.

"Troy…" His name faded to nothing as Mara took a step back, a hand held up pleadingly as the other continued to grip the can of Mountain Dew.

He had known, *worked with,* this woman for years, but Troy had no interest in listening to anything Mara had to say. White-hot rage filled him, and he exploded out of his chair.

As if in slow motion, Troy watched the can slip through Mara's fingers, exploding on the floor as she reached for the gun holstered at her waist. He grabbed the chair, twisting as he lifted and swung at the same time.

Mara ducked, but she was a split second too late, and the leg of the chair cracked against her shoulder, causing her to grunt in pain. The gun clattered to the floor as she reached for her injured arm. Troy didn't reach for the gun. He never felt raw hatred like he did at that moment, and he embraced it fully.

Out of the corner of his eye, Troy saw his phone flash with Caitlin's name, but he was already moving, launching himself forward as Mara struggled backward toward the door of the kitchen. He hit her at the waist in a full tackle, and they both became airborne as they sailed through the doorway.

* * * * *

Caitlin's hands shook violently by the time they roared into the front parking lot of *Nightwatch.* So much so that the wheel to the car slipped, bouncing them over the curb with a bone-jarring thump.

To his credit, James didn't say a word. He simply tore off his seat belt, adjusting the gun at his back as he stepped out of the car. Caitlin slammed her car door and rounded the front of the vehicle, gun in hand.

"Whoa," James said, putting a hand out to halt her dash to the front door.

"*What?*" Caitlin snapped, her patience already ragged.

"Tone it down," James snapped back.

Caitlin stopped cold, her hand tightening on the grip of her gun as her eyes narrowed. "Excuse me?" she ground out through clenched teeth.

"We don't know what's going on in there," James said, his eyes cold. "If you go in with your gun drawn, Mara could panic and start shooting. People could die, Caitlin. *Your* people."

Caitlin took a deep breath, forcing down the anger threatening to take over. James' eyes were cold, but so was his voice. This was no longer her employee standing before her; it was a soldier. One who wasn't going to let her walk through that door if it meant endangering other lives.

"Fine." Caitlin sighed grudgingly, slowly sliding her gun back into the holster at her shoulder. "Fine," she repeated a little more softly. She knew James was right, but she hated admitting when she was wrong.

They turned toward the glass doors of *Nightwatch* just as it exploded into thousands of fragments, a gunshot reverberating through the air. Caitlin felt the rush of air as the bullet narrowly missed her head. The loud crack of the car windshield shattering made her hunch forward instinctively. Eyes wide, she met those of James Walker.

"Feel free to pull your gun now," James said grimly as he pulled his own weapon from the holster at his back.

Caitlin glared as she yanked her gun back out from its place at her shoulder.

"Stay behind me," James ordered as he began moving forward in a half crouch, gun extended.

She wanted to argue, but there wasn't time. Caitlin fell into place behind him. Two steps later, they both hit the gravel as another shot kicked up dust mere feet from their position. Then Troy and Mara crashed through the broken doorway, the remaining glass tinkling as it landed on the concrete walkway, followed closely by Troy and Mara.

Caitlin felt glued to the ground as she watched her closest friend grapple with Mara, struggling to keep the investigator's weapon away from him while simultaneously attempting to gain control of the gun. James was back on his feet, gun pointed at the duo as he tried to find a shot.

Troy and Mara rolled off the walkway, still tangled together, arms and legs thrashing violently. James edged closer, trying to find an opening. Caitlin's head snapped up as more bodies crashed through the broken door. Loretta, Rick, Bryce, and Logan halted immediately, guns drawn and trained at their co-workers on the ground. It was obvious they had no idea who they should be pointing their weapons at.

Throwing up her hand, Caitlin scrambled to her feet, yelling, "Wait!" She didn't want Troy getting shot because someone felt trigger-happy. Bryce quickly put his gun away, but Caitlin knew it wasn't because he planned to stand down. Her head of security was inching forward, looking for a way to break up the fight without getting shot.

Troy finally managed to land an elbow across Mara's jaw. It stunned her long enough for the forensic scientist to slam the hand holding the gun against the hard ground. Mara's hand went slack, and the gun fell into the dirt. Teeth bared in a growl, Mara lashed out with her fist, catching Troy in the temple. He fell to the side, eyes dazed. Released from his weight, Mara rolled and came up on her feet.

James instantly trained his gun on the female investigator, Caitlin quickly following suit. Seeing their reaction, the remaining employees of *Nightwatch* did likewise. Mara's chest heaved as she fought to catch her breath. If the woman was bothered by the multitude of guns pointed at her head, she didn't show it.

"You're in over your head, Caitlin," Mara shouted. Her gaze flew over her former friends and co-workers, then returned to land on Caitlin. "If you shoot me, you won't get the answers you're looking for." Mara reached back as if to pull something from a back pocket, or from under her shirt.

An explosion of sound made Caitlin lurch forward, her shoulders rolling inward instinctively as her mind tried to process the red blood now staining Mara's shirt. The woman staggered back, shock lining Mara's face as she touched the blood at her side. She looked up at Rick, betrayal in her eyes, the hand that reached behind her back falling limp and empty at her side.

Caitlin watched in amazement as Mara turned on her heel and ran, her thin form stumbling. She vanished around the side of the building before the employees of *Nightwatch* could act. "Why did you do that?" Caitlin yelled at Rick as she ran toward the side of the building. "We need her alive!"

James rounded the corner of the building first, barely pausing before making the turn. Hot on his heels, Rick's eyes flashed fire at Caitlin's rebuke. He remained silent, choosing instead to focus on the task at hand. Caitlin held up her hand as Bryce began to follow.

"Call 911; make sure Troy's okay," she ordered, then took off after the other two men.

Rounding the corner of the building, Caitlin bolted down the alley, gun clenched tightly in both hands. She could see the tall forms of James and Rick disappear around the corner to the right, barely pausing to make sure the way was clear. Her breaths rapid and harsh from adrenaline, Caitlin burst out of the alley, squinting as the shadows of the passageway turned into piercing sunlight.

There. A split second after Caitlin caught sight of her query, she saw Mara turn, a small pistol in her hand. Caitlin swore. She forgot the woman always carried a back up piece in an ankle holster.

The private detective dove behind a parked car, catching a glimpse of James doing the same. Rick ducked into a recessed doorway. The shot sounded deafening to Caitlin and kicked up concrete mere inches from where she stood seconds before. Rick swung out in a low crouch, but quickly dove back to cover when Mara's second shot splintered the brick near his head.

When the third shot *thunked* into the car parked between the ones James and Caitlin were hiding behind, the detective suddenly knew what was happening. Spinning around to the other side of the car, Caitlin began moving along the road in a fast crouch, continuing to use the parked vehicles as cover. One car ahead, Caitlin could see James doing the same.

Four, five. Caitlin silently counted the shots as Mara continued to fire. *Only one more – she can't use it unless she has a guaranteed shot.* Rick must have had the same thought, because Caitlin heard a quick succession of shots from his 9mm. A car door slammed, and Caitlin and James dispensed with cover and stood to their full height, sprinting toward the car Mara had disappeared into.

Tires squealed against dark pavement as the SUV with darkened windows pulled away. Caitlin raised her gun, but James put his hand firmly on her wrist as he shook his head. Coming to her senses, Caitlin noticed the people crouched behind benches and huddled in doorways, their eyes wide as they stared at the people involved in a shootout on their street. There were too many innocent people around to risk a stray bullet.

Fury and helplessness collided as Caitlin watched the SUV take a corner to the left a few blocks from where they stood; they had been so close. The bigger question looming in Caitlin's mind was... *who was the owner of the vehicle?* It was now apparent Mara wasn't working alone.

Chapter 18

"I'm *fine*, James. Go home."

"Not a chance," the retired soldier said as he followed Caitlin up the driveway.

The stress of the day proved too much, and when James moved to follow Caitlin into her house, the former police officer swung to face him, her expression mutinous. "Back off," she hissed, hand twitching as she fought the urge to reach for her gun.

James paused but didn't back away as she hoped he would. "Troy is fine. He has Britt to tend his bruises and a gun to protect his family. And that's if Britt doesn't get to it first. I've met her, and wouldn't want to cross her on a bad day."

A smirk began lifting the corner of Caitlin's mouth until James moved a step closer.

"Troy and I have an agreement. *You* are my first priority, Caitlin O'Reilly. Mara Dunn is in the wind, and we still have no idea who the driver of that SUV is; so whether you like it or not, *Aednat*…you better get used to me being around."

Caitlin flushed red, hands clenching into fists. "I told you not to call me-"

"Try it." James's eyes flashed hot enough to match the flames burning in her chest.

Fury clouding her mind, Caitlin fought to think clearly. James wouldn't leave until he checked her house and made sure Mara wasn't lying in wait somewhere. If that's what it took to get rid of him, so be it.

Without speaking, Caitlin broke eye contact and unlocked her front door only to find herself unceremoniously shoved to the side once the lock released. "What the-"

"Don't kid yourself. There's no way you're going in first."

James brushed past her, gun drawn and held in front of him as he swept the door open. The feeling of violation after having someone enter her home for the second time without permission grated on Caitlin. Rick was bad enough. She didn't even know James.

"You leave the lights on like this when you're gone?" James asked, his voice fading slightly as he ducked into a room.

"Yes." Curt, to the point. He didn't deserve anything more.

Caitlin followed as James moved to the kitchen area. They heard the soft scraping sound at the same time. "Don't-" she yelled just as James spun around the edge of the counter, finger tightening on the trigger. He pulled up short, and Caitlin simultaneously breathed a sigh of relief and snickered. She could tell much didn't surprise James, but King Tut gave him a shock.

"A turtle?" James asked in disbelief as he shot a look at Caitlin over his shoulder.

She merely shrugged one shoulder, not feeling the need to explain. No one understood her choice of pet. No one except Troy.

James must have figured it would be better not to ask, because he stayed silent, moving to the door leading into the backyard. He disappeared from view and Caitlin let him be, taking the time alone to prepare Tut's dinner. James came back through the door, gun finally holstered, as Caitlin put the bowl of shredded lettuce on the floor.

"Thanks for checking everything out," Caitlin forced through a tight jaw. "I'll see you tomorrow."

James smirked. "Just to warn you, I'm up early."

Squinting, Caitlin looked through her lashes at the man standing in her kitchen. Then the light bulb flashed in her head.

"Oh, *hell* no," she spat, her hand actually finding the gun at her shoulder this time.

James was on her before she could pull the weapon. Pinning Caitlin's arms to her sides, James leaned in close enough she could smell the hint of peppermint on his breath. "You forget, Caitlin O'Reilly, this isn't happening on your terms, whether you like it or not. Someone is out for blood, and it very well could turn out to be yours. That couch in the living room is mine for the rest of the night – unless you'd like me to share your bed." His eyebrows rose.

Caitlin couldn't quell the shiver of horror that racked her body.

"I didn't think so," James said quietly. He slowly released her arms and stepped back. "I know you sleep with the lights on; that won't be a problem. I'll see you in the morning."

Without another word, James turned and walked out of the kitchen. Literally shaking with terror and rage, Caitlin snatched her phone from the counter.

WTF?

Troy's response pinged back so quickly, she knew he had been waiting for her. *You wouldn't stay here. You know that as well as I do. Get over it.*

Exhaling harshly, Caitlin fought the urge to slam the phone down on the floor and shatter it with the heel of her boot. The most irritating thing was that Troy was right – if he had asked, she would have refused to stay at his house.

Caitlin slowly made her way to her room, closing the door behind her for the first time in seventeen years. Her thumb hit the lock, only feeling mildly satisfied when she heard it *thunk* into place. The one thing worse than not being able to see what was coming at her was the tangible threat in the living room of her home; the place that should feel like her haven. She had to pick her evil tonight and there was no way in hell she was leaving open access to a man she barely knew.

Fully clothed, Caitlin fell into bed, hand clutching her gun. It was going to be another long night.

* * * * *

"Do we need to move the girls? Take them to my parent's?"

Troy winced as he pulled his shirt over his head. He didn't answer Britt's question right away, but he wasn't ignoring her concerns; he was trying not to groan from the aching muscles and bruises that covered his body. Troy wasn't in the habit of brawling in the street, and his body wasn't hesitant in telling him that Mara had gotten the upper hand a few times.

Sitting cross-legged in the middle of their bed, Britt's face went ashen when she saw the bruises marking her husband's torso. "Troy…"

"I'm all right, Britt." He met her gaze firmly. "Really. I'm okay. And we don't need to take the girls to your parent's house."

Britt forced her eyes from the marks on Troy's body. "But Mara is still out there. She knows that you know about her."

Troy sank down on the edge of the bed and took one of her hands in his. "Everyone at *Nightwatch* knows about her betrayal. There's no reason for her to single me out."

Still not looking convinced, Britt reached out and traced the length of a deep scrape high on Troy's shoulder. "I'll get some antibiotic ointment for that," was all she said, and Troy felt relief that she wasn't going to push the issue of Mara any further.

"What about Caitlin? Should she be alone at her house right now?" Britt asked as she gently rubbed the antibiotic cream into the wound on her husband's shoulder. She ripped open the packaging to a large bandage and pressed it over the scrape.

"James Walker is with her. She'll be all right."

There was a pause as Britt put the top back on the ointment then rested her hands on his shoulders. Troy could feel the tension radiating from her palms.

"You don't sound very confident," Britt said finally.

Troy stayed quiet. There wasn't any use trying to hide anything from Britt, and he wouldn't be able to convince her that everything would be okay when he still hadn't been able to convince himself.

* * * * *

Her alarm system triggered at three o'clock. It uttered no more than a soft *ping* from the monitor near her bed, but for Caitlin it was tantamount to a train whistle going off in her ear. She crouched next to her bedroom door, squinting down the barrel of her gun, free hand resting on the lock, before her body realized it was awake.

Caitlin pushed her shoulder even harder against the wall as she quietly sprang the lock. The well-oiled hinges allowed the door to coast inward silently as Caitlin quickly took in the empty hallway, both hands gripped around her gun. Still in a squat, Caitlin swung out slightly to take in the other end of the hallway – and almost pulled the trigger.

James crouched along the wall right next to her, obviously in the process of coming for her. His eyes bored into hers, fear non-existent as he stared down the barrel of her gun. Instead, he raised one finger to his lips in a shushing gesture as Caitlin fought to bring her heart rate back under control. She could feel the heat of his body as he moved past her, still staying low. Caitlin fell in behind.

Feeling exposed in the brightly lit hallway, Caitlin was nevertheless thankful for the light. She needed to see what was coming. Sweat began to build on her palms, and Caitlin mentally cursed as she felt her grip on the weapon slide.

The living room and kitchen lights were off. James paused at the opening to the kitchen, his eyes connecting with hers for the briefest second before he spun around the archway. A black boot connected with James's wrists, and his arms snapped to the side, the gun clattering across the hall as he lost his grip. He wasn't down, however, and James immediately lunged through the doorway.

Heart racing, Caitlin spun back down the hallway and turned into the living room, racing past the dark shapes of furniture as she bolted into the dim kitchen. Two shadows wrestled near the island, and Caitlin took aim, knowing the smaller form had to be Mara. Suddenly, James grunted as Mara managed to land a glancing blow to his temple. As he staggered back out of range, Caitlin began pulling the trigger. At that moment, Mara turned toward her, and Caitlin saw the briefest flash of metal before white-hot pain whipped across her cheek.

Stunned, Caitlin's gun lowered as she put a hand to her bleeding cheek. That was a mistake. Mara was on her before she could react, and Caitlin felt the tackle to her midsection pound all air from her lungs.

Caitlin's gun went flying as she landed hard on the floor, Mara on top of her.

Just as quickly, Mara's weight was gone, and Caitlin could see her writhing form as James pulled Mara hard against himself, arm locked tightly around her neck. As Caitlin rolled to her side, she saw Mara drag the heel of her boot down James's shin. The soldier grunted, and his hold slackened enough for Mara to land an elbow in his abdomen. With James' hold now weakened, Mara lurched forward.

Panic rolled in Caitlin's chest as she realized too late that Mara was going for the knife that grazed her cheek only seconds before and was now lodged in the wall of her living room. With one fluid move, Mara jerked the knife from the wall, spun, and threw it at James.

"No!" Caitlin screamed as James roared in pain, the blade sinking deep into his shoulder. The former soldier sank to his knees, Caitlin's eyes glued to him in horror. Suddenly, Caitlin saw movement out of the corner of her eye. Mara was heading straight for James, blood staining the shirt covering her abdomen, her eyes hard.

Caitlin reached for a gun that wasn't there as Mara reached behind her and pulled her own weapon. On her hands and knees, Caitlin scrambled for the coffee table in front of the couch, lunging the last few feet. Slamming her hands down on the front edge of the table, the top flew back on a metal track, revealing two 9mm handguns, two knives, and a shotgun.

Grabbing the first 9mm her hand touched, Caitlin spun on her knee and squeezed off three shots just as the barrel of Mara's gun lined up with James' forehead. All three bullets found their mark center mass, blood blossoming across Mara's chest as the former *Nightwatch* agent's eyes widened in shock. Her body slammed back against the wall and stayed as if suspended there for several seconds before slowly sliding down to land on the floor, gun falling from her limp hand.

Harsh breaths rasping from her lungs, Caitlin kept her gun trained on the woman bleeding out on her living room floor. When she was sure Mara wouldn't move, Caitlin glanced toward James. The retired military officer looked from Caitlin to the open coffee table and back again.

"I think..." he grimaced, hand going to the handle of the knife sticking out of his shoulder. "I think I just fell in love with you a little bit."

Reining her breathing back into a normal cadence, Caitlin smirked. "In your dreams, Walker."

James gave a half grin as he staggered to his feet. Caitlin followed suit, her attention now fully on the woman sagging against her bloodstained wall. Her jaw locked with determination, Caitlin knelt beside the dying woman. A woman she had trusted. The barrel of her gun pushed hard into Mara's forehead, pinning the woman's head to the wall.

"Who are you working with?" Caitlin asked harshly.

Mara's breathing was guttural; blood seeped from the corner of her mouth. She stared at Caitlin. "Rick...Rick...hired me...asked me...to help...at *Nightwatch*." The words were bleak, all fight gone from the woman who only moments before tried to kill the two other people occupying the room.

A curl of disgust lifted Caitlin's lip. Rick *had* been the one to find Mara, to hire her and bring her into the fold of *Nightwatch*. Now Caitlin's father was dead because of her. "You betrayed him. You betrayed all of us."

A cough racked Mara's thin form as her eyes once again sought those of the woman holding a gun to her head. "This...is much...bigger..." The thin, reedy words faded to nothing, then Mara seemed to rally for a parting blow. "Your father...should have left...it...alone..."

Mara's head sagged forward, putting pressure on the barrel of Caitlin's gun, her eyes staring blankly at the floor. Caitlin felt the faint flare of hope die within her chest. Mara had been their only lead. She couldn't die; they would have *nothing*.

Caitlin dropped her gun and grabbed the front of Mara's shirt, slamming her limp body back against the wall. "What does that *mean?*" she screamed at the dead woman, shaking Mara's body. "*Who are you working for?*"

"Caitlin." James's hand fell heavily on her shoulder, and Caitlin forced herself to take a deep breath and uncurl her fingers from Mara's leather jacket. Just then her eyes fell to the blood staining the side of Mara's shirt. Caitlin's eyes flew over the rest of Mara's clothes. Suddenly, Caitlin leaned forward, grasped the neckline of Mara's shirt, and pulled her hands apart, ripping the shirt down the middle.

"What the hell-"

She chose to ignore James and his shock, instead looking for the bullet wound from earlier that day. It took one glance and Caitlin was back on her feet, cell phone in hand.

"You mind telling me-" James began.

"She's wearing different clothes than when she fled *Nightwatch* and her bullet hole is stitched up. The fight caused the wound to leak."

Comprehension dawned on James' face as Troy finally picked up the other end of the call. "Troy, you need to get over here. Now."

Caitlin ended the call and began walking around, turning on the rest of the lights.

Chapter 19

"The stitching was done by an amateur," Troy said, stripping off his gloves. "Nothing revealing. Except we know she had help."

Caitlin turned away as her closest friend rose to his feet, frustration lining his face. If Troy was frustrated, that meant there wasn't much hope. Caitlin couldn't handle the loss of hope. She had lived without it for too long.

"She was too young to have been involved in my abduction," she said quietly, her thoughts tumultuous. "She was brought in after."

"Sounds about right," James said, wincing as Troy removed the gauze bandages from his shoulder to inspect the wound he had stitched up only moments before. Troy's removal of the knife from James' shoulder had caused a bellow loud enough to wake the neighbors.

"Why?" Caitlin asked, a fingernail firmly lodged between her front teeth as she thought. King Tut slowly made his way toward her, completely unbothered by the addition of a dead body and blood in his living room. "It had to be money, right? Someone had to be paying her. Did she need money for something?"

"Or revenge?" Troy suggested from the vicinity of James' shoulder.

"Watch it," James hissed, his eyes hard as Troy probed the wound.

Caitlin snapped her fingers. "It has to be one of the two. I can't see love figuring into it anywhere. Love, money, and revenge are the three biggest reasons for crime and murder."

"On it," James said, choosing to ignore Troy's ministrations and pulling his laptop closer to him.

Caitlin eyed the computer as James began typing one-handed. "She was here to kill me," she murmured, lost in her thoughts. "But why? What would that accomplish?"

Troy looked over his shoulder at her as he adhered the last bit of medical tape to the gauze that swathed the arm of the soldier in front of him. "Whoever kidnapped you had seventeen years to right their mistake," he said, his voice clinical though his eyes were filled with fury. "Why send an outsider to do the job? Why tonight?"

"It doesn't make sense." Caitlin began pacing. The click of the laptop keyboard was grating on her nerves. She spun on her heel and glared at James as she crossed the length of the living room.

"You must look outside the obvious, Aednat," Donovan admonished, *looking at her over the crime scene photograph covering his desk. "It's never the reason you are looking for…"*

Caitlin strode over to Mara's body, closing her mind to the fact she was dead, that a woman she trusted for years lay lifeless in her home – and by Caitlin's own hand.

"I already searched her," Troy said quietly, his warm presence suddenly at her shoulder.

"I know," Caitlin said grimly, her fingers plying the lace at Mara's chest. "I watched."

Troy's eyes narrowed as he watched Caitlin work. "Are you saying you don't think I did a good enough job?"

"No," Caitlin said as she pulled the thumb drive from the depths of Mara's bra. "I'm saying you're too much of a gentleman."

James whistled. "Remember that comment I made earlier? Double that."

Troy looked curious as Caitlin blushed red. "Something I should know?" he asked quietly.

Caitlin looked at him sharply. She had only heard that tone of voice from Troy twice before. Neither time ended well for the person on the receiving end. "No," she stated bluntly, and pushed to her feet.

Her mind working overtime, Caitlin turned the small device over and over in her palm. "This is the drive that contained the last message from my father," she told Troy quietly. "It was still in the laptop on the kitchen table."

Suddenly, the man at her side was much more interested in the flash drive than in James' comment. "Why would she…"

"I know why." Caitlin had her car keys in hand before either man could blink twice.

"Now wait a minute-"

"Keep up or be left behind," Caitlin shouted over her shoulder as she jogged to her car. She knew there would be hell to pay when the authorities arrived at her house. Caitlin could already hear the sirens. Dear Mrs. Walsh from across the street never missed an opportunity to indulge in her need for drama. Caitlin was sure her neighbor made the phone call summoning the authorities.

Both men barely made it into the car before Caitlin threw the gearshift into reverse. Rubber burned as she tore down the driveway. Caitlin made sure to toss Mrs. Walsh a wave as she passed the small blue house across the street.

* * * * *

Caitlin threw caution to the wind and charged into her father's home without the usual precautions she would have taken after almost being murdered. James and Troy protested loudly as she threw open the front door and strode into the hall.

Making a beeline to the kitchen, Caitlin threw open the refrigerator door. Scanning the contents, she quickly withdrew the mayonnaise jar and slammed it down on the counter. "He never liked mayo. Never had it on a sandwich. Ever."

Troy quickly pulled a pair of gloves from his pocket and unscrewed the lid. Giving a low whistle, he withdrew a plastic Ziploc bag with an envelope inside. "Nice work."

Caitlin wasn't there to be congratulated. She moved to the pantry door next to the archway leading into the living room. Pulling on the door, her eyes narrowed as it gave the familiar catch before acquiescing to the pressure of her hand.

"Here."

She turned to find James holding a small step stool in his good hand, injured arm pressed close to his side. Caitlin took the stool and scaled it rapidly. Her fingers slid across the top edge of the door. It took less than three seconds to find the small latch. Caitlin wasn't tall enough to see into the hollow area at the top of the door, but her fingers became her eyes. The small vial caught as she lifted it from the small depression at the top of the door, but a firm tug was all it needed to relinquish its hiding place.

Descending the stool as rapidly as she went up, Caitlin tossed the vial to Troy who snatched it from the air with his gloved hand. A few more strides had her at the hall closet where she unceremoniously pulled the door open and yanked the vacuum out into the living room. The front compartment opened easily, and Caitlin withdrew a small Ziploc bag from where it was tucked between the bag and the wall of the vacuum. Instead of immediately handing it over, however, Caitlin paused. Her thumb smoothed the clear plastic over the enclosed photograph.

Squinting, she looked closer. "What the…" her voice trailed off, unaware she had verbalized her surprise.

"What is it?" The words were spoken in unison as Troy and James moved closer.

"It's Gia," Caitlin breathed. Her lungs constricted and she felt panic edging in, though she wasn't sure why.

"Gia VanMaar?" Troy asked, moving close enough Caitlin felt his breath feather across her cheek as he stared at the picture in her trembling hand.

"Who is she and why is she important?" James' voice held traces of irritation and confusion.

"Marci's mother," Caitlin said flatly as she allowed Troy to take the wrapped photograph from her hand.

James' eyes registered recognition, but he wisely kept silent.

"It looks like she's watching someone," Troy mumbled as he scrutinized the picture of Gia VanMaar sitting in a dark sedan, binoculars held close to her face.

"You think?" Caitlin snapped, irritated by Troy's statement of the obvious.

Troy looked up and shot her a glare plainly stating he understood she was stressed and would overlook her comment. This time.

"So we need to find out who Gia had under surveillance and why," James said. Caitlin snapped her mouth shut before she reiterated her snappy retort from before. "I can ask Charlie to take a look at the photo."

Caitlin shot him a sidelong look. "We have people at *Nightwatch* who can do that."

James looked back, his expression void of emotion. "Not as fast as Charlie."

Troy looked at Caitlin. His expression remained neutral, but she knew him too well. She sighed. "Fine."

They had her dead to rights, and Caitlin knew it; Mara had been *Nightwatch's* best technical asset. The others could do the job, but not as well as the newly departed Mara Dunn. Definitely not as well as James' mysterious Charlie.

James headed for the door, injured arm held stiffly at his side, photograph clenched tightly in the other hand.

"Where is he going?" Caitlin threw her hands up in the air, feeling exhaustion creep in. It had been slinking nearer, stealthily moving closer under the flow of adrenaline.

Troy shrugged. "He'll find a ride."

Caitlin glared at her closest friend. "He needs a *doctor*."

"Charlie can help him with that."

"I'm sure she can," Caitlin muttered.

Troy's eyes narrowed. "We have the authorities to deal with," he said, the words clipped.

Great. Caitlin could imagine how much fun *that* was going to be.

Chapter 20

Caitlin leaned back in the chair and crossed her ankles, peering over her booted feet to where Troy worked steadily at the other end of the table. The beer in her hand was cold, and Caitlin was thankful for the discomfort against her fingers – it kept her awake. Exhaustion threatened to pull her under, but the newest owner of *Nightwatch* had no intention of slowing down. Not until she had some answers.

Watching Troy for several minutes, Caitlin was once again struck by his love for science. She would watch him for hours when she was younger, entranced by the steady, methodical way in which he approached his work. When she asked why he didn't leave *Nightwatch* to work in a government forensic lab, Troy had looked at her like she was crazy.

"I get to do it all here. Why would I go somewhere else?"

"What do you mean?" Caitlin asked, spinning the stool she sat on from side to side.

"By working in a private lab, I get to work all the instruments. In a government lab, I'd only get to work one or two. Not to mention, I'm able to work all kinds of cases and analyze all types of evidence, sometimes even going into the field. Most scientists are only allowed to work certain types of cases and are stuck in the lab all the time."

Though Caitlin didn't understand much of anything about forensic science, she was grateful to her father for giving Troy the freedom he craved. It meant he would never leave *Nightwatch*. It meant he would never leave *her*.

"By the way," Caitlin said quietly as Troy squinted at the envelope in his gloved hands, "thanks." She tipped the bottle to her lips.

Troy didn't bother to look up. "Yup," he drawled, his attention elsewhere.

They aligned their stories on the ride back to the house; the reception there was what they expected.

Hands held above their heads as they exited the vehicle, Troy and Caitlin were immediately forced to the ground and handcuffed by the Healey PD. Hours later, the look on Derek's face still haunted Caitlin. His was a visage of a man betrayed by someone he trusted; Derek knew there was more to the story than Caitlin and Troy revealed.

Like any good lie, there were elements of truth sprinkled amidst the falsehoods. They found out Mara Dunn had been betraying *Nightwatch*, leaking information, and confronted her. She pulled her gun, and that's when Rick shot her. Why she was in Caitlin's home…Caitlin and Troy looked at each other and shrugged. Maybe she was looking for more information to sell?

They could tell Derek and the other officers – many Caitlin knew well – recognized something didn't line up right, but there wasn't enough for them to figure out what that was. Caitlin was just glad that everyone was out of her house. Thinking about that many people wandering through her sanctuary still made her skin crawl, and thoughts about the mess waiting for her when she returned home made her feel even more exhausted than she already did.

"Any word from James?"

Troy shook his head. "We'll hear from him when he has something."

The beer bottle rolled between Caitlin's palms as a flash of irritation spiked through her. She had never been good at waiting.

"Relax, Cait." Troy didn't bother looking over, absorbed by the envelope in front of him. With tweezers, he carefully removed the paper inside through the slit he made at the end of the envelope.

Caitlin fell silent. Why the shortened nickname from Troy? He rarely varied from *Caitlin* or *Aednat*. She felt uneasy, and the irony wasn't lost on Caitlin that the nickname issue bothered her more than what Troy might find in the paper he was unfolding. There wouldn't be any point in asking, however. Troy could be just as stubborn as Caitlin when he wanted to be.

"What is it?" Caitlin leaned forward, letting her boots slide from the countertop as Troy's eyebrows pulled down.

"It's an invoice for a rental payment." Troy's voice was distant as he concentrated on the paper.

"For what?"

"For a residence. From the address it looks like the high-end lofts across town."

"What's the name?" Caitlin was on her feet now, the adrenaline humming through her blood. Had they finally found something legit?

"Gerald Marcine." Troy looked up at her. "Mean anything to you?"

Caitlin's forehead wrinkled as she thought. "No. You?"

Troy shook his head.

"So why would Dad have this?" Caitlin mused. "Were there any prints?"

"Just your father's, and the employee who mailed the envelope." He shrugged when Caitlin's eyebrows rose. "The employee had a rap sheet, so her prints popped up."

"What else are you going to look for?"

"I'll give it the whole treatment," Troy said, already beginning to move toward the instruments lining the counter. "Surface contamination, indented writing, concealed writing, drugs, poisons. Anything unusual."

Caitlin blinked rapidly at the mention of poison. "Right. And, uh, how long will this take?"

"Settle in; it'll be a good three hours."

Sighing, Caitlin slid off the stool. "I'm going to find something to eat."

Troy didn't answer, his attention focused on the work before him. Caitlin shook her head; she could feel the excitement radiating off him. Troy was definitely in his element when in his lab.

Three hours later, Caitlin had gone through two cans of Sprite, three bags of chips, and was bored out of her mind. Boots propped up on the edge of the counter, she slouched down in her chair and leaned her head back. She was dozing lightly when Troy clapped his hands together, startling her upright.

"Done!"

"Great." Caitlin cleared her throat and tried to get her bearings. "Find anything?"

"Well, I've looked at it by stereomicroscopy, ESDA, ATR, fluorescence microscopy, XRF, SEM-EDS, and then did solvent extractions for GC-MS and ion chromatography."

Caitlin cleared her throat and forced her eyebrows down to a normal level. "Um, right. So…find anything?"

"Just mayonnaise," Troy said, wrinkling his nose.

The automatic door to the lab whooshed open, and Caitlin reached for the gun that was no longer at her shoulder. The police had taken all of her weapons as part of the investigation. She hated how helpless that made her feel.

"Just me," James said as he strode into the lab. Somewhere along the way he had found a new plaid shirt. His arm was in a sling made from what looked like an old, torn t-shirt. His goatee stood out in stark relief against his pale face. Caitlin mentally cursed him for not going to the doctor.

"Hey, man, find anything?" Troy was already eyeing the Ziploc encased photograph hanging from James's beefy hand.

The soldier tossed the photograph on the lab table. "All prints on the photo are Donovan's," James said, glancing at Caitlin as he spoke. "Picture was taken about six weeks ago, up near St. Jorge Street. Gia is looking to the east, and the closest building that meets the trajectory of the binocular's angle are the high-rise apartments a block over on Mathers Avenue."

Troy immediately stiffened, but Caitlin eyed James with a narrow gaze. "How could you possibly know all that?"

James watched Troy grab for the piece of paper he had been examining seconds earlier, then jabbed at the photograph with a large finger. "See that crane?"

Caitlin squinted. It took her a minute, but she finally caught the outline of a construction crane in the background of the picture.

"They began construction on St. Jorge nine weeks ago. By the amount of completed work, Charlie was able to deduce the picture was taken six weeks ago."

"How was she able to deduce that?" Caitlin asked suspiciously.

James looked at her with placid features. "You don't want to know."

Probably not, Caitlin mentally agreed.

Turning his attention toward Troy, James waved his hand in a general motion around the lab. "You might want to take a look at it with your fancy do-dad machines to make sure there isn't anything Charlie missed though."

"Don't call them machines," Troy and Caitlin chorused in unison.

James blinked slowly. "Right."

"They all have specific names and functions," Caitlin said testily. Troy had already resumed his perusal of the invoice, looking from the paper to his computer as he used one hand to type. She didn't feel it necessary to share with James the fact that she mistakenly called the lab equipment "machines" when she first met Troy. The ensuing lecture took an hour and left her glassy-eyed.

"Mathers Avenue is the address on this invoice," Troy said suddenly. His eyes burned with the intensity he always had when pieces began linking together.

Caitlin looked at him sharply. "Yeah?"

"Yeah. How much you want to bet that whoever Gia was watching lived at this address?"

"I guess we know where our next stop is," Caitlin said, once again reaching for a weapon that wasn't there. She gritted her teeth in frustration.

James reached behind his back and pulled a .45 Glock from under his shirt. Wordlessly, he held it out to her. "I picked it up on the way over."

Caitlin eyed the gun with trepidation. "Where did you-"

Dark eyes stared.

Sighing, Caitlin tucked the gun into the waistband of her jeans. "I don't want to know, do I?"

James shook his head.

"Has this always been a thing with you?" Caitlin grumbled as she waited for Troy to take his lab coat off.

"You don't want to know that either. Let's go." Troy strode toward the lab doors.

James motioned for Caitlin to go next. As she followed Troy out of the lab, Caitlin began wondering if hiring someone as enigmatic as James was a good idea.

Chapter 21

"Well, now what?" Caitlin planted her hands on her hips, thoroughly annoyed. Their knock at the loft on the nineteenth floor of Hager Towers had been met with silence. She wondered how hard it would be to break the door down.

James cocked his head to the side. "Hear that? I thought I heard something."

Rolling his eyes, Troy threw his hands up in the air. "Here we go," he muttered.

Caitlin eyed the retired soldier. James looked back, raising an eyebrow slowly. She smirked. "Yeah. I hear it. Sounds like someone calling for help."

"You two were made for each other," Troy snapped.

Caitlin glared at her best friend. Troy rarely lost his temper, but had seemed on edge several times in the last twenty-four hours; her patience was wearing thin. "Got a better idea?" she shot back.

They stared at each other so long James finally cleared his throat. "Getting a little awkward, and I'm getting hungry. A decision in either direction would be great."

"Fine. Whatever." Troy sighed and broke eye contact with Caitlin.

"Great." James backed up a couple of steps, his gaze on the door.

"No!" Troy yelled, putting himself between James and the imminent destruction of the door to the loft. "Geez, guys, all it takes is a little finesse." He pulled a small leather case from his back pocket.

"You know how to pick locks?" Caitlin asked in amazement.

"There are a couple things you don't know about me yet," Troy said, the words short. He turned his back to her and bent to the task at hand. Seconds later the door swung wide, and Troy glanced behind him with raised eyebrows before entering the loft first.

"He can be insufferable when he's right," James said flatly.

"Tell me about it," Caitlin muttered, stepping through the door.

They separated quietly, as if from previous agreement. Caitlin was scanning the kitchen when James spoke from the large picture window to the left.

"This could definitely be the loft." He jerked his thumb toward the darkening sky. "There's a park a quarter mile away with line of sight to this window."

Troy walked over and peered out the glass. "The question remains – why was Gia VanMaar spying on Gerald Marcine?"

"Let's find out," Caitlin said grimly, turning back toward the open loft. "What did you find out about this guy, anyway?" She began working her way through the books lining the wall at the far end of the living space, wondering if her questions would spark another annoyed response from Troy. Thankfully, he seemed too distracted to be irritable.

"I couldn't find much on him," Troy said absently as he rifled through a designated junk drawer in the kitchen. "Been living here over fifteen years, drives a midnight blue Mercedes sedan, no record, self-employed."

James grunted. "That usually means living off family money or drugs."

Glancing at her newest employee, Caitlin turned back toward the books, her fingertips pausing on the spine of a book. *Oliver Twist*, she mused. Her finger traced the crease running the length of the spine. It was a title Caitlin had seen often, though where eluded her; she never owned the book, and hadn't even read it.

Moving on, she forced her mind back to the house they were illegally searching. Adrenaline coursed through her as she realized Gerald

Marcine could walk through the door at any time and have them all arrested for breaking and entering.

"It doesn't *always* mean money or drugs," Caitlin finally said in response to James' earlier comment. She abandoned the bookcase to look through the nearest end table. "Did it mention what kind of work he did?" she asked Troy.

"Not really." Troy closed the junk drawer and started opening and closing cupboard doors in the kitchen. "Financial computation, I think the file said. I couldn't find any record of anyone who had employed his services, or taxes filed."

Not finding anything of interest in the main living area, Caitlin wandered down the hallway, thinking she might go through the bathroom. It was amazing what a person could learn about another just from what they had in their bathroom.

As she passed by a doorway, Caitlin looked in to see James had moved on as well and stood in the middle of a bedroom, a picture frame in his hand. She was about to continue down the hall when the frame tilted in his hand. Caitlin felt as if the oxygen had been sucked from her body, and the hallway tilted around her.

"Where did you get that?" It came out in a whisper, her eyes locked on the frame, unable to move.

"What?" James turned toward her, and the image behind the glass disappeared as his hand moved. It was enough to release Caitlin from the trance that claimed her.

"Where did you get that picture?" Caitlin demanded. Suddenly mobilized by a mixture of confusion and terror, she strode into the room, her gaze only on the object in James' hand.

"This?" James sounded as confused as Caitlin felt. He tilted the frame toward himself, then toward the woman coming toward him, but she was already beside him and snatched the photograph from his hand.

"Marci." The name escaped her lips in a hissing exhale. Caitlin felt as if someone had punched her in the stomach. There, looking up at her with the cocky smile Caitlin knew so well, was the face of her best friend. Forever suspended at age thirteen, Marci VanMaar's love for life was so clearly depicted by that smile, for an instant – for one second of time – Caitlin was sure she couldn't be dead. Then reality swooped in and crushed her like it always did.

"Where did you find this?" Caitlin didn't realize she yelled the question until she heard a crash from the kitchen and Troy was suddenly by her side, breathing hard.

"What? What's wrong?" Troy's gaze ping ponged back and forth between the man and woman before him.

Caitlin ignored him. She wanted an answer to her question, and she wanted it *now*. "Well?" The word was aimed at James and ground out through clenched teeth.

"On the dresser." James answered, obviously disgruntled by Caitlin's ferocity.

"What the hell is going on?" Troy's voice rose in frustration.

Caitlin shoved the photograph and frame at him, then immediately stepped away from the men to begin her own search of the room. It took Troy all of two seconds to register why Caitlin was so upset.

"You found this on the dresser?"

James grunted an assent, and an instant later Troy was beside her. "I'll check the nightstands," he said, tossing the frame onto the bed.

"Marcine will know we've been here," James said a few minutes later as he watched Troy and Caitlin toss the room, leaving items spread haphazardly behind them. They didn't bother to respond; neither cared anymore.

"Either help or get out of the way," Caitlin said, her voice oddly deadened as she swept past James and into the hall. She headed for the bathroom, desperation edging the periphery of her emotions at the knowledge nothing else in the bedroom revealed why Marcine had a picture of Marci. Caitlin heard the men's voices rise and fall behind her; she didn't bother to tune in, knowing Troy was explaining the meaning of the picture to James. At least she and Troy seemed to be on the same page again.

An hour later, the loft looked as if it had been ransacked, Marcine still hadn't shown up, and all three stared at each other, discouragement mirrored on each face. "Why the hell does he have a picture of Marci? Who is this guy?" Caitlin whispered. Seeing that picture ripped open a part of her that she valiantly tried to hide every day of her life. She felt as if someone had used her as a punching bag.

James broke the silence first. "I'll set up across the street. He has to come back sometime."

Caitlin glanced at him, hoping her gratitude showed on her face. She didn't trust herself to speak. Troy shifted beside her, and Caitlin's eyes slid closed. She could tell she wasn't going to like what he planned to say next.

"Caitlin, I'm going to take you home, and you're going to rest. We'll talk to Gia in the morning, see if something shakes loose."

Dislike was too strong a word. *Loathe* was much more appropriate.

She found her voice. "Not a chance."

Troy shifted so he was standing in front of her. "It's late. You haven't slept all night. You come home and sleep, or I go alone to talk with Gia."

Caitlin glared. "You wouldn't."

Troy simply looked at her.

"Go, Caitlin. I've got this covered here; I'll call if he shows up." James' voice barely registered, but his words finally got through.

"Fine." Caitlin headed for the door. "Let's get this over with."

"You really have to stop viewing sleep as the enemy," Troy said as he trotted after her.

"When the nightmares stop I'll consider it." Her voice came out flat, anger burning that Troy was forcing her to stop the investigation for something so trivial as a few hours of shut-eye. He knew what was going to happen. He *knew*.

A half hour later, Troy stood at the open door to his guest room, Britt having just left after making sure Caitlin had what she needed. His expression softened as he looked at her.

"Aednat."

There was so much in that one word, but Caitlin didn't care. "What are you going to tell the girls when they hear me screaming in the middle of the night?"

It was a rhetorical question, and Troy knew it, the look on his face stricken. Caitlin swung the door closed and flipped the lock.

* * * * *

"Just go."

Britt felt Troy's body jerk in surprise at her words. She knew he thought she was asleep, but the tension radiating off her husband made that impossible. She felt Troy roll toward her, his arm finding its way around her and pulling her close against his chest.

"Britt-"

"It's okay," she said, turning in his arms to face him in the darkness. Britt could barely make out his features, but she could hear the worry in her name, she could feel it in his arms. "I understand. The nightmares are going to come, they always do. And I don't want the girls to wake up scared if they hear something."

Troy sighed as he rested his forehead against hers. "In case I don't tell you enough, you are amazing. Not many wives would be this understanding."

Britt's lips curved in a soft smile. "I know, but feel free to keep telling me."

Troy's lips found hers in the darkness, and then he was gone, his pillow tucked under one arm as he padded toward their bedroom door.

"Take Thunder with you," Britt called after her husband, "or he's going to be whining at the door all night."

There was whispered word and the jangle of the Rottweiler's collar as he followed Troy toward the door.

"Love you," Troy said softly as he closed the door against the light in the hall.

Britt mumbled some semblance of a response, already half asleep with her head deep in the pillow.

Chapter 22

Marci's screams ripped through the walls. Caitlin huddled in the corner, the blindfold pressed to her knees as she rocked back and forth, the cloth wet from her tears.

"Why? Why? What do you want?"

Caitlin yelled the questions, hoping they could hear through the walls, that they would stop, just for a moment, and show a shred of mercy to her friend.

"Unless you want to join her, shut up."

Caitlin's body jerked in fear at the closeness of the voice. She wasn't alone; how had she not known she wasn't alone? Taking a deep breath to steady her racing heart, Caitlin worked up all the courage she could muster.

"What do you want? We don't have whatever you're looking for!"

"We know."

Stunned by the bare truth offered so readily, Caitlin fell silent. She listened for Marci; she could hear sobs through the wall.

"Then why are you doing this?" It came out as a whisper.

"Because Daddy has what we're looking for."

"What good is it going to do to torture Marci?" A sob caught in her throat. "Just leave her alone!"

"Don't you get it, girl? It's all a show for Daddy."

Caitlin's mind spun. What? Understanding dawned a second later, and horror ripped through her. "You're recording that?"

A laugh was the only response.

Fury surged within, and Caitlin found a reserve of audacity she didn't know was there. "You're a monster!" she screamed, and spit in the direction of the voice.

The blow tossed her head to the side, slamming the side of her face into the wall. Pain was instant, every nerve ending screaming with fire.

"You forget yourself, girl," the voice rasped.

New tears soaked the blindfold, but still, Caitlin had to try.

"Just leave her alone," she sobbed.

The second blow brought darkness.

———————

She woke sweating, barely able to keep the scream between her clenched lips. It took several seconds for the image at the end of her gun to register. The door was still closed, the lights still on, the lock still snug in its chamber.

Hands shaking, Caitlin lowered the weapon, continuing to stare at the bottom of the door. A shadow blocked the light from the hall. She knew Troy left it on; he knew she *needed* it on. So what was blocking the light?

Gun still clenched tightly in her fist, Caitlin slid from the bed in one fluid move. Feet silent on the thick carpet, she crossed the room quickly, one hand resting on the lock while the other held the weapon ready. The lock rotated slowly, silently. Her hand dropped to the doorknob, twisting carefully.

The door swung inward, grazing the carpet as Caitlin found herself pointing a gun at Troy, stretched out in the hallway in front of her room. A pillow cradled his head, a blanket was pulled up to his shoulders; it was too small for his long form. He was fast asleep.

Thunder lifted his head and whined from where he lay on the other side of Troy. Caitlin and the Rottweiler stared at each other for several seconds. When Thunder judged there to be no emergency, he settled his wide head back on his paws.

The gun dropped to her side, her grip loosening. Quietly, Caitlin turned, pulled the pillow and blanket from her bed, and walked back to the door. Leaving it open, she lay down on the carpet, facing Troy, and covered herself with the blanket. Her gaze locked onto Troy's still features, Caitlin forced herself to breathe deeply, again…and again. Finally, she closed her eyes against the light.

The gun remained clenched in her fist under the blanket.

* * * * *

"We got distracted."

Caitlin looked over at Troy's profile. His eyes never wavered from the road. "What?"

"We got distracted." Troy flipped on the blinker to turn left. "The address, the loft, the picture…we forgot about the vial."

Caitlin sucked her breath in sharply. He was right; the vial she found in the pantry door…where was it? "Where is it?" Caitlin asked, giving voice to her thoughts.

"I remembered to grab it before we left for Marcine's loft, then forgot about it. Found it in my pants pocket last night and put it in the safe room."

Breathing a little easier, Caitlin nodded, then looked at Troy out of the corner of her eye. "I still can't believe you went through with building a panic room in your basement."

Troy was silent for several seconds. "I've seen too much evil to *not* have a panic room."

Touché. Caitlin let it go. She had something she needed to confess anyway.

"I asked Rick to meet us at the VanMaar's house."

Troy glanced at Caitlin, then back at the road. "You sure you want to bring him in on this?"

Caitlin nodded even though Troy wasn't looking. "He was Dad's partner, and part of the family; he wants to find my father's killer as much as I do. He also worked for Grant VanMaar when this all went down. If anyone can read Gia, it'll be him."

"Good point."

Before Troy could say more, Caitlin's phone chimed from where it sat on the console. "It's James," she said, snatching up the phone.

"Just texted you a pic," James said without waiting for a greeting. "Might not have gone through yet. I think you'll find it interesting."

"Was it Gerald Marcine? Did he come back to the loft?"

"Something like that."

Caitlin's brow furrowed. What the hell was that supposed to mean?

"He walked in, then left ten minutes later."

"Wait, he didn't stay? Didn't he call the police? It looked like someone robbed the place after we were done."

"No cops." His voice was flat.

Caitlin's mind spun. No cops meant Marcine didn't want the police involved in…whatever this was.

"I'm going in to look around. He was there long enough, maybe he left something that will give us another clue as to what the hell is going on."

Just then, Caitlin heard her phone ping with a message. "You're text came through. I've gotta go."

"Remember things aren't always what they seem."

What?

James hung up before Caitlin could clarify what he meant. Swiping over to her text messages, she clicked on the one from James. As the picture filled the screen, Caitlin felt the world tilt around her, and swore.

"What? Caitlin, what is it?" Troy swerved as he looked over at her, and hastily corrected the wheel.

Caitlin felt the phone drop to her lap, her hand numb. Everything felt as if it was in slow motion, yet moving so fast she couldn't keep up. *What the hell was going on?*

"Gerald Marcine is Grant VanMaar," she whispered.

Chapter 23

Rick grabbed her arm as she prepared to pound on the front door of the palatial VanMaar residence. "Hold on, Caitlin. You can't just barge in like you're on the warpath."

"Why not?" Caitlin demanded. "I want to know what's going on!" She glared at the man who was like an uncle to her. Out of everyone, *he* should understand.

"Because this may not have anything to do with your kidnapping," Troy snapped. "What the VanMaars do with their personal time is *their* business."

Caitlin hesitated for a moment, then rounded on both men. "If it doesn't have anything to do with my kidnapping, why did Dad hide the invoice and the surveillance photo of Gia?"

Rick opened his mouth to answer, then stopped, sighed, and motioned for Caitlin to knock. "Just try to stay calm, all right?"

The brass knocker pounded against the front door several times. "Yeah. Calm. Sure." Caitlin tapped her foot impatiently as she waited for someone to answer.

An eternity later, Gia VanMaar swept the door inward, a smile gracing her elegant features. "Caitlin! What a wonderful surprise!" Her eyes widened and her voice trailed off as she caught sight of Rick and Troy standing behind Caitlin. Gia's hand tightened on the door. "I take it this isn't a social visit." Her voice held a question, as well as a hint of resignation.

"I'm sorry, not this time," Caitlin said, stepping into the foyer. "Is Grant here as well?"

"Yes, he's in his study." Gia's eyebrows pulled down in confusion. "Have a seat, I'll go get him." She gestured toward French doors standing open, revealing a spacious sitting room with two couches and several chairs. Gia turned her back on her guests and continued down the hall.

"Breathe, Cait," Rick whispered in Caitlin's ear as they walked into the room.

Caitlin took a deep breath, trying to heed the advice. Troy stood in the middle of the room, his eyes moving over the expensive paintings and antiques. He wasn't curious about how the VanMaars decided to decorate; he was looking for clues. A glance in Rick's direction told her he was doing the same.

"Caitlin! It's so good to see you again!"

She spun at the sound of Grant's voice, barely able to get her arms up before the tall man engulfed her in a hug. Grant released her quickly, probably feeling the tension in Caitlin's body; he was an intelligent man and didn't miss much. He reached to shake Rick's hand, then Troy's.

"Please, sit down." Grant turned to place his hand at the small of his wife's back, gently leading Gia to one of the couches.

Caitlin perched on the end of a chair. Rick chose the couch, but Troy remained standing, hands in his pockets. Caitlin looked at the VanMaars closely. They were both smiling, but was that tension tightening the skin around Gia's eyes? Was that uncertainty in the slanted tilt of Grant's lips? Now that Caitlin had their attention, she wasn't sure how to begin. Troy was watching her closely, and Caitlin cleared her throat, the silence becoming awkward.

"Dad thought he had a lead on the kidnapping when he died."

The entwined hands of the couple on the couch tightened at her words, then relaxed. Grant was the first to speak. "We knew he never stopped looking for the bastards who killed our daughter," he said quietly. "We would never have been able to repay the debt we owed him for his dedication."

"You could start by explaining why you have a loft across town under a different name," Caitlin said, unfolding the invoice and sliding it across the coffee table.

Grant's face remained impassive. "I'm not sure I understand. What loft?"

Caitlin regarded the father of her dead friend, her instincts flaring with unease. Why was he lying? "The loft James Walker saw you walking out of earlier today. He's there now."

Rick stiffened beside her, as did Grant and Gia in front of her. Caitlin glanced at Rick to signal that James was capable of handling himself if needed. She then took the surveillance photo of Gia and placed that next to the invoice.

"We were also curious why you needed to keep your husband under surveillance."

Grant's face paled, and Gia pulled her hand from beneath her husband's. *Interesting,* Caitlin thought. She glanced at Troy and could tell the action hadn't been missed by the forensic scientist.

Silence stretched, enveloping the seconds, pushing them into a minute, then two. Caitlin's heart beat against her ribs as she waited. She had trusted these people, the parents of the girl she missed every day, who she remembered every day. *What had they done?*

Finally, Grant VanMaar cleared his throat, his gaze on the picture of his wife, binoculars held to her eyes. "You said you have a man at the loft?"

Caitlin leaned forward. "Yes."

Grant looked up, his expression as heavy as his voice. "You should tell him to fall back. There will be nothing to find; I am afraid this has all been a misunderstanding."

"Yes," Gia said quickly, careful not to look at her husband. "Just a misunderstanding. It can easily be explained."

Easily, huh? Caitlin kept her gaze on the couple who suddenly looked very uncomfortable. Then why was there sweat forming on Grant VanMaar's upper lip?

* * * * *

Frustrated, James tore off the makeshift sling and tossed it onto the nearest chair. He hated feeling hampered, and trying to search someone's home with one working arm was the very definition of hampered. He didn't care how badly it hurt, James knew he'd be done in a lot less time if he could use both arms and hands.

As he moved from room to room, however, nothing seemed any different than how they left it after searching the place. Until he opened the hall linen closet. It took James a minute to realize what he was looking at. He had to admit, it was well done, disguised in a way most would miss. So when recognition finally clicked in his mind, only one thought had time to form.

Damn.

Chapter 24

"It was hard after Marci died."

Grant and Gia were no longer the loving couple sitting close together on the couch, shoulders touching, fingers entwined. Several inches now separated them, and Gia shot a venomous look at her husband after he spoke.

"After she was *murdered*, you mean." Gia's words were scathing, her fingers clutching tightly at the hem of the skirt covering her knees.

Caitlin wasn't sure what she had been expecting, but this wasn't it. The VanMaars had always been the perfect couple, generous, kind, loving, standing strong together through Marci's kidnapping and death. What happened to drive them apart?

Grant glanced quickly at his wife, then focused on Caitlin. "There were times when I felt as if I was suffocating after her death. It wasn't anyone's fault," he continued, his gaze sliding to his wife once again. She refused to return his gaze. "I think…I think there were times I just needed…to escape reality."

Caitlin's eyebrows pulled down in confusion. "How did the loft help you do that?"

Sighing, Grant leaned back. "It allowed me to be someone else, even if only for a few hours. Gerald Marcine hadn't lost his daughter. He didn't have a strained relationship with his wife."

"You sound like a child," Gia snapped, twisting the large diamond ring encircling her finger.

Grant's jaw tightened, but he remained silent. Gia, however, tapped the picture with her image. "I thought he was having an affair, all right? I began following him, I wanted to know where he went." Her eyes shifted toward her husband. "I wanted to know who she was."

"There was never another woman," Grant said. It was obvious they had had this conversation many times before. The words were flat, resigned.

After several beats of silence, Gia sighed. "I know."

Grant looked at his wife in surprise.

Gia met his gaze, but her own was unforgiving. "Yet you still had a mistress. A secret, a way to have another life. Without me, without…our *daughter*." She spit the words as if they tasted foul. "How *could* you, Grant? How could you pretend, even for a second, that Marci didn't exist?"

Marital dysfunction? That's what this amounted to? Caitlin didn't know whether to be disappointed or relieved. She felt Rick's gaze and turned to look at him. He raised his eyebrows and shrugged.

Troy stepped forward. "We found a small vial in Donovan's house."

Everyone turned to look at the scientist. Even to Caitlin, his expression was unreadable.

"It contained a microchip. I haven't had time to look closely at it yet. Any thoughts?" Troy kept his eyes on Grant.

Grant didn't hesitate. "It was probably the recording I gave Donovan. It contains the voice of Marci's killer."

Caitlin's heart leaped, her stomach rolling in confusion and uncertainty. Her father had known her kidnapper's identity – *the identity of the man who killed Marci* – and locked it away without telling anyone?

Even Gia was paying attention now. "What?" she whispered. "You know who killed our daughter?"

Holding up a hand, Grant shook his head. "Let me explain; it was unrecognizable. Donovan was trying to clean it up, but the voice was so distorted, it was impossible to make it clean enough to begin looking for a match." He looked away, his fingers tapping on the arm of the couch. "Not that we knew where to start looking, anyway," he added bitterly.

"Are you sure he never got it clean enough to find a match?" Caitlin moved to the edge of the chair. She ran through scenarios in her mind, trying to think why her father would keep the microchip hidden for so long, only to mention it in the recording he made for her, if it was useless.

Grant shrugged. "He hadn't mentioned it in years. I assumed he gave up on it, that it was a dead end."

Desperate to understand, Caitlin sat so far forward she almost fell off the chair. "But – how did you *get* the recording?"

It was as if a vacuum had sucked all sound from the room. Caitlin's eyes darted from person to person, shocked to see every gaze locked on her.

"What?"

"You really don't remember?" Grant's voice came out quiet, sympathetic.

"I-I don't remember a lot of things," Caitlin said, her gaze beseeching as she sought out Troy, then Rick. "What's going on?"

Rick reached out and placed a hand on her knee. "Somehow you managed to hide the small recorder you used for journalism class at school." Rick's eyes searched hers. "The kidnappers never found it, and at one point you got a recording of one of them speaking."

Her mind spinning, Caitlin bit her lower lip. "But...why is it distorted? I don't remember them disguising their voices or doing anything to hide what they sounded like to us."

"The recorder got wet." Troy jumped in, hands still shoved deep into his pockets. He seemed tense, watching her carefully.

"Wet?" Caitlin repeated, confused.

"We don't know how, but the recorder got really wet, probably soaked in water at some point. It was almost impossible to restore as much as we did."

Caitlin looked away from Troy and stared blankly into space. Her brain clicked along furiously, trying to remember even one second of what they were describing, but her memory remained a black void.

A muted buzzing broke through the speculative quiet that ensued, and Caitlin looked over to see Troy fumbling in his pocket for his phone. "Sorry," the scientist muttered. He put the phone to his ear and walked a few steps away.

Though still feeling like she was in a fog, Caitlin looked over at Rick and raised her eyebrows, silently asking if there was anything he wanted to ask or add. Her father's former partner shook his head ever so slightly. Caitlin looked back at Marci's parents. So, it all seemed legit to Rick then. She trusted his instincts and needed to take time to process everything. As she got to her feet, Rick followed suit.

"Caitlin."

Troy walked quickly toward her, his face ashen. "We've got to go."

"What happened?" Caitlin felt her heart rate pick up. Troy rarely seemed so rattled.

Troy's gaze shot to where Grant and Gia remained on the couch. "There was an explosion at the loft. James was inside."

Grant slowly leaned forward, but Gia's jaw fell open. "What? Is someone targeting my husband now?"

Caitlin felt her thoughts spinning out of control. She opened her mouth, but no sound came out. Thankfully, Rick stepped forward. "I'll stay until we know what's going on," he said. He put a hand on Caitlin's arm and squeezed lightly. "Go. I've got this."

Caitlin felt Troy's hand under her elbow, felt him propel her toward the door. Her legs were heavy, her feet unable to keep up, tripping over the Oriental rug in the foyer. Finally her mind unglued enough to ask, "Is he alive?"

"Yes, but I don't know how bad it is."

Troy helped her into the car, then jogged to the driver's side and slid behind the wheel.

"What happened? Was it a gas leak? Or -" she couldn't bring herself to finish the thought.

"Think more on the *or* side," Troy said grimly.

Caitlin looked at him sharply. "A bomb," she breathed. She grabbed onto the door handle as Troy took a corner with tires squealing.

He didn't respond to her statement in the affirmative, but he didn't need to. "So the question begs…is someone after Grant VanMaar?"

"Or did Grant blow it up after finding out someone was on to him?" Troy's expression was hard. "It would be the easiest way to destroy evidence of his second life."

Caitlin shot a look at her friend. "Gia seems to think someone is after her husband."

Troy returned her look quickly, then looked back at the road. "But that wasn't *your* first thought."

She looked out the windshield blindly. "No," Caitlin said quietly. "No, that wasn't my first thought."

Chapter 25

They sprinted through the hospital halls until they came to the Intensive Care unit. "Four-oh-five," Troy said, his eyes scanning the plaques outside the rooms as they hurried past. "Here." He grabbed Caitlin's hand and pulled her inside a room.

Caitlin inhaled sharply when her eyes landed on the burned and bruised body of James Walker. She walked slowly toward the bed, guilt raging within as she took in the patches of burned skin on his face and arms. Machines clicked and hummed, protruding from various parts of his body.

With a feather-light touch, Caitlin rested her hand on the bandages around James' arm. "I'm so sorry," she whispered, feeling as if his wounds were her own fault.

"How bad is it?"

Caitlin turned at the sound of Troy's voice, startled to see a shadow in the corner of the room. The shadow stepped forward, and Charlotte Vance's face became illuminated in the harsh light from the hall.

"Could have been worse," the tech genius said flatly, then shook the bag of chips in her hand before drawing one out and popping it into her mouth.

"Any internal injuries?" Troy asked, turning back to where James lay.

"Not that they can find."

Caitlin stared at Charlie, oddly entranced by the sight of this woman answering questions in a monotone, her jaw moving rapidly as she devoured the chips from the bag. She wanted to look away; the woman irritated her more than she wanted to admit. But Caitlin couldn't seem to tear her eyes from Charlie's face.

"I'm in on this now."

Caitlin blinked. "What?"

Charlie's gaze didn't waver. "I'm part of this investigation now. I'm going to find out who did this to him."

That snapped Caitlin out of it. "No." It was her turn to pull out the monotone.

Charlie popped another chip into her mouth. Caitlin caught the briefest glimpse of a tongue ring.

"I don't think you understand," Charlie finally said. "It's non-negotiable."

"You're right." Caitlin stepped away from James' bed, her temper flaring. "It *is* non-negotiable; the answer is *no*."

Tossing the bag of chips into a trash can by the wall, Charlie kept her eyes on Caitlin as she wiped greasy fingers down her shirt. Caitlin fought hard to keep from shuddering in revulsion.

"I've cloned and hacked my way into every tech and digital thing you own, sweetheart." Charlie's eyes were the coldest blue Caitlin had ever seen. "Just try going somewhere without me knowing about it or hearing it."

Fury whipped through Caitlin, her vision actually turning red for a split second. "You-"

"Aednat!"

Her nickname cracked through the air with shocking force. It stopped Caitlin in her tracks, but she continued to stare at Charlie, her chest heaving.

"Aednat." It came softly this time, and Caitlin tore her gaze from the hacker to look at Troy. His eyes were dark and unreadable. "We need her."

Her eyes slid closed for a brief moment. She knew they did. And she hated Charlie for it; she hated Charlie for a lot of reasons. Caitlin's eyes narrowed. "Why is James so important to you, anyway?"

Charlie put one hand on her hip, head cocked to the side. A smirk lifted the corner of her mouth. "Well, aren't you cute."

"What?" Caitlin blinked rapidly, caught off guard by the statement.

The hacker rubbed at the diamond stud embedded in the side of her nose. Then she leaned forward and whispered, "I think you should be asking yourself why my relationship with Jimmy matters to you."

As Caitlin stood by James' bed, mouth hanging open, yet somehow speechless, Charlotte Vance winked and headed for the door. "See ya around, sweetheart. I have work to do."

* * * * *

Relieved to have him gone, Gia VanMaar pressed her hand to the glass as she watched Rick back down the driveway. *Seventeen years.* This had gone on long enough.

Backing away from the window, Gia straightened her shoulders and smoothed back an errant strand of hair. Turning, she walked down the hall until she reached her husband's study. Resting her hand on the smooth wood surface of the door, Gia closed her eyes briefly, then pushed until the door swung inward.

Grant looked up dully, the glass of bourbon on his desk already three quarters gone. She had loved him once. Years ago. That time had passed, and Gia VanMaar looked at her husband with nothing but contempt and loathing in her gaze.

"You killed our daughter." The words were laced with hatred and derision. Her eyes were hard, brown flints of stone.

At one time, Grant would have been stronger than those words. He would have risen from behind the desk and put his wife in her place. No longer. No longer was Grant VanMaar a force to be reckoned with. He simply stared at Gia, a man adrift.

Gia swept into the room regally, her head held high. Placing the fingertips of each hand on the desk, she leaned forward, composed, uncaring and unfeeling. "You know what you need to do." It was stated with authority. Gia then turned and strode back toward the door, control evident in every line of her body. One hand resting on the doorframe, Grant's wife turned to look at him for the last time. Then she was gone.

Grant VanMaar stared at the empty doorway for several minutes. With a hand lined with age and appearing much older than his fifty-eight years, Grant reached for his bourbon. One deep swallow and the amber liquid was gone, just like his resolve, just like the strength that had seeped from his soul over the last seventeen years.

Staring at the light glinting off the ice in the tumbler, Grant rested his hand on the drawer handle. It seemed his wife was right; it was time. The drawer slid open under his touch, and Grant looked down at the gun resting within its depths.

Chapter 26

Couldn't get more from VanMaars – coming in.

Caitlin glanced down at the text from Rick, then pocketed her phone and walked the hall toward the front entrance of *Nightwatch*. The glass doors had been replaced; Loretta had been busy. Loretta herself sat behind her desk, long red fingernails clacking along the keyboard of her computer.

"What's on your mind, sugar?" Loretta's fingers never stopped, yet Caitlin knew she would pause in a heartbeat if she thought Caitlin needed her full attention.

Shoving away from the wall she leaned against, Caitlin found a bare section of desk and hopped onto it, legs dangling. It instantly brought her back to her childhood and countless hours spent chatting with her father's secretary as she worked.

"Troy's upset with me, but I don't know why." Caitlin found a pen and began twisting it through her fingers.

That got Loretta's attention. The woman who had become a stand-in mother to Caitlin leaned back in her chair and rested her hands on her ample abdomen. Ebony skin glowed under the lights, and Caitlin thought for the millionth time how she wished to be as beautiful as Loretta Lewis. Instead, her body was marred by scars, and her soul by the ugliness of evil.

"That boy adores the ground you walk on. What'd you do to rock his world?"

Caitlin stared blankly at the far wall, fingers still moving over the pen. "I don't know, but I can tell something's off."

"Ever think to ask the man himself?"

Rolling her eyes, Caitlin glanced at Loretta. "Like he'd tell me."

Mama Lewis tilted her head in acquiescence. "Yeah, he's a hard case, that one. Kind of reminds me of someone else." Her look became pointed.

Caitlin ignored the jibe and swung her dangling legs back and forth. "Has he said anything to you?"

"Sugar, do I *look* like I have time to be a mediator between children who can't sit down and have a conversation with each other like adults? Mm-mm. No, ma'am." Loretta's gaze was stern.

Sighing, Caitlin hopped off the desk. She hadn't expected any other answer; it never hurt to try though.

"How's that lumberjack boy doin'?" Loretta asked, swiveling her chair to keep Caitlin in sight.

Caitlin felt a pang in her chest at the thought of James. "Hanging in there," she said, thoughts shifting to wonder how he *really* was doing. Maybe she should call the nurse.

"Mm-hm," Mama Lewis murmured, her gaze direct.

Snapping out of her musings, Caitlin glared at the woman swiveling back and forth in a gentle arc. She knew that tone. "What is that supposed to mean?" she snapped.

Loretta swiveled to face her desk fully, long fingernails once again resting on the keyboard. "Nothin', sugar," she drawled. "Just observin', that's all."

Observing *what*? Asking would be useless, so Caitlin tossed the pen back on the desk and headed back down the hall. Thoughts of James now had her mind locked on the man lying in the hospital.

"Caitlin!"

Jerked out of her thoughts, she glanced to the right as Landon exited his office, sheaf of papers clutched in his hand.

"Hey, Rick filled us in on what happened with James." The firm's financial expert ran his free hand through his hair. "What can we do?"

"Nothing for now." Caitlin shook her head. "I'll keep you posted." She kept walking, feeling Landon's eyes on her as she continued down the hall. Landon meant well, but Caitlin didn't feel like having an in-depth conversation.

Approaching the door leading to James' office, Caitlin walked in without hesitation, then paused once over the threshold. The newest member of *Nightwatch* barely had a chance to settle in; if you could even call it that.

Caitlin felt her chest tighten, and her eyes darted around the small room, trying to ascertain what brought on the feeling of anxiety. The room was well lit, the door open behind her. She was in her father's – no, *her* – firm, with people she trusted.

You trusted Mara Dunn, a small voice whispered in the back of her mind.

Her body went still. She brought James here, and now he had been injured twice. The responsibility and guilt were suffocating.

The contents of the room were sparse. A computer filled one corner of the desk, an open notepad in front of the keyboard. A large box with a few papers scattered across the bottom was near the door where Caitlin stood. The contradiction of the size of the box and its contents made her smile. A guitar stood sentinel in the corner behind the desk. Caitlin stared at it for a moment, not sure what to make of the instrument. Somehow the idea of James holding the guitar and singing didn't jive with the image she had of him.

Propelled forward by a primal need to understand the man who risked his life for her, Caitlin moved behind the desk and lowered herself to the chair. Resting her hands lightly on the desk, she stared at the dark computer screen, then the pen lying near her fingertips. Her mind was blank; she was unsure what to think.

After a moment, Caitlin opened the drawer to her right. She felt like she was snooping, prying into James' life, but Caitlin didn't really expect to find anything. She knew that by how surprised she was when her gaze landed on the three leather bound journals stacked neatly in the drawer. Lifting out the top book, Caitlin flipped it open without hesitation. The need to know the enigmatic man lying in the hospital drove out any qualms.

Slanted writing covered the pages, the words sometimes veering off the lines, then merging back where they belonged, as if James was in a hurry to get his thoughts down before they disappeared. Caitlin squinted, trying to make out the more hurried portions.

The night closed in around him, the fog allowing minimal visibility. He must hurry, but the bullet lodged in his thigh made that impossible. Limping silently from tree to tree, the soldier ignored the blood soaking his uniform, the weakness that threatened to overtake him. They were too close; he couldn't stop now...

Her fingers flattened over the page as Caitlin leaned in closer, her mind immediately taken with the flow of the words, the feeling of desperation and despair seeping from the page. Caitlin was so engrossed that she jumped, the book falling to the floor, when Bruce knocked on the doorframe.

An eyebrow rising, Bruce stepped into the office. "Everything okay?"

Flustered, Caitlin bent to retrieve the book. "Yes," she snapped, her rattled nerves showing in the short answer.

Bruce clearly didn't believe his boss, but didn't pry. "I was able to shake loose some answers on the bomb."

That got her attention. Caitlin leaned back in the chair. "Let's hear it."

"The bomb was homemade, nothing fancy. It also wasn't intended for major damage."

Caitlin thought about that. "The perp didn't want the whole building to go down, just destroy Grant's apartment."

Bruce inclined his head, affirming her statement. "Turpentine was placed next to the bomb. The small explosion was supposed to ignite the solvent, causing a fire that would wipe out any evidence, but allow other residents time to evacuate the building once fire alarms went off."

"But there wasn't a fire."

"No. Something went wrong, and the turpentine never ignited."

"That saved James' life," Caitlin said thoughtfully, her thoughts turning inward.

"That, and the fact that he was able to turn slightly to the right, swinging the door partially between him and the blast. He still ended up across the room, burned, and with a bad concussion, but if he hadn't moved, the blast would have killed him, no question."

Caitlin shuddered at how close James had come to dying – and on her watch. Anger flared hot. "Was this an attack on Grant?"

Bruce hesitated and rubbed the scar between his eyes. Caitlin glanced at him, her eyes narrowing. "What?"

"In my experience, if someone was going after Grant, they wouldn't have cared who got hurt. They would have gone for maximum power, wanting to make sure the job was done."

"What are you saying?" Caitlin asked.

Bruce shrugged. "It sounds more to me like Grant was trying to cover his tracks without hurting anyone."

Caitlin felt her chest constrict. "What would he be hiding?" She had a hard time believing Marci's father would do something that could have resulted in another person's death.

Eyes hard, Bruce folded his thick arms across his chest. "Any man with a secret apartment has *something* to hide. Can't say what that is at the moment."

Feeling sick to her stomach, Caitlin swiveled the chair to the side, suddenly done with the conversation. "Thanks. Let me know if you find anything else."

"Will do, boss." Bruce backed out of the room, leaving the door open as he left.

Running a hand down her face, Caitlin bit her lower lip. What the hell was going on? Was Grant really responsible for blowing up his own loft? Her mind moved backward in time, going over every word spoken during their meeting with Gia and Grant earlier that day.

"You should tell him to fall back…"

Ice formed in Caitlin's veins as she recalled Grant's words after finding out James was searching his loft. Was that his way of warning them? Yet, he didn't say more; if Grant was responsible for the explosion, he allowed the bomb to go off with James inside the loft.

Confused and needing to clear her head, Caitlin grabbed the journal and left James' office. She would go back to the VanMaar's house and have another chat with Grant. But first, she needed to see James and see with her own eyes that he was still breathing.

Chapter 27

Her phone buzzed for the fifth time, but Caitlin ignored it. Both Troy and Rick had sent multiple texts after realizing she wasn't at the firm. Too bad for them; she needed a break from Troy's dour mood and the questions she knew Rick would have. Charlie would be able to ping her phone and know her location in a few seconds anyway, Caitlin thought crudely.

Pressing the pages of the journal flat, Caitlin continued reading aloud, her voice merging with the hums and clicks of the machines surrounding James. His appearance was worse than reality. The prognosis was good; he had a concussion and some burns, but the doctor assured Caitlin he would live. Internal damage was limited to bruising on a few organs. He was in a lot of pain and medicated accordingly, but they expected James to heal quickly enough to be discharged in a few days.

Caitlin had been reading for several minutes, hoping the familiarity of James' own words would bring him some comfort, even in sleep. The stories in James' journal were gripping. As she read, Caitlin realized it was a collection of short stories, all in the genres of thriller and horror. Most people she knew would have been turned off by such gruesome writing, but Caitlin could relate to horror – she had *lived* horror, and therefore drew an odd comfort from reading about someone else's problems, even if they were fictional. It made her feel like she wasn't so alone.

One story had her so engrossed it was several minutes before Caitlin realized James was awake and looking at her. She immediately lowered the journal and leaned forward, a smile lighting her face.

"Hey, stranger. For the record, there are easier and less painful ways to get attention."

James blinked slowly, the bandage on his cheek wrinkling as the corner of his mouth turned up slightly. That effort at a smile did Caitlin's emotions a world of good. Not sure if James could talk well just yet, Caitlin searched for something to say. Her eyes fell on the book in her hands.

"I hope you don't mind that I found these stories in your desk. I had no idea you write in your free time." Caitlin moved closer to the edge of her chair. "These are really good, James. I mean, *really* good."

James moved his fingers over the blanket, his head shaking slightly. Caitlin could tell he was trying to speak, but couldn't get the words out. Gently laying her hand over his, Caitlin stood up, leaning over him. He seemed upset that she had the book.

"Don't try to talk. I'm sorry if I shouldn't have read these; I'll put the journal back when I go to *Nightwatch*."

"No..."

The word was nothing more than an exhale of air, and Caitlin bent even closer, afraid James would hurt himself.

"St...or...ies..."

"I'll put them back, James, I'm sorry. I shouldn't have read them without your permission first."

James began moving his head back and forth over the pillow, clearly agitated. "No."

The word was clearer this time. His mouth moved, but no sound came out. Caitlin put a hand lightly on his shoulder, then realized it was the shoulder with the knife injury when James grimaced.

"Sorry," she muttered, removing her hand. She felt like she had made a mess of things and didn't know how to make James calm down. His blood pressure and heart rate monitor were rising slightly, and Caitlin was afraid he was going to hurt himself.

"Not...stories."

Caitlin frowned. "Okay," she said, not sure what James was getting at. At least his voice sounded stronger the more he tried to talk.

"Night...mares."

"What?" Caitlin narrowed her eyes as she locked gazes with James. He went still, no longer trying to speak, simply holding her gaze. The machines hummed and clicked while Caitlin searched James' eyes, wanting to know what he meant. Then, from one second to the next, she knew.

"These aren't stories." She said it slowly, watching James and his reactions. He blinked slowly. "These are nightmares." James kept his eyes on hers. "*Your* nightmares." James nodded.

Stunned, Caitlin sank back down into the chair. "But...you dreamt all these horrible things?"

James simply looked at her.

Caitlin splayed her fingers over the cover of the journal. She had unknowingly violated James' mind, had crawled into the most private place in his thoughts and set up shop where she didn't belong. She looked at him, not sure how to tell him how sorry she was. Caitlin knew the vulnerability that accompanied nightmares. They laid bare your soul while simultaneously tearing it apart.

The two investigators silently looked at each other, a new understanding between them. Caitlin suddenly didn't feel quite as alone as she used to...she also understood more of why James had offered to help her.

"Hope we're not interrupting."

Caitlin whipped her head toward the door. Troy and Rick stood in the doorway, their expressions unreadable. Troy looked away when Caitlin met his gaze. Glancing back toward James, Caitlin realized his eyes were closed, his breathing deepened in sleep. Standing slowly, she placed James' journal on the table next to his bed; she had no right to his private thoughts and wouldn't be reading it again.

Walking toward the two men, Caitlin faltered as she saw a look in their eyes she had seen only once before. "What happened?" she asked, already resigned to the new horror waiting.

"Grant VanMaar." Rick was motionless as he spoke.

Caitlin looked at him questioningly. "I was just about to go talk to him. What's going on?"

Rick and Troy exchanged glances. This time, Troy delivered the news. "Grant is dead."

* * * * *

"Are they sure it's suicide?" Caitlin adjusted the strap of her seatbelt, still trying to wrap her mind around the fact that Marci's father was dead.

Troy insisted on driving Caitlin's car from the hospital, not trusting driving skills that had already proven dangerous to her own health, much less that of her passengers. Driving while in shock, he stated firmly, would only make her driving worse. Caitlin thought briefly about decking him, then decided she didn't want to waste the time and threw him her keys instead. Rick followed in his truck.

"That's what Gia claimed when she called. The body has already been moved and evidence collected, so there's no need to worry about that."

Caitlin stared out he windshield, not willing to admit how much she had been dreading seeing Grant's lifeless body surrounded by blood.

Troy glanced at her out of the corner of his eye, then turned back to the road. "Gia was insistent that she talk to you."

"Me?" Caitlin tore her gaze from the scenery to stare at Troy in surprise. "Why?"

"She wouldn't say. Just that she had to talk to you. Today."

The car fell silent, each lost in their own thoughts.

"I'm sorry, Aednat."

Caitlin's eyes slid closed at the sound of her nickname on Troy's lips. She hoped whatever had been bothering him had passed; she hated being at odds with him.

"There are just so many things that don't make sense. So many holes and questions."

"It will come to you."

"It's been seventeen years, and I still can't remember half of what happened. Just enough to give me nightmares every night," she said bitterly.

"What is it you think you should remember?" Troy shot her a glance, fingers tightening on the wheel.

"I don't know." Caitlin slammed her hand down on the armrest of the door. "But I obviously didn't remember recording my kidnappers, so who knows what else I've blocked out? I might have the key to this whole mess locked away in my head, Troy, and I can't get it out!"

Reaching over, Troy folded his hand over hers. "Don't do this to yourself, Caitlin. None of this is your fault."

Choosing not to respond with the biting answer rising to her lips, Caitlin fell silent. She knew her irritation wasn't with Troy, and she didn't want to take it out on him now that he was acting normal toward her. A sudden thought occurred to her, and Caitlin shifted in her seat to look at him.

"Where's Charlie?"

Troy's hand slid from hers as he placed it back on the wheel. "Back at the lab, working on the microchip."

"You left her alone in your lab?" Incredulous, Caitlin tried not to show how shocked she felt. Troy never left anyone alone his lab. Not even Caitlin.

Troy shrugged. "Work still needed to be done."

Caitlin stared at his profile, not sure what to think. In a way, she felt betrayed, though that thought made her feel ridiculous. Thankfully, Troy turned into the VanMaar's driveway at that moment.

"This way," Rick said quietly as they entered through the unlocked front door.

Neither Caitlin nor Troy bothered to ask how he knew where to go. Caitlin took a deep breath as she followed Rick, sweat gathering at the back of her neck from the tension. Suddenly, she wasn't sure she could do this. Then, it was too late.

Rick moved to the side, and Caitlin saw Gia standing at the doorway to her husband's study, her features twisted as she stared at a scene Caitlin couldn't see. Not sure what to do, Caitlin finally cleared her throat.

"Caitlin."

Gia's eyes were red, her usually flawless makeup smeared as she held out trembling arms to Caitlin. Without a second thought, Caitlin stepped into the older woman's embrace, suddenly feeling as if she might begin crying as well.

When Gia finally released Caitlin, she wiped at her eyes with a mascara-stained tissue and turned back toward her husband's study. "He loved you."

Caitlin stared at Gia in surprise. "What?"

Gia offered a small smile. "We so enjoyed having you girls here, playing, hearing your laughter…it was so nice to hear the innocence of youth." Her voice ended in a whisper, and Caitlin automatically leaned closer. "He thought of you as another daughter. I know he never told you." Gia placed a hand on Caitlin's arm, her eyes searching those of the younger woman. "We both did. We mourned the loss of you almost as much as we mourned Marci. The loss of that innocence, the loss of laughter in our home."

Gia turned back toward Grant's study, and Caitlin blindly followed her gaze, a lump in her throat constricting the airflow. She remembered coming here as a kid; she *loved* coming here. It was a real home, with both a mother and father, and a warmth lacking in the house she shared with Donovan.

The office she and Marci used to play hide-and-seek in was roped off with yellow crime scene tape. It was the office Caitlin remembered, the late afternoon sun throwing long shadows onto the carpet near the door. Her eyes traveled farther, unwilling, yet drawn to the black fingerprint powder coating all surfaces, the blood sprayed across the back of the leather desk chair and staining the window and drapes behind the desk. Closing her eyes, Caitlin turned her face away.

"Come." Gia gently put pressure on Caitlin's arm, turning her back down the hallway. "I need to ask you something."

Caitlin followed, eager to leave the macabre sight behind her. Rick gently touched her shoulder as the women passed, then he and Troy fell into line behind them. Gia stopped in the same sitting room they met in before, lowering herself to the same couch she sat in earlier.

Caitlin hesitated, not wanting to sit where Grant had only hours ago, but Gia's hand on her arm didn't give her a choice.

Once Caitlin was perched on the edge of the sofa next to her, Gia released the arm of the younger woman and entwined her own fingers together. Caitlin could tell Grant's widow had something specific on her mind, but after clearing her throat twice, Gia still had not spoken.

"We're all friends here, Gia," Rick said suddenly, though he kept his voice at a low level. Marci's mother looked up at her old friend and seemed to gather strength from his direct gaze.

Offering a small smile, Gia turned toward Caitlin. "This may seem an odd request, but it's something I thought of before, but kept putting off. Now, with Grant's…passing, I feel the need to ask."

Her forehead creased in bewilderment, Caitlin studied the woman beside her. "What is it?" She was oddly tense as she wondered if Gia planned to ask something about Marci, or about their captivity. Caitlin didn't think she could handle that, not today.

Gia's fingers twisted together until they appeared bloodless. "Do you remember a day, about two weeks before you were…taken, when you came to stay here, at this house?"

Caitlin frowned as she thought, then nodded. "Dad had to work a case in Florida. He was gone for a week."

Her admission seemed to relax Gia, and the other woman's shoulders lowered slightly as she gave a small smile. "Yes. You missed him a great deal, do you remember?"

Caitlin offered her own sad smile. "Yes."

"So much so that you failed a math test because you couldn't concentrate enough to study."

"I was upset."

"Inconsolable would be a more accurate term," Gia said with a small laugh. "You were always a perfectionist."

Troy and Rick snorted a laugh from the other couch, and Caitlin shot a glare in their direction.

"Caitlin," Gia reached out a hand to touch Caitlin's knee lightly. "I know Marci's death drove a wedge between Grant and me. We…had unresolved issues, and did a lot of fault-finding."

Caitlin shifted, not comfortable with talking about the VanMaar's personal lives.

"Though things were not perfect between us, I still loved him." Tears dampened Gia's gaze, and she blinked rapidly. "There was a necklace he gave me. It's missing now."

Now Caitlin was really confused. "I don't understand."

"Right before your father came back from Florida, I gave that necklace to you, to cheer you up after failing that test."

Caitlin stared at a spot over Gia's shoulder, thinking, trying to remember. Suddenly, her eyes widened. "The gold locket with the diamond in the center." She remembered now; she had never owned anything with a real diamond before, and was so excited to have such a fancy and expensive piece of jewelry.

"Yes. You...you were wearing it the day you and Marci were...taken." Gia took a deep breath. "When they found you," her gaze shifted to Troy, "you weren't wearing it."

Caitlin's hand went to her throat as if she would feel it there. "Are you sure? I admit, I haven't thought about it in years."

Gia patted the younger woman's knee. "I wouldn't expect you to. I wouldn't even be bringing it up if it weren't for Grant's...death." She took a deep breath. "It was just such a special piece of jewelry, and the last gift he ever gave me." Her fingers began twisting together again. "Like I said, we grew apart after Marci's death."

"You would like it back," Caitlin said quietly.

"I'm so sorry to ask-"

"I understand." Caitlin waved her hand in the air to cut off Gia's apology. "I'll look through some things at home. If it's not there, I'll see if there is any possible way to find it. Troy and Rick will help." She looked at the two men, who nodded in the affirmative.

"Thank you, dear. You have no idea how much it would mean to me."

Caitlin leaned over to wrap her arms around Gia in a quick hug, then stood to her feet. "If you need anything else, please let me know."

Gia nodded. "Yes, thank you."

As the three visitors showed themselves out, Rick looked at Caitlin out of the corner of his eye. "If you don't find the necklace at your home or at Donovan's house, how in the world do you expect to find it?"

Caitlin stopped at the passenger side of her car and rested her hand on the roof, knowing Troy still wouldn't let her drive. "I have absolutely no idea."

Chapter 28

Caitlin sank down on the edge of the Daniels' guest room bed, completely exhausted. After stopping home to feed King Tut, she completed a thorough search of both her house and her father's, poking into every nook and cranny she could find. If the locket was anywhere in either residence, it was hidden well enough Caitlin didn't think it would ever be found. To top it off, a phone call revealed that the "amazing" Charlie still hadn't been able to clear up the recording of the kidnapper's voice.

On the upside, Troy had found someone to do a crime scene cleanup of her living room, and there was no sign of Mara Dunn's blood. The hole in the wall from her knife remained, and Caitlin got a headache just thinking about trying to re-drywall and paint. She didn't have to worry about it for a while; Troy still wouldn't let her stay at her own house.

Driving back to the Daniels' house, Rick called and asked if she wanted to meet for a beer. She wasn't in the mood for company, but knew her godfather had to be hurting over Grant's death. Caitlin realized Rick had not only lost his two closest friends, but that the years of friendship between Donovan, Grant, and Rick surpassed that of any other friendship her godfather had.

So Caitlin met Rick for a beer.

Sitting across from each other in Rigg's Tavern, their favorite bar, Caitlin and Rick stared at each other, suddenly at a loss for words. She couldn't ever remember a time when she didn't know what to say to her godfather. Finally Caitlin sighed and said the most clichéd words ever to be said in those situations.

"I'm sorry, Rick."

The corner of Rick's mouth turned up and he nodded, knowing how much she hated saying wasted words. What good did being "sorry" do? It had never helped anyone move past his grief.

"I know, Aednat." Rick lifted his beer to his lips, then regarded the woman across from him. "How are you doing with all of this?"

Tucking a strand of dark hair behind her ear, Caitlin shrugged and picked at the label on the bottle. "I'm a little numb, I think. I don't really know what to feel."

"It's hard when you find out things aren't always as you thought, isn't it?"

Caitlin nodded absently, her mind flashing back to the hostility Gia held toward her husband while he was alive. She had never known their marriage suffered so much.

"Remember when we took you and Marci shooting?" Rick bent his head until he caught Caitlin's gaze. A crooked smile bent his lips. "Your father, me, and Grant, we had these inflated ideas of teaching our girls how to shoot guns."

Caitlin leaned back, a grin parting her lips at the memory. "I had forgotten about that."

Rick snorted. "Then you and Marci outshot us like you had been doing it your whole lives."

"No way. You guys missed those shots on purpose," Caitlin scoffed, though her eyes sparkled as she looked across at her godfather. How long had it been since they had really sat down and talked? Caitlin couldn't remember the last time.

Shrugging, Rick took a swig of beer. "Okay, maybe one or two."

Caitlin laughed outright. "All of them is more like it. Come on, Uncle Ricky," she goaded. "Like you've ever missed a shot at thirty feet."

Widening his eyes innocently, Rick looked across the table. "I've missed at thirty feet. It was when I was six years old, but I've missed."

Caitlin smirked. "Keep gloating, old man, and I may challenge you to another shooting match. You won't win so easily this time."

"No, I don't think I would." Rick's smile faded as he continued to look at her across the table. "Thank you for meeting me, Caitlin."

"Yeah." Caitlin shrugged it off, and started picking at the label on the bottle again. She cleared her throat. "I think I needed this as much as you, I just didn't realize it."

Silence fell for a few minutes as they turned to watch the other patrons of the tavern. Finally, Rick spoke.

"I'm sorry that life didn't turn out the way we had all hoped it would."

Caitlin forced her eyes back to the man she had looked to like a second father her whole life. Lifting a shoulder, she let it fall, not knowing what to say. "You have to live with the hand you're dealt," she said finally.

Rick pushed his empty bottle away and leaned across the table. "We'll make it through."

Lifting her gaze from her bottle, Caitlin gave Rick a lopsided smile. "Family first, right?"

Rick leaned back in his seat, nodding. "That's my girl."

Now, kicking off her shoes, Caitlin flopped back on the bed and stared at the ceiling. Fatigue was moving in quickly, but her mind continued to spin with the things they had learned over the last few days, as well as with a multitude of questions. After several minutes, Caitlin's thoughts landed on James. He was still in the hospital, and she planned to visit him again tomorrow.

Caitlin allowed her tired eyelids to slip down over her eyes. She just needed to rest for a few minutes, then she would work out the next steps of the investigation…

———————

She shivered, the cold, damp air penetrating through skin and down to bone. Caitlin lay on her side, hands tied in front of her, the ever-present blindfold barring her from sight. Caitlin's immediate thought was to lift the blindfold; they had never tied her hands in front of her before. Fear trampled that thought as quickly as it had sprung to life. There were too many times when Caitlin thought she was alone, only to bite back screams of terror as she suddenly realized one of the kidnappers was mere feet away.

She was somewhere new; they must have moved her when she was unconscious, that's the only thing she could think of. But why? And where was Marci? Caitlin couldn't even roll onto her back, the place where she lay was so cramped. The top of her head brushed against wood, her feet doing the same. She couldn't stretch out her legs; her knees were pulled up to her stomach.

Fear churned. Where was Marci? What had they done with her? Caitlin felt nauseous, and realized it felt as if she was swaying gently. The motion didn't stop. Why did it feel as if she was moving? Were they driving her somewhere? It didn't feel like that type of movement.

Something bumped her chin as her body rocked, and Caitlin reached up with fingers almost too numb to feel. Wrapping her heart-shaped locket in her cold hands, Caitlin fought off the urge to cry.

"Crying never got anyone out of a life-threatening situation, Aednat." Her father's voice echoed in her head. "Clear thinking is what will save you if you are in danger."

Caitlin closed her eyes, even though she couldn't see anyway. When had he told her that? He had been describing a case he just closed. It had ended with a woman held hostage by her husband. She was so hysterical, crying and screaming for hours, that her husband finally shot her just to shut her up. Caitlin shivered at the thought. No crying – don't cry, Caitlin ordered herself.

The swaying motion got worse, and suddenly her body lifted an inch off the hard floor, then slammed back down, the wood planks unforgiving. Caitlin cried out, her hands jerking away from her body as she searched for something to hold on to.

The chain of the locket pulled against her neck, then released. She heard it hit the wood, and she ran her fingers over the smooth surface, trying to find it. No, no, no. Not this; don't take this, too. Despite her own previous admonishment, Caitlin felt tears leak beneath her blindfold as she frantically tried to move her body enough to keep searching for the necklace.

Apparently she was making too much noise.

Something opened in front of her and Caitlin felt a rush of frigid, wet air. She cried out and shrank back, but there was nowhere to go as the fist reached in and connected with her temple.

———————

Caitlin jerked awake, yanking the gun from her shoulder holster as she rolled onto her side. She trained the weapon on the closed bedroom door as she blinked sleep from her eyes and brain.

When she finally remembered where she was and that she was safe, Caitlin lowered the gun, her heart still beating double time. What would it be like to wake up without fear, without pointing a gun at an empty doorway? She couldn't remember what that was like.

Sitting up, Caitlin ran a hand through her hair and glanced at the clock on the nightstand. One in the morning. Great. There was no way she would be able to sleep again for a while. Thinking she could find some bourbon or whiskey to help take the edge off and get her body and mind to relax, Caitlin headed toward the kitchen.

She was so busy mulling over the nightmare and the realization that it was about the locket Gia asked about, Caitlin didn't notice Britt sitting at the counter until she was already halfway across the large kitchen.

"Sorry. I didn't see you there."

Britt smiled. "Couldn't sleep either, huh?"

"Nightmare," Caitlin said shortly, hoping Britt wouldn't ask for details.

"Ah. Well, there's cake to ease the soul and coffee to soothe the nerves, decaf of course."

Caitlin looked at the counter and noticed the large round cake in front of Britt for the first time. Troy's wife had one hand wrapped around a coffee mug and the other clutching a fork. She was eating the cake right off the platter.

Laughing, Caitlin nodded. "I'll join you on the cake. Need something stronger than coffee though."

"You know where it is," Britt said as she swiped another fork from the drawer next to her and tossed it on the counter.

Caitlin found the whiskey and poured a generous amount into a glass. Snatching the fork, she settled onto the stool next to Britt and dug into the cake.

"Did you make this today?" Caitlin asked around a mouthful of cream cheese frosting.

Britt licked an errant crumb from her fork and nodded. "Seems I can always tell when I'll need a midnight snack – the baking urge comes on full force."

The women ate in silence for a few minutes. Caitlin sipped the whiskey and felt warmth move through her body. Thunder padded into the room and positioned himself between the two women, his look expectant. When Britt wasn't looking, Caitlin swiped a finger through the frosting and held it down near the big dog's mouth.

"If we manage to refrain from devouring the whole cake, you can take some to James tomorrow."

Caitlin glanced at Britt in surprise. "How did you know I was planning to go?"

"Troy mentioned it."

Emitting an unladylike grunt, Caitlin jabbed her fork at the cake. "No offense, but I don't get your husband lately."

Britt raised an eyebrow, but didn't seem bothered. That was one of the things Caitlin liked about her so much; Britt didn't get offended or annoyed easily. "Wait 'til you get married, sweetheart. You just described marriage in a nutshell."

Caitlin took a sip of whiskey. "Usually we're on the same page about things, even if we don't agree. Does that make sense? Even if I get annoyed with something he does, I know *why* he does it."

"You guys have a special connection that way, always have."

"Well, something in that connection went haywire."

"What do you mean?" Britt put down her fork and wrapped both hands around her coffee cup.

Caitlin shrugged. "I'm not sure how to explain it. He called me 'Cait' the other day, was irritable most of the day too. Then he seemed annoyed when I mentioned visiting the hospital tomorrow. You'd think he'd want to know how James is doing."

Britt winked over her coffee cup as she brought it to her lips. "Hold down the fort, the world is ending."

Blushing, Caitlin shoved a forkful of cake into her mouth. It *had* sounded rather inane as she listed off her complaints. Maybe she was stressed to the point she was imagining things.

"Caitlin, I'm kidding." Britt put her cup on the counter and leaned forward. "Troy has been the only man in your life, besides your father and Rick. Along comes James, and my husband is realizing you might have a connection with someone else."

Stunned, Caitlin carefully put down her fork so she wouldn't drop it. "I don't have a connection with James."

Britt eyed her friend patiently. "Would you consider him a friend?"

"I – haven't really thought about it like that," Caitlin stammered.

"You read by his bedside at the hospital yesterday."

Caitlin glared. "How do you know these things? I'm pretty sure Troy didn't tell you that."

Shrugging, Britt sipped her coffee. "Let's face it, Caitlin. You're not thirteen anymore. You're going to have other relationships besides the one you have with Troy."

"That just sounds weird," Caitlin mumbled, rolling her glass between her palms. "You're making it sound like Troy is jealous."

"He is."

"But Troy and I are just friends! It doesn't make sense."

Bored with the conversation and resigning himself to the realization he wouldn't be getting any more treats, Thunder walked over to the end of the counter and let his large body sprawl across the tiles.

"You and Troy are more than friends, you always have been." Britt put a hand on Caitlin's arm to get the other woman to look at her. "What you have is something most people don't experience in their lifetime. Something between friendship and family, but that runs deeper."

Caitlin was quiet as she eyed the amber liquid between her hands. "Are you jealous?" It came out as a whisper. She wasn't sure why she asked; and wasn't sure she wanted to know the answer.

"No."

Relief swept through Caitlin, and she looked at Britt. "He loves you so much. You should have seen his face when he told me he proposed to you."

A gentle smile curved Britt's lips. "I know he loves me." She slid off her stool and walked her mug to the sink, rinsing it out before putting it in the dishwasher. Turning, she faced Caitlin across the counter. "What *you* need to realize is the true nature of what you have with my husband."

It felt like Britt slapped her. "What?"

Holding up a hand, Britt's eyes held Caitlin to her place with a firm gaze. "Relax. I'm simply saying, again, that you're not thirteen anymore. You aren't a kid swinging her legs while sitting on a stool watching him run samples through the GC-MS."

Caitlin felt like her tongue was glued to the roof of her mouth. She had no idea what to say, or even what Britt was getting at.

"Caitlin, like all relationships, yours and Troy's will shift and change. You're a young woman now, not a child. Now that someone new has come along – whether as a friend or more," Britt said, holding up a hand to stave off Caitlin's arguments, "Troy is trying to figure out where that leaves him."

"But that's ridiculous," Caitlin sputtered. "He's *Troy*, he's my-" She stopped abruptly, not sure how Britt would react to what she had been about to say.

Britt, however, didn't miss much. "He's your everything," she finished quietly.

"But that doesn't mean I'm in love with him-"

Shaking her head, the corner of Britt's mouth turned up. "I'm not saying you are; I understand that what you have with my husband and being in love are their own entities and not necessarily the same. What I'm trying to say is that you guys have a complex relationship. You're family, but more, and also different. You both will figure it out, it just may take some time."

Moving around the counter, Britt stooped to give Thunder a pat on the head before she stopped by the stool where Caitlin perched. "Drink enough whiskey that when you fall asleep it will be dreamless."

She headed for the hallway. "And stop worrying so much," she called over her shoulder.

Caitlin downed the rest of the whiskey in her glass like a shot and let her head fall to the counter as she prayed for oblivion.

Chapter 29

Violent pounding at the door jerked Caitlin out of the oblivion she had desperately longed for and had finally acquired. Her body flailed as her mind tried to remember where she was and what was reality. She swore as she tilted to the side, realizing too late that she had fallen asleep at the counter and was still sitting precariously on the counter stool.

Caitlin hit the floor and let out another bout of profanity as her arm took the brunt of the fall. Deep-throated barking rent the air as Thunder raced into the kitchen, gaze intent upon the door. Pounding feet matched the drumming at the entrance, and Troy raced past Caitlin before realizing his guest was sprawled on the floor at an awkward angle.

"Caitlin! Are you okay?"

The fear Caitlin heard in his voice made her realize Troy didn't realize she had just fallen off a stool; he thought someone had broken in and done her harm.

"I'm fine," she groaned. "My pride is more wounded than anything."

"What?" Troy looked confused as his head ping-ponged between her and the door rattling in its frame at the front of the house. Thunder's ears were back, a growl emanating from deep in his throat.

"Just answer the door," Caitlin snapped, rolling onto her side and staggering to her feet. She looked up toward the stairs to see Britt, feet spread shoulder-width apart, ready to run for Ranae and Rebekah if the hammering at the door turned out to be a threat.

Troy threw the door open before Caitlin fully got her wits about her and could draw her gun as a precaution. She was equally relieved and annoyed to see Charlie stride into the kitchen, laptop in hand. Thunder immediately set about sniffing the newcomer, but when Troy gave a strong pat to his side and a soft command, the Rottweiler gave Charlie some room and stationed himself in the corner.

Massaging her sore arm, Caitlin glared at the woman. "Was that really necessary?" Caitlin snapped, her heart still galloping in her chest.

"Not if any of you would answer your phones," Charlie shot back, setting her computer down on the counter. Her eyes lit up at the sight of the half-eaten cake. Grabbing the fork Caitlin used the night before, the hacker speared a large piece of cake, not seeming to be bothered that the fork obviously had another user before her.

"What's so important at six o'clock in the morning, anyway?" Caitlin said, shuddering as she watched the cake and fork disappear into Charlie's mouth.

"I found your guy." The fork once again impaled the cake.

"What guy?" Troy asked, moving toward the coffee maker. Britt joined him, pulling down mugs from the cupboard.

Charlie rolled her eyes, then fiddled with her nose ring. "The guy on the recording," she mumbled around more cake.

A coffee mug hit the counter harder than intended, and all three turned to stare at the hacker. Caitlin found her voice first. "You got him? You know who kidnapped me?"

Charlie licked the fork and set it down on the counter, then opened the top of her computer. "One of them, anyway. There's a second voice, but it's muted in the background and I haven't had much luck with it yet."

"Who is it?" Caitlin and Troy both crowded around Charlie as she tapped at the keys.

"Meet Josiah Hudson."

A picture flashed up on the screen. Caitlin got an impression of short graying hair and cold black eyes before Charlie began talking again.

"Do you recognize him?" Troy asked Caitlin quietly. She shook her head.

"How did you find him?" Caitlin studied the picture as she waited for Charlie's response.

"So. The fun really started when I began digging. I mean, CIA level digging."

Eyes glued to the woman at the counter, Caitlin waited impatiently. She refused to beg for the information.

"The CIA has a voice database from…I'll say it bluntly – cell phone spying."

"You hacked the CIA?" Caitlin's voice rose an octave on the question.

Charlie looked irritated at the interruption. "Yes. Why wouldn't I?"

Well, I could think of several reasons, Caitlin thought, but didn't have a chance to voice them; Charlie was on a roll.

"I got a hit in the database, which helped me ID him. I was also able to pull up standard info using more conventional methods."

Charlie looked pointedly at Caitlin as if to say *conventional = boring.* Caitlin rolled her eyes.

"You ready for this?" The hacker paused dramatically. "Josiah works for Redman's Slats."

It took a few seconds, but the connection finally sank in. "Where Donovan was killed?" Troy asked as his eyebrows pulled down, his expression dark.

Charlie nodded, and Caitlin sucked in her breath sharply. Her father knew. Somehow he found out who kidnapped his daughter and Marci.

"It gets better."

Caitlin forced her attention back to the hacker. Charlie pulled out a stool and sat down. Britt began placing mugs of steaming coffee on the counter; no one touched them.

"He worked for Grant VanMaar."

"What?" It shot out of Caitlin's mouth before she was conscious of yelling the word. Troy looked as stunned as she felt.

Charlie nodded. "Not recently, but he was on the payroll for Grant's security firm…what was it called?"

"*Shadow Guards*," Caitlin answered flatly.

"Yeah. He was on the payroll for *Guards* for five years before the kidnapping. He suddenly stopped accepting contracts – get this – the week before you and the other girl disappeared." Charlie's gaze landed on Caitlin and stayed there.

"Her name was Marci," Caitlin said coldly, but her mind was moving along rapidly, processing the new information.

"Well, here's the biggest thing."

Troy and Caitlin glanced at each other. There was more? Something bigger than working for Grant VanMaar?

"Josiah's partner for a lot of missions? It was Rick Bannan."

The kitchen tilted around Caitlin, and Troy pushed her in the direction of a stool before she could fall.

"Think clearly, Caitlin. There were a lot of men at that firm, and they worked in various groupings depending on what the mission was. I've talked to Rick about it before, after he left. Charlie isn't saying Rick is part of this."

"Nope," Charlie said as she slapped the top of the computer down. "But your guy Rick can probably help us get Josiah. He'll have the inside info on our man, and Josiah will trust him."

Caitlin took a deep breath. She felt horrible for even thinking Rick would have something to do with her kidnapping and Marci's death. "Let's go. Now. Right now." She was already sliding off the stool.

"Hold on." Troy held his hand out to hold Caitlin in place. Looking at Charlie, he said, "I need the original drive with the recording, and also a drive with the cleaned up recording and everything you found out."

Charlie produced two flash drives, seemingly out of nowhere. "Way ahead of you."

Troy took them, then immediately handed them off to Britt across the counter. His wife nodded. "You guys go. I know what to do with these."

Charlie slid off her stool. "I'm headed back to my place. I want to nail the second bastard's voice."

"Thanks, Charlie." Troy and Caitlin headed for the stairs to get dressed.

Chapter 30

Caitlin let Troy drive this time; she had a call to make.

"Hi, Gia. I hate to bother you so early in the morning, but I need you to go through Grant's files and find an address for Josiah Hudson, one of the old employees of the firm."

There was a beat of silence, then, "Does this have something to do with Marci's killer? Is this man involved?" Gia VanMaar was an intelligent woman, and her ability to read between the lines had come in handy over the years.

Caitlin glanced at Troy as he drove, debating what to tell Gia. Finally, she opted for the truth. "Yes."

"You have evidence that will nail this bastard?" Gia's voice was hard.

"We do. Troy has it where it can't be tampered with." Caitlin paused. She ached for Marci's mother and wanted to give the woman hope. "The second kidnapper's voice is on the recording as well. We haven't been able to identify him yet, but we will. I can explain more later, but I need that address right now."

"I'll call back in a few minutes."

The call disconnected and Caitlin leaned her head back on her seat. "Did you call Rick to let him know we're coming?" she asked Troy.

"Yeah. He said he'll be waiting."

* * * * *

Gia paced the length of Grant's office, studiously ignoring the bloodstains yet to be cleaned. The folder bearing Josiah Hudson's name tapped against her palm as she thought.

Finally, she flipped open the folder and pulled her phone from her pocket.

* * * * *

"I worked several missions with Josiah." Rick ran a hand over his short silver hair, clearly agitated. "Are you sure you have the right guy?"

Troy nodded firmly. "Yes. Charlie wouldn't have given us the intel if she wasn't positive."

"When was your last contract with him?" Caitlin shifted her weight, feeling antsy. She couldn't bear to sit, but she couldn't stand still either.

Rick looked at his goddaughter, still in shock. "A few weeks before your disappearance," he finally said. "We provided protection for an executive of a pipeline company in Kenya. He had to be on site, but there had been several attempts at blowing up the line in the previous weeks. He was concerned for his safety – and rightly so."

"What can you tell us about Hudson?" Troy asked. "Anything that can help us approach him would be helpful."

"You won't be going without me." Rick's tone left no room for argument. "If he's responsible for this, I'm going to bring him down."

Caitlin wasn't about to argue; they could use all the back up they could find. "What would make him desperate enough to kidnap Marci? You've mentioned several times yourself that Grant treated his contractors well. Why risk kidnapping Marci for a ransom?"

Rick looked to the side, then sighed. "I should have seen this."

"What?" Troy leaned forward. "Seen what?"

"He gambled. Heavily. He wasn't very good at it, either. I knew he had gotten himself into some trouble, but I didn't realize it was that bad. I never imagined he would kidnap a young girl; during the whole situation, he never even occurred to me as a suspect."

"Does he know who I am? Would he recognize me?" Caitlin wanted to know what she was walking into when they approached Hudson.

Rick regarded his goddaughter for several seconds. "Yeah, if he's responsible for this, then he knows," he said finally. "He'd want to be prepared in case this day came. We can't let him see you coming."

* * * * *

"531 Vernon Street. In the Division suburbs."

"Thanks, Gia. I owe you one."

Gia disconnected the call with Caitlin, then calmly closed the file and leaned back in her chair. Looking at the mantle, she began watching the clock. When ten minutes had passed, she flipped the folder open for the last time and dialed the number listed on the second line of the form.

"They're coming for you. They can't know I tipped you off; you'll have to fight your way out."

Gia ended the call and then opened the small notebook she had placed by the file folder containing Josiah Hudson's contract with *Shadow Guards*. Running her manicured nail down the page, she stopped at the name she was looking for, then tapped a number into her phone with a manicured nail.

Chapter 31

Troy parked a block from Josiah Hudson's house. The car was silent as he, Caitlin, and Rick took in the small home with peeling paint. The yard had been mowed recently, but weeds choked the overgrown garden at the side of the house.

"Let me lead," Rick said. "He'll recognize me and won't feel threatened. Caitlin, you go around back. It'll take him longer to realize you're here if he doesn't see you right away. Weapons ready?"

Troy and Caitlin nodded, though Troy didn't look too happy about packing heat. Rick hadn't given him a choice; carry a gun or stay home.

"Don't draw them unless we have to. Let him think this is a social visit."

Caitlin raised an eyebrow. "This early in the morning? You really think he's going to assume it's social?"

"No, but I can hope. Just be ready."

They got out of the car, closing the doors quietly. Caitlin peeled off quickly, jogging through the neighbor's yard and hopping the short hedge to enter Hudson's backyard. Her heart hammered against her ribs as she glanced over to see Rick and Troy heading toward the front of the house, trying to appear casual. Feeling vulnerable and defenseless,

Caitlin drew her gun even though she had agreed not to; the weight of the weapon instantly calmed her nerves.

Creeping toward the back entrance to the house, Caitlin had just pressed her back to the peeling paint of the rear wall when she heard the muted sound of Rick's knock at the front door. Caitlin shifted her feet, getting ready. If Hudson spooked, he'd head for the back door first.

The walls were thin, and Caitlin could hear movement inside the house. Erratic movements, not those of someone casually walking to the door to meet a friend. Mentally, she swore. Rick knocked again, harder this time.

She was wrong about Hudson heading for the back door.

He decided to start shooting first.

* * * * *

Britt slid cereal bowls across the counter to her girls, grinning as Ranae tried balancing a Cheerio on her nose before digging in with her spoon. Rebekah blindly reached for her own bowl, eyes glued to the book in her other hand.

"I'm going to toss a load of laundry in, loves," Britt said as she began walking toward the back of the house. "I'll be back in a sec."

"Wash my princess shirt!" Ranae yelled, the words garbled around her mouthful of Cheerios.

"Always," Britt called over her shoulder. *Every. Day.* If she could squeeze her youngest into any other shirt, it was a miracle.

"And my soccer shorts, Mom!" Rebekah said without lifting her nose from her book.

Right. Britt had forgotten about soccer practice that afternoon.

Walking into the mudroom, she opened the washer and tossed in the detergent packet. Then she searched the laundry baskets piled at her feet for the beloved princess shirt and soccer shorts; heaven forbid she forget to put those in first.

When she was confident the shirt and shorts were being shaken and tumbled amidst the other clothes in the washer, Britt headed back toward the kitchen. As she passed the large picture window in the living room, a gleam of sunlight flashing off an object caused her to pause.

The Daniels' front lawn was several acres, the dirt driveway cutting a path through green grass before winding through trees bordering the edge of the property and joining with the road. There was a slight curve at the tree line, and it was there Britt had seen the flash. Squinting, she studied the area. When recognition came, the first feeling to accompany it was confusion.

Why would anyone park that far from the house instead of driving up to the garage? It was a long walk when other options were available. On the heels of that thought came another, more ominous in nature.

Maybe it was the events of the morning and Charlie's announcement about finding the kidnapper. Maybe it was the flash drives Troy had given her to tuck away in their safe spot. Or maybe it was simply from living with a forensic scientist and hearing stories that would keep even the most unruffled person awake at night. Whatever it was, Britt felt every hair on her arms stand on end, and she began to run.

"Rebekah! Ranae! Get out of the kitchen! Now!" Britt was screaming, something she had never done with her children before, and it rattled them. She heard a bowl crash to the floor, splitting into three pieces and splashing milk and Cheerios across the floor as her girls turned on their stools to stare at their mother in confusion and fear.

"Come with me – now!" She grabbed their arms, pulling them with her because they weren't moving fast enough, dear God, they weren't moving fast enough.

Britt could hear them now, she could see the shadows as men moved to surround the house. How had she not noticed them before? How could she have been so blind?

"Mommy, you're hurting me!" Ranae sobbed, trying to pull from her mother's grasp.

They'll kill them, they'll kill them, they won't care that they're children. Britt's thoughts scattered, her daughter's cries threatening to undo her. Taking a deep breath, Britt knew if she didn't pull it together, her girls were as good as dead.

Pulling Ranae and Rebekah to a halt just short of the stairs, she knelt down in front of them. Ranae was crying, but Rebekah looked too shocked for tears. Her babies, her life. Britt speared Rebekah with a firm look.

"I need you to take Ranae to the hiding place, okay? Just like we practiced. You have to do it *now*."

Her oldest daughter nodded jerkily.

"You don't open the door for anyone. *No one*, do you understand?"

Again, Rebekah nodded. Britt put Ranae's small hand in Rebekah's slightly larger hand. "I love you both. Remember Mommy loves you. Go!"

Rebekah and Ranae sprinted for the of back the house and the stairs leading into the basement. *Not enough time, there's not enough time*, Britt thought, racing back toward the kitchen. She had to stall them, she had to give the girls enough time to get there.

Britt's mind raced as she thought about her options. Her phone was still upstairs in her room, as was the gun Troy kept in a lockbox at the top of their closet. As Britt heard the first sounds of splintering doors, she ran full out for the kitchen.

Chapter 32

The echo of the gunshots still rang in the air when Caitlin heard yelling from Troy and Rick at the front. *Time to improvise,* Caitlin thought, and ripped open the back door. Gun held ready, she entered the house – and was met with the sight of Josiah Hudson running toward her down a narrow hall.

Looking over his shoulder, Hudson squeezed off two more rounds, which were returned by the men at the front of his house. Caitlin ducked instinctively, and that was her mistake. As she straightened back up, she was looking down the barrel of Josiah's gun.

"Who are you?" The former Marine was extremely pissed off.

Caitlin didn't lower her weapon, hoping it wouldn't get her killed. "We just need to talk to you, Josiah. That's all."

"I don't talk," Hudson grated. In the next instant, his look became more intense. "Wait a-"

If possible, his looked became even darker, and Caitlin squeezed the trigger a split second before Hudson pulled his. Caitlin's bullet hit Josiah high in the right shoulder, causing him to stagger backward. She felt the heat from his bullet as it whizzed by her cheek.

"Drop it, Hudson! The next one won't be so friendly."

"I knew we shouldn't have let you live," Josiah spat.

His words created a vacuum in her chest, and Caitlin found it hard to breathe. Despite the bullet in Hudson's shoulder, his gun rose steadily until it was aimed directly between her eyes. Suddenly, a shot echoed down the hall, and Josiah Hudson's body jerked violently. His eyes went wide in shock, then the gun in his grasp fell to the floor, his body following its path.

Without Hudson's body blocking her view, Caitlin stared into the eyes of Rick, gun still in firing position, and Troy, standing behind him. Relief warred with dismay.

"We needed him," she whispered. "We needed him." She fell to her knees, searching for a pulse. Hudson's heart, however, had stopped pumping blood and was still. Caitlin sagged in defeat. They couldn't question a dead man. As she stared at Hudson's still features, Caitlin felt the answers she longed for slipping away.

"He would have killed you." Rick said, the words steel. "I couldn't let that happen."

Before Caitlin could reply, a ringing cell phone startled them all. Troy's hands slapped at his pockets. "Sorry. Sorry." He pulled his phone from his pocket, then frowned as he looked at the name on the screen. He punched the speaker button. "Charlie?"

"You can't ask me how I know this." Charlie's words were rushed, her tone as close to panicked as Caitlin imagined she could sound.

"What's goi-"

"They're at your house, Troy. I'm sorry. I tried calling Britt, but she's not picking up. The police are on their way, but they won't make it, Troy, I'm sorry." Charlie was crying now, and all three in the hallway stared in shock at the phone in Troy's hand. "I'm sorry, they won't make it-"

The phone hit the floor as Troy turned and ran for the door.

* * * * *

The large butcher knife barely cleared the wood block when the patio door shattered into a million pieces by an explosive device Britt didn't even know existed. She turned to see a man dressed in dark clothing, his face hidden by a black mask, enter her home.

Terror had no room as fury at the danger to her home, to her *children*, took hold. The man was mere feet away and didn't stand a chance. Britt crossed the distance in one heartbeat of time and swung, sinking the knife deep into the man's neck.

Britt Daniels had never taken a life before – had never expected the need would arise where she would be forced to – and as the knife shuddered in her hand as it entered the intruder's neck, Britt felt a mix of emotions. Relief, terror, self-loathing, and a hatred like she had never known before for the man whose blood now stained her face and clothing, warred within.

There was no time to analyze emotions, however, as Britt yanked the knife free and turned to see another man entering her kitchen. Her grip on the knife shifted, her fingers tightening on the handle now slick with blood. How *dare* he? How dare they violate her home, her sanctuary, her *children*? Britt glared at the man, her chin tilted at a downward angle, almost as if she was looking down her nose at an insignificant bug.

The man's gun was raised, but Britt ignored the weapon, choosing instead to look into his eyes. As if from a distance, she heard more glass breaking, more doors being shattered, her home being invaded. *I just have to get through you,* she silently communicated to the man before her, *and then I'll move on to the next.*

It was going to hurt, Britt had no illusions about that. Sifting back in her memory to only moments earlier, the young mother called up images of her daughter's faces; scared, tear-stricken, uncertain. Britt's teeth ground together as she raised the blood-smeared knife in front of her. *You won't get them,* she vowed.

She was numb as she ran forward, the butcher knife held ready. The first bullet simply made her feel like she ran into a wall. Britt slowed, looked down, saw the blood spreading on her abdomen. A warning shot. *Keep moving,* Britt admonished her mind and body. *Before the pain starts…keep moving!*

The look on the shooter's face was priceless as Britt uttered a guttural yell and once again began running across the tiled kitchen floor.

His gun exploded for the second time, and that one hurt. It was fire in her chest and lungs, and Britt staggered. She forced one foot forward, then the other; it was then her legs betrayed her.

Her knees hit the tiled floor hard, but Britt didn't feel any pain except for the fire in her chest. *No, he can't win. He can't be left to find my girls...* She was on her knees, looking up at the intruder through a red-tinted gaze. It was only by pure stubbornness Britt managed to keep hold of the knife.

Warm metal pressed to her forehead, and Britt lowered her gaze just enough...just enough. Yes, there. She leaned forward, half falling, half in control. The barrel of the gun pressed into her forehead, then slipped upward, the man too surprised to react. Bringing her other hand to bear with the first on the knife handle, Britt lunged, driving the wide blade into the man's inner thigh and jerking downward, carving a large gash through skin and muscle – and severing his femoral artery.

Warm blood washed over her hands, and Britt finally relinquished the knife. Bellowing in pain and rage, he dropped, the floor shaking with his weight. She fell with him, her head coming to rest on his shin, the coarse fabric of his pants and the leather of his boot cutting into her cheek.

Britt's eyes were open, her breathing shallow, as she felt the last quiver of life leave the man beneath her. She had that, at least. She had outlasted him.

It was getting harder to breathe, and it was so cold. Her fingers scratched at the tile, dragging through thick blood as she fought to draw breath. A pair of boots came into view, then moved on, assuming her dead.

Don't let them get our babies, Troy...don't let them get our babies...don't let them get our ba –

Chapter 33

Against their better judgment, they let Troy drive. They didn't have much choice; Troy reached the car first, already had the keys, and Caitlin and Rick barely managed to get the doors closed before Troy punched the accelerator.

Rick was in the backseat, talking with Charlie on the phone. "The police are there, Troy," he relayed to the passengers in the front.

Caitlin glanced at Troy, who remained stoic. She could see the muscle jumping in his jaw, and his hands gripped the wheel so hard it looked like he planned to rip it from the steering column. Caitlin knew better than to say it would be all right; there was no one who hated that trite saying more than she did. Instead, she checked one more time to make sure there was a bullet in the chamber of the .45 in her hand and that the safety was off.

They roared up the driveway at a speed that kicked up dust, and Troy had to slam on the breaks to avoid hitting the police and emergency vehicles that usually weren't in his yard. Caitlin and Rick grabbed for hand holds as the car fishtailed wildly, then ground to a halt.

The wind had picked up since earlier that morning, and as they ran toward the house, Caitlin could feel heaviness in the air indicating rain wasn't far away. There was confusion and yelling as the police officers on the perimeter saw the drawn weapons, and it took a lot of fast talking and flashing of credentials before things calmed down. Even then, they were reluctant to let the three into the house.

"You can let me through, or my fist can rearrange your nose placement – your choice." Troy's fists were already clenched, and the officer must have valued his nose right where it was, because he let them pass.

The biggest crowd was in the kitchen, easily visible from the front entryway. Caitlin felt her chest tighten as she caught sight of the shattered patio door. Another step in, and a man dressed in black came into view. He was laying among the shards of glass, dead, a large gash in his neck. Blood was everywhere.

Panic began to set in, and she could tell Troy felt the same as he yelled Britt's name. The police officers and EMTs in the kitchen fell silent as they turned to look at the three newcomers. Caitlin moaned as she caught a glimpse of blond curls on the tile between booted feet. She reached out for Troy, not wanting him to enter the kitchen and see what they had both feared since the call from Charlie. Her hand met empty air, Troy already rushing forward, shoving people out of his way.

"No, Britt, no," Troy moaned. He fell to his knees beside his motionless wife.

Caitlin felt weighted down as she fought to move forward through air that suddenly seemed too thick. She ignored Rick as he called her name, concern in his voice.

Britt's eyes were open, sightless as she stared past those gathered around her body. She was lying on her side, her shirt drenched in blood. A butcher knife lay nearby, as did another black-clad man. His mask had been pulled up to reveal his face. Caitlin didn't know him.

Troy gently moved a curl near Britt's temple, his shoulders shaking with quiet sobs. His fingers moved over her cheek, her lips. "I'm sorry," he whispered. "I'm so sorry, Britt."

A police officer began talking, but the words sounded as if they were traveling down a long tunnel, and Caitlin couldn't grasp them, couldn't make them stay long enough for her to understand.

"She fought hard...shot twice...took out two..."

The girls. *Where were the girls?*

Caitlin whipped her head toward the nearest officer. "Were there two girls in the house? Did you find Ranae and Rebekah?" She had to force the words out, fear of the police officer's answer choking her.

"Children?" the officer looked confused, and glanced at the others gathered around him. "We swept the house and didn't find any children."

Hearing Caitlin's question, Troy stood. "You didn't find them anywhere?" His gaze was direct, his voice hard. Finding his children was what mattered now.

The officers and EMTs in the kitchen all looked at each other, their heads shaking. Caitlin and Troy looked at each other, then turned and began running toward the back of the house.

"Guys? What's going on?"

Rick was hot on their heels, his questions ignored as Troy and Caitlin raced down the stairs to the basement, skipping the last four and jumping to the carpet below. Making a beeline for the back wall, Troy moved a heavy book from a shelf and pressed the button hidden in the wood paneling.

"What the-" Rick's mouth fell open as a large portion of the wall swung out toward them, revealing a vault-like door behind the wood.

Caitlin immediately began pounding on the door with her fist, gun forgotten in her other hand. "Rebekah! Ranae! Are you in there? It's Auntie Caitlin, open the door!"

"They won't open the door for anyone," Troy mumbled, his fingers moving over the keypad embedded near the handle of the two-foot thick door. His hand shook so much, his fingers slipped, and Troy swore as he was forced to enter the code a second time. "Come on, come on," he muttered. Only someone who knew him as well as Caitlin did would hear the thread of panic lacing the words.

A beep sounded, and Troy jerked on the handle even though the door was already swinging open on hydraulic hinges. When there was a space large enough to squeeze through, Troy slid inside, Caitlin and Rick right behind him.

"Daddy!"

At the sound of the girls' cries, Caitlin felt her legs give out, and she sank to her knees on the carpet. Rick's hand settled on her shoulder, and they both watched as Troy also fell to his knees, wrapping both girls in his arms as tightly as he could.

The girls were alive. They were scared and crying, but they were alive.

Caitlin felt her gun slip from her fingers and land with a soft thud on the carpet next to her knee. Tears welled hot in her eyes, and a sob tore from her throat.

Oh, Britt, your girls are alive. They're safe. Can you hear me, Britt? They're safe. I'm so sorry...

Rebekah looked over her father's shoulder, her face streaked with tears. There was no way for her to know yet that her mother lay lifeless in the kitchen, no way for her to know how hard her mother fought to keep them safe. Yet, as Caitlin stared into the eyes of the young girl only feet away, she watched the innocence slowly fade from her gaze.

Chapter 34

It wasn't a simple home invasion gone wrong; that became apparent simply by looking around the Daniels' home. The house had been torn apart. Nothing had been left unturned, no mattress or cushion had been spared a slashing knife. While the devastation was hard to stomach, it told them two things.

One, Britt's killers were looking for something. Two, there had been more intruders than the two Britt managed to kill in the kitchen. Some of Britt's attackers were still at large, running free, and Troy, Caitlin, and Rick were pissed as hell.

Adding insult to injury, Thunder was found dead at the edge of the rear property line with two bullets in his broad chest; it explained why Britt never heard him bark a warning. It would later be realized that the perps used a silencer to kill the dog, also making it harder for Britt to realize something was wrong until it was too late.

The police detectives assigned the case grilled the three hard. Did they know what the perps were looking for? Did they get what they were looking for? Why would they kill Britt instead of just tying her and the kids up? How did Britt know to hide the girls in the safe room?

Caitlin, Troy, and Rick played dumb, acting bewildered that someone would break into the Daniels' home, that anyone would choose to kill Britt when they could have just wounded her. In the back of their minds, the flash drives in the hidden safe in the panic room haunted them.

Charlotte Vance proved to be more valuable to *Nightwatch* than they could have anticipated. While crime scene investigators collected samples, Charlie suddenly appeared with her own collection kit and got to work right beside them. When asked to see her credentials, Charlie whipped them out confidently and rattled off a name of a CSI who was supposedly sick. She was filling in; Mark Weatherly sent her. Where she snagged a CSI jacket and badge, and knew names of people that would make the other CSIs nod knowingly, Caitlin, Troy, and Rick didn't know – and they didn't ask.

When the panic room was empty, Charlie slipped in and, with the code Troy gave her, removed the flash drives from the safe. She also made a copy of the house and property security cameras, making sure the originals were there for the police to collect for their own investigation.

After Britt's body was removed and on the way to the morgue, Caitlin turned around to find her former partner staring at her. Derek's face was expressionless, and Caitlin wondered how long he had been there. It was unlikely he had been one of the first responders to the scene as the Daniels' property was outside the city limits.

"What are you doing here, Derek?"

"Trying to figure out what's going on with you." Derek's voice was as flat as his expression. "And why people are dying all around you."

Caitlin glared at the man she had worked side-by-side with and trusted with her life only weeks before. He had delivered a low blow, and Derek knew it; he had the good grace to look somewhat ashamed. As much as she wanted to turn and walk away, Caitlin stopped herself as she caught a glimpse of the blood-smeared kitchen behind Derek. Though she hated to admit it, she needed him.

"I need you to keep me in the loop on what they find," Caitlin said, nodding in the direction of the crime scene techs.

"Can't."

Caitlin stared at her partner in disbelief. "What?"

"Chief would fire me, you know that."

Taking a step closer so no one else could hear, she ground out, "We are talking about *Britt*, Derek. I have to know what's going on."

Derek stood silent, his eyes searching hers. After a few seconds, his gaze clouded over again, and the line of his jaw hardened. "So you can track down the people who did this and kill them?" He shook his head. "I may not be able to stop you from whatever path of destruction you're on, but I can stop you from committing murder."

Fury engulfed her, and Caitlin drew herself up to her full height, which still only brought her to the level of Derek's chin. Even so, she speared him with the look she reserved for the wife-beaters and child molesters she had arrested while working the beat. She saw Derek swallow hard.

"Do I need to remind you of an incident two years ago? About six months after you got married?"

Derek's face went white. "You wouldn't."

Watch me, Caitlin thought venomously. "I kept your little one-night stand with that court reporter a secret while your new bride picked out curtains for your baby's nursery. Somehow I don't think the passage of time will dull the pain and fury of betrayal if she finds out about that night."

Anger moved in, darkening Derek's gaze, and he took a step closer to Caitlin. She stood her ground, glaring up at him with a matching level of wrath. This was for Britt; she wouldn't back down.

"You do this, and I'm done watching your back."

"Just get me the information, Derek."

A muscle near his eye twitched, then Derek pushed past his former partner and walked out the door. Caitlin watched him go, feeling the loss of what had been a good friendship. Derek would never forgive her for blackmailing him; he wasn't the forgiving type.

"What was that about?" Rick had come up beside her.

Caitlin took a deep breath. "Nothing," she said, turning to face him. "Where are Troy and the girls?"

"I took them out the back so the girls wouldn't see the kitchen. Troy is checking into a hotel for the night."

Caitlin gave a short nod. Britt's parents lived close by, but they wouldn't be in any shape to have people in their home after hearing the news of their only child's death. Troy wouldn't want to be around anyone right now anyway; she knew that, but it was still hard to keep her place and not race after him to help with the girls.

Her cell phone rang, and Caitlin pulled it from her pocket. "Yeah, Mama." It was a testament to how shaken she was that she reverted to the firm's nickname for Loretta instead of using her first name.

"I have that uppity young blond thing Troy brought in here earlier at my desk saying she needs to put something in my boy's lab."

Caitlin couldn't help a small smile from curving her lips at Loretta's exasperated tone and possessiveness of Troy's lab; she knew his rules about letting people in when he wasn't there, and she abided by those rules religiously.

"Her name is Charlie," Caitlin admonished gently, thoroughly surprised she was coming to the other woman's defense. Seeing her collect evidence to help find Britt's killers had made her look at Charlie in a new way. Sort of. A little bit.

"I don't care if she's Joan of Arc, sugar. She's about to meet Mr. Heckler and Mr. Koch if she keeps bein' so dang pushy."

Caitlin bit her lower lip to keep from laughing. She could imagine it now – Mama Lewis and Charlie glaring at each other across the front lobby desk, Loretta's wide girth blocking the way into the firm.

"Let her in, Mama," Caitlin said quietly. "And keep Bruce and Landon there for a while, okay? Rick will be heading in to brief everyone."

Loretta's voice softened. "Count on it, sugar. You take care of yourself."

Caitlin ended the call and turned to look at the thinning crowd in the kitchen. Rick's hand rested on her shoulder, and Caitlin touched it lightly before moving away and walking out the door without looking back.

Chapter 35

The next two weeks were hell.

Charlie was nowhere to be seen as she hunkered down in her fortress and set to work analyzing all data she could get her hands on as they searched for Britt's killers. There were no boundaries in Charlie's mind, and Caitlin didn't try to hold her back, not even after finding out she had hacked her way into the Healey PD's computers. Who knew if Derek would hold to their agreement and pass along intel on the case; Caitlin was more than willing to have Charlie be her backup in case Derek fell through.

The only time Charlie surfaced was to call and check on James. Caitlin knew this because she had set up camp, so to speak, at the soldier's bedside. James had been discharged from the hospital, and Caitlin helped him settle back into the small house he owned several miles outside of town. Though recovering quickly and gaining strength, James wasn't talkative; which was right up Caitlin's alley. Hours were spent in silence, playing chess or checkers on a portable board Caitlin hauled to the house, or staring into space as they both pretended to watch the endless talk shows and sitcoms flashing across the television mounted to the wall.

Caitlin found solace in James' quiet presence, especially after the revelation that they were both haunted by nightmares. They had become a team, Caitlin reaching out to touch his arm as James fought his demons, thrashing under the covers of his bed or under the blanket on the couch. James likewise would reach out to rest a hand on either Caitlin's arm or leg as the demons came for her while dozing in the chair beside him.

There were times when Caitlin ventured from James' home, though she always returned emotionally beaten and bruised. Troy refused to take her calls, or return her voicemail messages since Britt's death. He had shut her out, and Caitlin floundered. Never in the past seventeen years had she felt so alone. Troy had been her constant, her rock, yet now was a stranger, and Caitlin felt panic deep in her soul. That terror drove her to his lab over and over again, though the silence was more telling than when Troy turned away from her for the first time.

Britt's funeral was a different kind of hell, one Caitlin endured only for Troy and the girls. Caitlin grieved for the loss of innocence in Rebekah and Ranae's eyes as much as she mourned the loss of the woman who had become one of her closest friends. As the girls watched their mother's body lowered into the ground, forever taken from them, Caitlin longed to will innocence back into their small souls, but she had none to part with herself. How could she provide what she did not have? So she hugged the girls hard, wrapping them close to her chest until they grew restless and squirmed away, futilely imagining that her arms could protect them from the evil touching their lives.

Caitlin desperately wanted to help Troy as well, to provide comfort like he had so many times for her. She waited for hours as friends and family expressed their condolences, crying on Troy's shoulder as he stood silent and haggard. Caitlin wanted to push them away and wrap her arms around him, and finally it was her turn.

Caitlin looked deeply into Troy's eyes as she stepped forward. The pain she saw there threatened to drown her as deeply as it was drowning him. Caitlin was helpless to relieve his suffering, and she loathed that powerlessness with everything in her. She reached out to place her hand on Troy's cheek, to offer what little comfort she might have…and watched, stunned, as he turned from her and walked away, leaving her hand suspended in the air between them.

That night, Caitlin went home to feed King Tut, then stood in her kitchen, arms dangling by her sides, as the tears came. The people who kidnapped her so many years ago had taken everything from her. Happiness, confidence, her best friend, her father, Britt…and now Troy.

Rage slammed through her, and Caitlin picked up the glass of water she poured for herself upon returning home. Her fingers tightened on the glass, and suddenly she screamed, throwing it against the nearest wall. The glass shattered, the pieces scattering across the floor. Water sprayed the wall, forming arcs until the fluid lost its momentum and dripped straight down. It summed up her life.

Caitlin grabbed the bowl of dried fruit and chocolate, hurling it toward the same wall. Crystal broke apart, releasing the chocolate and fruit to join the glass shards on the floor. Her hands shaking, Caitlin ran to the cupboard, ripping open the door and grabbing glass after glass, hurling them one by one across the room until her hand came down on bare wood. There were no more.

Chest heaving, Caitlin grabbed the hair at her temples, the air in her chest squeezing until it locked there, suffocating her. They had taken everything, and she hated them. They had taken *everything*.

Don't let them.

The voice was so clear, the words so succinct, Caitlin whirled, her heart pounding as she searched for the person who had managed to break through her locks and into her home. But there was no one there. Gripping the counter, Caitlin closed her eyes. The words raced through her mind again and again. *Don't let them, don't let them, don't let them…*

Her eyes snapped open, the stubbornness and determination that earned her the name Aednat burning in her chest. They had taken everything from her. She wouldn't let them take Troy. She couldn't; she would never survive.

Chapter 36

Troy finally relinquished care of Rebekah and Ranae to Britt's parents. They had been begging, and Caitlin understood. They no longer had their daughter, and the girls were a part of Britt that continued living. They needed to be near their grandchildren; and Troy needed time to track down his wife's killers.

Caitlin now divided her time between James' home and Troy's lab. She would sit on a stool, booted feet on the counter, watching Troy pour over the evidence samples Charlie had locked in his office. The flash drives were locked in a safe deposit box Charlie set up the day after Britt's murder.

Troy never spoke to Caitlin, but he didn't tell her to leave. So Caitlin stayed, watching, silent, because that is what Troy would do for her. He would be there, even if Caitlin didn't want him to be. The silence, however, cut as deeply as a knife, and finally James had had enough.

"You're not going to lose him."

Startled, Caitlin looked up from the chessboard where she was getting a sound beating. "What?"

The board shifted, pieces toppling over as James shoved his chair away from the small table by the living room window. "Hey," Caitlin protested. "I was winning that game, you know."

"Hardly." James crossed his arms, only wincing slightly at the tug to the healing knife wound in his shoulder. "You need to liven up a little. And by that, I mean you need to live. You're the walking dead around here, and that's saying something."

Stung, Caitlin sat back in her chair and glared at the man who somehow had managed to become one of her closest friends in the last few weeks. She certainly wouldn't have put up with just anyone saying that. "I don't know what you mean," she mumbled, but had to look away, unable to meet James' eyes. He was beginning to know her too well.

"Come on, Cait. You've been walking around the last couple weeks like the very soul has been ripped from your body. I know you loved Britt, but I also know that you didn't love her *that* much."

"Excuse me?" Caitlin's hackles rose, his words pricking at her conscience, mostly because they were true.

James regarded her with the most direct look she had ever received from him. "He loves you."

The words were like a balm and a torch combined. Caitlin felt her eyes immediately fill with tears, and she swallowed hard to keep them back. "I'm not so sure anymore."

"He loves you." The words were patient, but firm.

"Like a sister, sure."

"No."

Caitlin felt her breathing constrict, and her chest heaved as she stared at the man across the table. "He loved Britt."

James nodded. "Yes."

"She was his world."

"She was *part* of his world."

"Don't you dare," Caitlin whispered, anger causing the words to shake. "Don't you dare sully his reputation, his name, by suggesting-"

"By suggesting what? That Troy loves two women?"

Caitlin gripped the arms of the chair, her knuckles white. "He was *faithful* to her, he would *never-*"

"You're missing the point."

Confused, Caitlin fell silent. Her chest hurt, and for a moment she wondered if she was having a heart attack. Then she remembered heart attacks in women didn't cause chest pain. Pity. She would give just about anything to keel over and free herself from James and the look he bestowed upon her. He was looking into one of the darkest parts of her heart, her soul, and it terrified her.

"What's the point?" Caitlin finally whispered when James remained silent.

"He doesn't even know it, Caitlin."

Relief and hurt flooded her body in tandem, and Caitlin sank back against her chair, suddenly exhausted. Rubbing her forehead with her fingertips, Caitlin peeked at James from under her palm. "I don't get it."

Shifting on the chair, James looked like he was preparing to give a lecture. "The point, Caitlin, is that there is something between you and Troy that has yet to be defined. Love is the only word close enough to describe it, but even that isn't right."

Caitlin looked down, once again in the Daniels' kitchen with Britt as Troy's wife tried to help Caitlin understand what no one seemed able to comprehend, herself included.

"It makes the rest of us jealous, you know."

Caitlin snapped her gaze up to James' face, uncertain what he meant. People were jealous of this mysterious, unexplainable bond she and Troy shared, or was James implying something else? Something more personal? She was afraid to ask.

Sighing, James fiddled with one of the chess pieces. "Caitlin, you didn't do anything wrong."

"He loved her. So much." Caitlin felt her voice catch. "His face…it just lit up when she was around, even when he just *talked* about her. It doesn't make sense…"

James waited, then spoke when Caitlin remained silent. "You've been asking yourself why Troy has been shutting you out."

It was a statement, not a question, and Caitlin felt as if her most private thoughts had been violated; she never told James she felt Troy was carving her out of his life.

"He feels guilty, Caitlin."

Her eyes slid closed painfully.

"Troy may not recognize the feeling for what it is, but that is the truth. He loved Britt, but his subconscious is telling him the truth about you now that she's gone. He doesn't know how to handle that, what to do with it. Troy feels like he betrayed his wife, but he isn't sure *why*. Buried deep down in his mind, he knows it has to do with you, and that's why he's shutting you out."

Caitlin leaned forward and let her face fall into her hands. She felt sick, and she breathed deeply, trying to contain the war of emotions running through her.

"Troy also feels guilty because he is the one who put the flash drives in the safe."

This was something Caitlin could fight. She pulled her hands down and shook her head vehemently. "No. He gave them to Britt, and she put them in the panic room safe."

James looked at Caitlin closely. "But Troy brought them into his home." He paused. "Britt knew what he wanted her to do with them, didn't she?"

Caitlin narrowed her eyes. "You think it's his fault too, don't you?"

"No, I'm explaining why Troy feels like he betrayed his family. He led the lion to his doorstep and opened the door. Any man would blame himself, even if there was no way to know what would happen because of his actions."

Pushing herself up from the chair, Caitlin walked to the window and crossed her arms over her chest. "I don't want to talk about this anymore."

Mercifully, James fell silent for several seconds. Then, "Just out of curiosity, how *do* you feel about Troy?"

Caitlin bypassed irritated and ran headlong into full-blown pissed. "Excuse me?" she asked, turning slowly on her heel to glare at James. "I don't believe that is any of your business."

James shrugged. His nonchalance grated on her raw nerves. "It's not. But maybe I'd like to know my chances."

Her eyes snapped wide, and Caitlin whirled back to face the window, her eyes closing as she fought to remain calm. This was *not* a conversation she could handle right now.

Caitlin jumped as her phone buzzed in her pocket. She had never been so glad to get a phone call as she was at that moment. "Hello?"

"It's Derek."

Caitlin turned back toward the room, her eyes coming back to James. He didn't look at all bothered by her reaction to his previous statement, but looked remarkably more interested when Caitlin mouthed Derek's name. She walked back toward the table and put the phone on the chessboard as she hit the speaker button.

"Go ahead." Caitlin kept her tone professional, hoping Derek would follow suit. He did.

"The two men Brittany Daniels killed were identified as Tate Fetterman and Hank Willard. They're part of Ghetto 40."

"Ghetto what?"

"It's a gang on the south end of town. They've been lying low, but seems like they want to start making a name for themselves. Ghetto 40 has come up more than once in the last month."

Caitlin was quiet for a minute, the tranquil silence of James' house a direct contrast to her racing thoughts. "How are we just now finding out their identities? It's been almost two weeks. If they're part of a gang, Fetterman and Willard would have records."

"You'd think so. They both had juvie records, but the courts ordered them wiped clean when they turned eighteen. Whatever Fetterman and Willard have been up to the last few years, they managed to keep out of the eye of the law."

"Who's the leader of Ghetto 40?"

"Local thug, Kobe Tyce. Got a rap sheet a mile long."

"You question him?"

"Can't find him."

Caitlin and James exchanged a glance. James mouthed Charlie's name. She nodded.

"So he's gone underground," Caitlin said, her mind already thinking of what needed to happen next.

"Tyce was smart, using at least two guys without records, but now they're dead. He had to know we'd eventually find the connection."

"Thanks, Derek. Keep me posted." Caitlin ended the call and immediately punched in Charlie's number, keeping it on speaker.

"What?"

Caitlin rolled her eyes. Charlotte Vance would never win any congeniality contests, that was a given. "Hey, Charlie. I just heard from my contact at the Healey PD. Seems the attempt to get the flash drives was orchestrated by a local gang, Ghetto 40."

"I knew that days ago."

A crunching sound came through the speaker, and Caitlin could imagine the huge bag of Cheetos being demolished by the hacker as they spoke. She looked at James, who grinned and shrugged.

"I'm guessing you also know the name of the gang leader."

"Tyce."

Caitlin felt a flare of irritation that Charlie hadn't bothered to keep her apprised of her findings. "Planning on telling me any of this?" she snapped.

Another Cheeto bit the dust. "The info doesn't do much good until I find Tyce, does it?"

Caitlin briefly closed her eyes, exhaling loudly. "*Can* you find him?"

"You all think I'm a miracle worker; it doesn't work like that."

"It's how you were sold to me," Caitlin raised her eyebrows at James who suddenly adopted a look she guessed was supposed to resemble angelic.

"Give me a few hours." The phone went dead.

"I'm going with you."

"What?" Caitlin's mind was still on the conversation with Charlie, and she had no idea what James was talking about.

"I'm going with you."

Caitlin eyed the large man in the chair across the table. "Just guessing here, but I'm pretty sure you aren't fully healed and shouldn't be chasing thugs around town."

"I'm not sitting in this house while you go on a suicide mission against an entire south side gang."

"James-"

"You let me go with you, or I tie you to that chair so you can't run out of here on your own. Those are your choices."

Caitlin stared at James for several seconds. She knew him well enough now to know he wasn't bluffing. She sighed. "Fine."

A few minutes later, Caitlin headed for her car parked at the curb. "Are you sure you're up for this?" Though James was walking normally and without any obvious pain, his face was a shade of white she hadn't seen before.

"Yes, and don't ask me again."

Caitlin threw up her hands in surrender and unlocked the Challenger. "Fine. Get in."

Their seatbelts just clicked into place when her cell phone rang. "It's Charlie." Caitlin hit speaker and put the phone between them on the console. "You got him?"

"I'm offended you had to ask, and I'm seriously thinking about not telling you now."

"Charlie…" Caitlin said warningly.

"7436 Harlem Drive. It's an abandoned strip club five miles east of Highpointe River."

"Got it."

"I'll meet you there. You'll need me."

"Why?" Caitlin turned the key in the ignition, already putting the car in gear.

"These guys didn't do this for fun, they were hired. If I can get my hands on Tyce's tech I can find out who."

"Sounds good to me."

"You want me to call the cops for backup?"

Caitlin didn't have to think about that one. "No."

"Good answer. I might eventually start to like you."

The phone went dead. Caitlin was beginning to think Charlie just liked hanging up on her. Shaking her head, Caitlin put the car into gear. "You remembered your gun, right?" she asked James.

The soldier's eyes held heat as he stared at her wordlessly. "I like you, so I'm going to pretend you didn't just insult me," James finally said, his voice a low growl.

"I was just making sure – never mind." Caitlin punched the accelerator and the car lurched forward.

"Is this going to be just the two of us?"

"No, we're stopping to get Troy. You may need to call him; he won't answer if it's me."

James glanced at her. "Do you really think it's a good idea to let him come?"

Caitlin turned the wheel, entering the flow of traffic. "No, but he'll never forgive me if I don't."

Thankfully, James didn't argue, just pulled out his phone. Caitlin felt the adrenaline start flowing. Kobe Tyce had no idea what he was in for.

Chapter 37

Troy was in his office near the front of the lab when Caitlin and James walked in. Hanging his lab coat on a hook behind the door, Troy nodded in greeting. "I need to grab my gun."

Caitlin and James exchanged a look, but remained silent as Troy went around his desk and extracted a nickel-plated .45 pistol Caitlin hadn't seen before. She bit the inside of her cheek so she wouldn't ask when he had gotten the weapon.

"It's good to see you on your feet." This was directed at James as Troy slid the .45 into a holster at his belt. The holster was also new. He didn't look at Caitlin once. "Let's get this bastard." Troy headed for the door.

Stepping in his path, Caitlin blocked Troy's way to the door, then nodded toward James. "We'll meet you at the car."

James nodded and left the lab. Caitlin looked at her best friend, hardening her gaze. "We need to talk."

"No, we need to get to Kobe Tyce before he disappears again." A muscle jumped in Troy's jaw, and Caitlin could tell he was trying to keep his temper.

"I need to know you're not going into this trigger-happy," Caitlin stated bluntly, hands on her hips.

Troy's hands clenched at his side. "I'm not planning to go easy on the man who ordered my wife killed, if that's what you mean. It would be in your best interest not to ask me to."

Caitlin blinked, the words small daggers. She fought not to reveal how much they hurt. "In case you haven't noticed," she said, lowering her voice and keeping it calm with an effort, "Rick has been a little trigger-happy himself lately. That's why he's not here. If I think for one second I need to worry about you too, you're not going."

Stepping closer, Troy's gaze turned ice cold. "You can't stop me from going."

Caitlin shook like a leaf inside, but managed to keep up the calm façade on the outside. "I'll shoot you in the leg if I have to."

It was Troy's turn to blink. "You wouldn't."

Caitlin hardened her own gaze. "Try me."

Troy took a step back in disbelief, and Caitlin softened her expression. "Look. I know you blame me for what happened to Britt." Her voice faltered, and Caitlin cleared her throat. "I blame myself. She would still be alive if it wasn't for me and what happened seventeen years ago."

"Caitlin-"

She held up a visibly shaking hand. She had to finish this. "Kobe Tyce could have the answers we need to crack this wide open. You can't go in there with guns blazing. And-" Caitlin took a deep breath "-I need to know you have my back."

Troy stood mere inches from her, and Caitlin could see his shirt moving over his chest with each breath. She hurt for him, for all he had lost; she hurt for herself, and for all she had lost.

"I need to know I can trust you, Troy." Caitlin felt the air in her throat catch, and fought the tears that wanted to spring free. "When this is over, you can hate me, you can walk away from me-" that thought nearly paralyzed her, but she pushed on "-but I need to know you've got my back right now. I need to know I can trust you."

For the first time in days, Caitlin saw emotion in Troy's eyes, in his face. He looked betrayed, devastated that she would even think to ask that question. But life had dealt them both an unfair hand, and they couldn't change the past, or take back actions and words spoken in the midst of grief.

"Aednat."

That name on his tongue almost brought Caitlin to her knees. Relief coursed through her at the softly spoken word. Troy's hand rose slowly as if to touch her face, and she willed him to; she needed to know, to really know, that he forgave her. Halfway across the space between them, Troy's hand fell back to his side.

"I will always have your back," he whispered, then moved around her and out the door.

Chapter 38

They found Charlie parked three blocks from the old strip club and pulled up behind her in Caitlin's car. As they unbuckled, Troy held out his hand. Three cylindrical objects lay in his palm. Silencers. Caitlin stared at them, then at Troy.

"Just in case. Tyce can't hear us coming."

Caitlin knew he was right, but she didn't like how much easier it would be for Troy to make the decision to pull the trigger, knowing his gun wouldn't be heard. Rationality won, and she reached for the silencers, passing one back to James. Troy was right. If Tyce heard them coming, he could bolt or launch a counter attack. Better to be safe than sorry.

"Tyce's men will be at each entry point, as well as directly outside the room he's in." James' military training came to the fore. "Some may be with him as well. Stealth is optimal since we don't know how many we're up against."

No argument from the front seat.

"I'll take the lead, then Troy, Charlie, with Caitlin bringing up the rear. There will be no arguing or second-guessing; we have each others' backs and work as a team."

Caitlin and Troy glanced at each other, then looked away, nodding.

"Let's move."

Charlie joined them on the sidewalk, laptop backpack straps firmly over her shoulders. Her eyebrows rose at the sight of the silenced weapons. "Do I get one of those?"

"No. You get to walk between Troy and Caitlin and keep your mouth shut."

"Jimmy," Charlie pouted, "when have I ever talked out of turn?"

All three nailed her with a glare, and Charlie put her hands up in surrender. "Fine. Just know that if a gun is pointed at me, I'm definitely using you guys as a human shield. I'm too valuable to die."

Caitlin rolled her eyes and moved to stand behind the hacker. James and Troy fell into place and they began walking, guns held ready.

The front entrance to the strip club was unmanned. Dark tubes that used to flash bright neon shapes and words to lure customers rested against windows darkened with adhesive film so no one could look into the building. James put a hand on the door handle and gave a gentle tug, then shook his head. Locked. Troy moved forward, pulling his locking-picking kit from his pocket. Seconds later, he stepped back into line.

James pulled on the door, which opened silently. Oiled hinges on an abandoned building. If they had any doubt the building was in use by Tyce, they disappeared. At the back of the group, Caitlin watched James disappear inside, followed by Troy. As Charlie neared the entrance, they heard two short whistles of air. *Pfft. Pfft.*

Coming through the door, Caitlin saw two men armed with assault rifles lying dead on the floor, round bullet holes decorating their foreheads. She quickly panned the rest of the room, but saw no one. Using hand signals, James directed them toward a stairway at the back of the main room.

They threaded their way through tables laden with stacked, dusty chairs. The bar on their left had seen better days, the mirrored shelves behind the counter cracked in several places. Discarded napkins and beer bottles littered the floor. A large elevated stage with two poles at either end stood silent, the burgundy curtain at the back laden with grime from years of neglect.

Making it to the stairs with no further casualties, the group began their ascent. James crept around corners, sighting down the barrel of his gun as the staircase wound around several times. Caitlin scanned the room behind and below them as they worked their way up, making sure no one suddenly appeared.

As they continued to climb to the upper level, they could hear music with a heavy bass beat. It grew louder as the group ascended, and Caitlin was thankful for it; Kobe Tyce just made their job easier. He wouldn't be able to hear them coming with that racket banging against the walls of the club. James reached the top and there were two more whispered gunshots.

Merging into a wide hallway, they eyed several closed doors, but when they remained shut they focused on the one surrounded by two dead thugs with assault rifles. James grabbed one guard and dragged him away from the door, Troy doing the same with the other. Caitlin continued to sweep the entire area, making sure the stairway stayed empty and the other doors remained closed.

The music was deafening even with the door closed. Tyce wasn't going to last long as leader of Ghetto 40 if he didn't exercise more caution. Caitlin kept eyes on James now as he moved into position outside the door. He motioned for Caitlin to break ranks and stand directly behind him. Troy now brought up the rear.

Three, two, one.

James swept the door wide and immediately moved to the left, Caitlin to the right. The room was empty of occupants except for a man behind a renovated bar. His back was to them as he made a drink and moved to the beat of the music. Using the few seconds before they ruined Kobe Tyce's day, Caitlin glanced around and noticed the room had been completely renovated and updated. This was Tyce's home base.

Moving forward quickly, they kept their guns held up and ready. It was more than likely Tyce had a gun on him, and one behind the bar. Caitlin felt her heart beat against her ribs, and glanced quickly at Troy who had moved up beside her. She prayed he would keep his cool. Charlie walked over to a digital control panel on the wall and punched a button. The silence was almost as deafening as the music had been as it cut off mid-lyric. Kobe Tyce spun around, glass of whiskey in one hand, the other reaching for the gun in his front waistband.

"I wouldn't." James spoke with a coldness Caitlin hadn't heard from him before.

Clenching his jaw, Tyce slowly raised both hands, still holding onto the whiskey. Tattoos crept out from the sleeves and neck of his t-shirt, covering all visible skin except for his face. Multiple earrings graced both ears, and his dark hair was cut close to his scalp. An intimidating figure, but they had the upper hand.

"Move." James gestured with his gun, and Tyce stepped out from behind the bar and walked to a black leather chair a few feet away. "Gun on the table."

Tyce obeyed, keeping his fingers on the butt of the weapon as he set it on the glass table and slid it across. He then set the whiskey on the table and put both hands on his knees where they would be visible.

"My turn." Kobe Tyce's voice was a hoarse grating sound. "Who are you?" His eyes darted toward Charlie as she sat down in a chair at a table across the room. Sliding her computer out of her backpack, she set it down next to the one already resting on the table, then began hooking them together with cables. "What's she doin'?"

"Who ordered the hit on the Daniels' home?" James stood on the other side of the table, directly in front of Tyce. Caitlin was more than happy to let him take the lead.

The gang leader smirked. "Don't know what you mean, man. My hands are clean." He brushed his palms together and held them up as if to show them that, indeed, his hands were free of dirt and blood.

Caitlin could hear Charlie's fingers moving over the keyboards behind them. She wondered how long this would take. Troy's eyes had grown darker with each passing second, and with Tyce's flippant tone, she could see her friend's jaw lock with fury. Before she could say anything, Troy moved to stand behind Tyce's chair and pressed the barrel of the silencer against the man's neck.

Kobe Tyce stiffened, his own eyes darkening dangerously. "What's the meaning of this, homie? I didn't have nothin' to do with that hit."

James' lips stretched in a slow smile. "Then how'd you know about it, *homie*? That's not something that would pop up on your radar unless you were involved."

Tyce's jaw moved from side to side in irritation as he realized his mistake.

Caitlin spoke for the first time. "We know you were involved, Kobe. We want to know who hired your gang."

Tyce shrugged. "I'll just keep repeatin' myself. Don't know what you're talkin' about." He grimaced as Troy shoved the barrel of his weapon harder into his neck. "Easy, man."

James shifted, lowering his weapon slightly. "Now, see, this is where it really sucks for you. I'm a fairly nice guy. So's this lady to my right. This guy though," he gestured with his gun toward Troy, "you killed his wife and went after his daughters."

It took exactly two seconds for that to register in Tyce's brain, and Caitlin could see sweat begin to form at the gang leader's temples. He shifted in his seat. His eyes flickered toward Charlie as she got up from the computers and walked toward the bar. She hunkered down and looked at the contents of the shelves. Seconds later, she popped back up with a bag of chips in her hand. Charlie ripped it open as she walked back toward the table.

Attempting to get them to believe he wasn't fazed, Tyce jerked his chin in her direction. "Hey, sweetheart. Yeah, help yourself. You can pay me later, if you know what I mean." He smirked.

Charlie ignored him and continued typing, pausing every few seconds to grab another chip. James, Caitlin, and Troy remained quiet, staring at the man in the chair. The silence stretched on, and Tyce began shifting in his chair, eyes darting from person to person. His eyes followed Charlie as she stood and approached the group.

"Phone." She held out her hand to Tyce, who suddenly looked mutinous.

"Give the lady your phone, Kobe," James said, the quiet words holding a promise of menace.

Lips pressed together tightly, Tyce dug into his sagging pants pocket and pulled out a cell phone. Charlie took it without a word and walked back to her table.

"Who hired you, Kobe?" Caitlin tried again, hoping the gang leader would give them the answer they needed; Troy was making her uncomfortable. His finger shook on the trigger, and Caitlin could tell he was nearing the limit of his patience.

"I ain't a snitch."

"No, but you'll be dead if my friend Troy here gets tired of waiting." James' gaze didn't falter as he stared at the man in front of him.

Tyce seemed to be thinking that over when Charlie spoke up from the other side of the room. "Got it." She started pulling cables and repacking her bag, sliding the gang leader's computer and phone into a separate compartment in the backpack.

"Hey!" Tyce protested. "You can't take my stuff."

"We can do whatever we want." James gave a warning glare to Troy, then turned and walked over to Charlie. She handed him a handful of black zip ties, then shouldered her bag. James walked back over to Tyce. "Get on the floor."

"What?" Troy's gun jabbed into his neck, and Tyce slid to his knees on the floor in front of his chair. "This ain't right, man." His gaze was hot as he glared up at James.

"Lay down on your stomach, parallel to the chair." James didn't seem bothered by Tyce's anger, separating zip ties as casually as if he was counting out money or tickets to a ball game.

Realizing what James was thinking, Caitlin holstered her weapon and grabbed the edge of the table, dragging it over a few feet so that Tyce was now lying between the chair and the table. "Arms out."

Tyce shifted his glare to Caitlin as she took two zip ties from James. Kneeling on the carpet, she quickly tied Tyce's wrist to the table leg, using both ties for extra insurance. James repeated the action with Tyce's other wrist, binding it to the chair leg, then moved to the gang leader's feet, forcing them together and then zip tying his ankles together.

"Caitlin, call your friend at the PD and tell him we've got a present for him. All wrapped up and ready to go." James grinned down at the back of Tyce's head.

"You're gonna regret this, man," Tyce hissed, straining to keep his face off the carpet.

"Nah. Cause if I find out you're still in action, I'm going to send my boy Troy over here again. And this time I won't keep a leash on him." James walked toward Charlie.

Caitlin watched Troy, who still had his gun aimed at the back of Tyce's head. She walked up beside him. "We're done here, Troy," she said quietly.

"He deserves to die." Troy's voice shook with rage, his finger now steady on the trigger.

"Yes. But I know you, and killing him in cold blood is something you will regret. Pulling that trigger goes against everything you stand for." Caitlin hardened her tone, desperate to get through to him. James was a soldier, trained to destroy the enemy; she knew taking out Tyce's men wouldn't make him lose sleep. To James, it was a necessary evil to ensure the group was safe and reached Tyce to attain the information needed. Troy, however…

Several seconds ticked by. James and Charlie watched from across the room. It didn't appear either one would interfere if Troy decided to play God with Kobe Tyce's life.

After what seemed an eternity, Troy lowered the gun and Caitlin felt the air in her lungs release in a long exhale. "Come on." She put her hand gently on Troy's arm and began tugging him away from Tyce.

"Yeah, that's what I thought, man," Kobe jeered from the floor. "You don't have what it takes. Your wife was tougher than you-"

Caitlin didn't have time to react before Troy brought his gun up and fired one shot. Tyce screamed as the bullet ripped into the back of his thigh. Blood immediately began pooling beneath the gang leader's leg.

"Try not to bleed out before the cops get here." Troy turned and walked quickly toward the door.

James and Charlie followed, and Caitlin took one last look at Tyce. She debated putting a matching bullet in his other thigh, but figured from the man's hysterical screams that he was in enough pain. She pulled her phone from her pocket as she joined the others at the top of the stairs.

"Derek. We've got Kobe Tyce for you." Caitlin rattled off the address of the strip club.

"You found him?" Derek sounded stunned.

"Charlie did." Caitlin glanced at the hacker as they descended the stairs. Charlie lifted a potato chip in salute, then tossed it in her mouth.

"Who's Charlie? We may need to hire this guy."

"It's a woman. And you can't have her; she's ours."

Caitlin ended the call and gave Charlie a lift of her shoulder in a small shrug when the other woman smirked in her direction. She wondered if she should have told Derek to call an ambulance for Tyce.

Nah.

They moved down the stairs quickly, though continued to keep their eyes peeled for any surprises. Caitlin had to give Troy credit; he waited until they were back on the street before pouncing on Charlie.

"Who hired Tyce?"

The hacker tossed another chip in her mouth. Around the crunching, she answered, bringing Caitlin's world crashing down around her once again.

"Gia VanMaar."

Chapter 39

Caitlin felt the sidewalk tilt under her feet. Charlie was wrong; she had made a mistake. "I'm sorry, I thought you said Gia VanMaar hired Kobe Tyce to search Troy's house for the flash drives." Her throat was dry, and she had to force the words out. Troy looked equally stunned. James' forehead creased, and he seemed deep in thought.

"I did say Gia VanMaar."

"You're wrong." Caitlin blurted the words, her mind spinning. The implications of what Charlie was saying…it meant Gia was involved in her own daughter's kidnapping and death.

"Listen, honey," Charlie snapped, the bag of chips in her hand suddenly forgotten. "I'm a lot of things, but wrong isn't one of them. Never have been, don't plan to start now. I'll hit the road if you accuse me again."

"Easy, Char," James said soothingly, holding a hand out toward the hacker.

"But-" Caitlin and Troy exchange a long look. For the first time all day, Troy didn't look angry; he was just as confused as Caitlin. "That doesn't make any sense."

"You didn't ask me to make sense," Charlie said, digging into the chip bag. "You asked me to find out who hired Ghetto 40."

Caitlin opened her mouth to ask more, but James put his hand on her shoulder. "Look, we need to figure this out, but not here. Unless you'd like to explain the four dead guys in the strip club." He raised an eyebrow in her direction.

"No," Caitlin mumbled, hearing the sirens in the distance for the first time. "Let's get out of here."

They all piled back into their vehicles after instructing Charlie to follow them to *Nightwatch*. Caitlin could make the drive to the firm in her sleep, and she was glad for the familiarity; she felt like her head was encased in fog, her thoughts muddled.

Troy ducked into the lab for a minute, coming back with a file folder in his hand. Caitlin went in search of the rest of her team, but according to Mama Lewis, Bryce and Landon were on site, fulfilling previous contracts. Rick was in his office.

"You find that SOB who killed my girl?" Loretta asked, the lines of her face hard and unforgiving.

"Working on it," Caitlin said, dropping a quick kiss on top of Loretta's headscarf.

"You nail him to the wall, you hear me, sugar?" Mama Lewis yelled as Caitlin headed back down the hall.

Rick was the one Caitlin really needed anyway; he knew Gia VanMaar the best, and right now they needed all the help they could get. Caitlin knew he'd be pissed they left him off the Kobe Tyce roundup, but he'd get over it.

Sticking her head in his office, Caitlin saw Rick at his desk. Stepping inside, she closed the door and – speaking quickly, but quietly – filled Rick in on what happened just a little while ago. She was right; he was pissed as hell that she'd gone off to find Tyce without him, but he also understood the bigger picture and followed her down the hall.

Once everyone had settled into the conference room, Caitlin took a deep breath and speared Charlie with a look. "Okay, Charlie, fill us in on what you found at the club."

The hacker already had her computer open. "Lots of goodies, that's what I found." Charlie reached absently for the bag of chips, then seemed to realize she had eaten them all; Caitlin had watched her throw the bag away as they entered *Nightwatch*. Sighing in exasperation, Charlie continued.

"Mr. Tyce needed to learn a few more things about the art of misdirection and concealment. Gia was better, but still made a couple of mistakes." Charlie looked around the table. Everyone was giving her their full attention, except Troy. Caitlin could tell he was listening, but he had also flipped open the file folder from the lab and was scanning the contents. "I won't explain the entire trail, but let's just say I found an extra offshore account in Ms. VanMaar's name."

"Extra?" Caitlin asked blankly.

"Sure, hon. Did you really think Grant VanMaar got as rich as he did playing by the rules? If I dig hard enough, I'll find some money skeletons in his closet, trust me."

Caitlin felt sick to her stomach. She had trusted these people, they were Marci's *parents*. For all intents and purposes, they had been *her* parents as well after Emelia died and Donovan checked out for half her life.

"Anyway, looks like Gia set up an account and kept separate records from her husband. To be clear, he had set up the previous accounts, with Gia's name added to all of them. Except one." Charlie paused to let that sink in.

Troy finally looked up from the papers, and James gave a low whistle. "Skeletons, skeletons, skeletons," James murmured.

Rick tapped his fingers on the table. "So you're saying both Grant and Gia had one separate offshore account that neither knew about?"

"Yup. Both with a few million waiting patiently, accruing interest. And one payment of fifty thousand dollars was wired from Gia's account to an account set up by Kobe Tyce. He used an alias, of course, but a flimsy one; I cut through that in less than a minute. The transaction was made hours after Britt Daniels was killed."

Rick rubbed a hand over his face. Caitlin glanced over at her godfather, noting he looked resigned, but accepting of the information. She still had a hard time wrapping her mind around it all. Troy's face was void of expression.

"Were there any other ties between Gia and Tyce?" Caitlin asked quietly.

"A TracFone. Took a couple minutes to find it, but Gia purchased one two weeks ago. The number on it is Tyce's cell. Called several times, usually short conversations of two minutes or less. Tyce's cell matches up with the TracFone number."

Caitlin looked at her godfather. "Rick?" She was asking if he believed all this to be true.

Rick sighed and shrugged. "I don't know. Marci's death rocked Grant and Gia hard. I know it affected their marriage; it wouldn't surprise me if the separate accounts were in case they divorced at some point. A tragedy like yours and Marci's..." Rick hesitated, his eyes searching Caitlin's pained gaze. "It can change people, Aednat. It can make people do things they never thought themselves capable of."

Troy spoke for the first time. "But all this evidence points to the fact that Gia was behind the kidnapping. Why else would she want the flash drives with the killers' voices on them? The bigger question is why she would kidnap her own daughter. Marci's death destroyed her; no one is that good of an actress. It's just not adding up." He hesitated. "On the other hand..." Troy placed a hand on the papers in front of him.

"What?" Caitlin's eyes narrowed. "What did you find?"

"Something in the evidence Charlie brought back from...the crime scene might also point to the VanMaars." Troy's voice was professional, borderline indifferent. Caitlin knew it was her friend's way of not breaking down as he talked.

Everyone waited quietly, not wanting to interrupt and break Troy's train of thought.

"There were the usual samples of blood, hair, glass. All corresponded with Fetterman, Willard, and Britt." His voice cracked on his wife's name, but Troy pushed on. "The glass was from the patio door. Tests on the slugs in Britt's body corresponded to Fetterman's 9mm. I couldn't find much else out of the ordinary except..."

"Except what?" Caitlin prodded gently. It was killing her to see Troy struggling through the analysis of his wife's crime scene – hell, it was killing her listening to it. But they needed to know.

"There were white scuffs on both Fetterman's and Willard's boots. You did a good job to notice and collect that, Charlie." Troy nodded in the direction of the hacker. Charlie gave a small shrug in response, but looked pleased.

"I completed a stereomicroscopical observation, then mounted a small amount in oil on a slide for polarized light microscopy. It turns out the substance was clear, not white like it appeared on the boots. So, I looked at the chemistry of it using infrared spectro-"

"In English, Troy," Caitlin begged.

Having gone into full scientist mode, Troy snapped out of it and glanced around to see everyone staring at him with dazed expressions. "Uh, sorry. Long story short, the substance was spar varnish, which is mainly used outdoors."

"Okay," Caitlin said blankly, trying to understand how that related to the VanMaars.

"The VanMaars have a boat," Rick said suddenly. He leaned forward in his chair. "Grant told me the other day they were having some work done on it."

Troy leaned back in his seat. "I'd have to get a sample from the boat to be sure, but I bet Gia met with Fetterman and Willard on the boat at some point recently. It'd be a lot less conspicuous than the VanMaar mansion or the strip club."

Caitlin got to her feet, feeling excitement for the first time in weeks. There were still a lot of unanswered questions, but this was a start. "Troy, go to the marina and get a sample from the VanMaar's boat. Rick, you're coming with me. We're going to pay Gia a little visit."

"What about us?" Charlie asked as everyone but her and James began rising from their seats.

Caitlin looked at them both intently. "James, I'm putting you on desk duty; help Charlie." She turned her attention to the hacker. "You dig. I mean, *dig*. I want to know every step the VanMaars made over the last twenty years. Something isn't adding up, and I want to know what it is."

Chapter 40

Dusk darkened the air as they pulled up in front of the VanMaar mansion. Fat raindrops landed casually against the windshield, intermittent and slow, as if they had other things to think about than nourishing the ground.

Caitlin felt her hands shake as they approached the front door. Never in her years at Healey PD had she confronted a friend before. This was uncharted territory, and one she wasn't looking forward to experiencing. She noticed Rick was uncharacteristically quiet as well.

The doorbell chimed, and Caitlin began questioning everything. Was Gia VanMaar really the instigator of the hit that took Britt's life? Could she possibly be that dangerous? If so, should she draw her gun? A thought hit Caitlin out of left field, stunning her to the point she felt everything go black for a few seconds. If Gia orchestrated her daughter's kidnapping, and the search of the Daniels' home...*that meant she was the orchestrator of Donovan O'Reilly's death.*

"Caitlin!"

Gia's voice was warm as the door swung open, but Caitlin heard it as if from the end of a long tunnel. She stared at the woman before her, this woman who had been a mother figure during her life, unable to comprehend how she could possibly be responsible for her father's death.

"Caitlin?" Gia's tone became questioning, her expression confused as the young woman on her porch merely stared at her, silent. Gia's gaze moved to Rick, standing off Caitlin's left shoulder and one step back, and the furrows in her brow deepened. "Please. Come in." She opened the door wider and stepped back.

With Rick's hand at the small of her back, prompting her to move forward, Caitlin stepped into the foyer. The lights seemed overly bright, hurting her eyes. The door swung closed on rain that decided to become more persistent.

"Have you found the necklace, Caitlin? Is that why you're here? You found the locket?"

Confused, Caitlin looked between Gia and Rick, both watching her carefully. It took a moment for her to remember the previous conversation about the locket Gia gave her shortly before her kidnapping. With the attack on Britt and the girls, Caitlin had completely forgotten about the necklace, and also the dream where she remembered wearing the locket.

"No," she said quietly, struggling to break free from the fog that encased her mind. She needed a clear head, she needed to find out the *truth*. Drawing comfort from Rick's presence and the knowledge she wasn't alone, Caitlin lifted her chin and spoke in a firmer tone. "Gia, we need to talk."

The older woman's eyes darted between Rick and Caitlin, but if Gia knew why they were there, she didn't give any indication. "Please, follow me."

Caitlin and Rick followed Gia into the sitting room. Gia took her usual place on the couch, but Caitlin remained standing, as did Rick. She hated thinking strategically while in the home of a friend, but she wasn't so sure Gia VanMaar *was* a friend anymore.

Gia folded her hands primly in her lap and looked up at the two people in her sitting room. "What do you need?"

"We found evidence linking you to Kobe Tyce, leader of Ghetto 40 – the gang that invaded Troy Daniels' home and killed his wife." Caitlin figured shock factor might work best on Gia. She was always so poised; they needed to shake her up.

Gia VanMaar's body was extremely still as she regarded the guests in her home. She showed no outward signs of surprise, dismay, or anger. After several seconds, she smoothed her palms over the legs of her slacks and sighed.

"Grant was always ambitious."

Caitlin narrowed her eyes. What did that have to do with the accusation she just threw at Gia? Caitlin looked at Rick out of the corner of her eye, but he remained still beside her, his gaze on the woman he considered a friend for many years.

Gia twisted her wedding band over and over on her finger. "He worked hard, and sometimes…sometimes I wondered if he had begun to look for a way to hook that one big contract, that one job that would pay enough to let him sell the company and let us move to a warm place with white sand." She laughed softly, removed her hand from her wedding ring, and placed a hand on each knee. Gia looked up at Caitlin. "After Marci's death, I thought he was having an affair."

Caitlin nodded impatiently. They covered that already. Why was Gia jumping all over the place with her stories?

"What I hadn't told you before…" Gia hesitated, "was that when I found out Grant rented the loft under another name, I began to wonder." Her gaze hardened, but she no longer looked at Caitlin – her eyes locked on a point somewhere over the young woman's shoulder. "Who rents a loft under a different name, just for an affair? No," she continued softly, "there was another reason."

"And that reason was…?" Caitlin prompted when Gia fell silent.

"It took several years, but I realized I was right – Grant *had* been looking for an easy payout; and he found it."

"What are you talking about?" Caitlin felt her shoulders tense at Gia's accusation against her husband. Again, something didn't seem right, and for the same reason the suspicions about Gia didn't add up. What father would put his daughter in harms way, simply for money?

With an indulgent smile, Gia stood and walked to a large painting that had hung in the sitting room for as long as Caitlin could remember. It depicted a horse in mid-jump over a white fence, muscles bunched, mane flying. The detail was delicate and precise, and Caitlin always loved studying the painting.

Gia pulled at a corner of the painting and it swung away from the wall, revealing a safe built into the drywall. Caitlin felt she should be surprised, but she wasn't. A glance at Rick told her he wasn't shocked by the revelation either. Gia punched several numbers into the digital display, but from the angle she was on, Caitlin couldn't see the keypad. After a soft click, Gia reached inside the safe and withdrew a small, leather bound book.

"Grant's contract journal," Gia said, holding it up for Caitlin and Rick to peruse. "He wrote every job in here, with complete details. Who the contract was with, the soldiers or contractors called into play, flights, daily reports…you name it, it's in there."

"May I see it?" Caitlin held her hand out. She would have been lying if she said it wasn't a test. She wanted to know if Gia would really hand over the journal. To her surprise, the other woman stepped forward and handed it off without hesitation.

"The entry I think you're looking for would be April fourteenth, six months before you and Marci were kidnapped." Gia's words were quiet, and she stepped back toward the safe, as if wanting to put distance between herself and her husband's journal.

Caitlin felt Rick move close behind her, looking over her shoulder as she flipped page after page of handwritten notes, names, and facts. She began to feel sick to her stomach, and Caitlin forced her mind to compartmentalize. This was just another job, another investigation. This wasn't personal.

Yeah, right.

Finally finding the entry for April fourteenth, seventeen years ago, Caitlin pressed the pages flat with her palm. She squinted, trying to make out Grant's hurried scrawl.

```
Damaris Machinery
CEO Mark Flannigan
Request for security team to accompany him to
Kenya
Reports of violent uprisings
```

It went on, but Caitlin didn't have the patience to decipher the rest. She looked up at Gia. "Give me the details."

Gia clasped her hands loosely in front of her. "Mark Flannigan was CEO of the largest international, upscale jewelry chain in the world. He had planned a trip to Kenya, where a large supply of rubies was being mined. Unfortunately, two days before Flannigan was to leave, violent uprising were reported. He called Grant."

"He wanted security, a team to protect him while he was there." Caitlin held the small book open in her hand, but she had eyes only for Gia. Until she heard and felt Rick move away from her. Caitlin looked at him in surprise.

"I was contracted for that job," Rick said flatly, in answer to her unasked question. "So was Josiah Hudson."

Caitlin inhaled sharply while Gia nodded. "The two best contractors Grant had," Gia confirmed, "and discreet enough no one would question them as part of Flannigan's team."

"That bastard," Rick breathed.

Caitlin's gaze darted between Gia and Rick. Then the proverbial light bulb went off in her head. "Grant had Josiah Hudson steal rubies while in Kenya."

Gia nodded, and her clasped hands began to turn white as her fingers tightened with the memories. "Then my dear, loving husband, father to my darling daughter Marci…decided to double-cross Hudson."

"Double-cross…?" It felt like she was in a dream. At the very least, in some sort of movie plot secretly being filmed using real people. Caitlin had to force herself not to scan the room for hidden cameras. This couldn't be real.

"It makes sense," Rick said, beginning to pace. "Grant fired Hudson a few weeks after we got back. We were all surprised; Hudson was one of the best. I remember having a beer with Josiah a few days later, and he was really bitter about the whole thing."

"I had to dig through Grant's office more times than I could count, but he finally slipped up – and I found it." Gia raised her chin defiantly.

"Found *what?*" Caitlin was beginning to feel incredibly frustrated. She didn't understand.

"The small notations in this book." Gia had reached back in the safe and pulled out another journal, this one half the size of the one

Caitlin held. "The details of the trade, or transaction between Grant and a black market dealer in New York." She tossed the book to Caitlin, who managed to catch it but didn't look inside.

"Why would Hudson let this go? It doesn't make sense. If Grant double-crossed him, why wouldn't Hudson go after him? It had been seventeen years, and Hudson sat on it?" Caitlin shook her head. "No way."

"Grant recorded the theft."

Rick stopped pacing and joined Caitlin in staring at the woman across the room. "How? He wasn't there."

"By doing his research and finding a miner whose daughter was dying of cancer. They had no money for treatments – until Grant wired money to this man from an account I previously had no knowledge of. The only stipulation was that the miner must follow Hudson and you, Rick. Discreetly. As part of the crew working in the mine Flannigan was inspecting – and film Hudson taking the rubies."

Caitlin felt overwhelmed, but the pieces were clicking together. "So Grant had proof that Hudson stole the rubies, and was blackmailing him. Hudson's hands were tied."

Gia nodded, keeping her gaze locked on Caitlin. "Until he found a way to get the money he had been promised."

Rick swore, and Caitlin joined him. "Hudson kidnapped Marci, blackmailing Grant for the money he believed he deserved." Caitlin felt her mind spinning, and she had a hard time keeping up. "That's why they were so specific about *the* money. It wasn't just a ransom. Hudson wanted *his* money."

Once again, Gia nodded affirmation.

Caitlin felt horror well up inside as she connected the dots. "But Grant didn't pay. He didn't pay Hudson, so Josiah killed Marci, and tried to kill me." Her eyes shot to Gia, fury riding her emotions to the point she took two steps toward the older woman until she felt Rick's hand on her shoulder. Caitlin shook it off, but stopped moving. Her chest heaved as if she had run several miles. "Why would Grant let Hudson kill his daughter?" Her voice was small now, once again a little girl who lost her best friend and wanted so badly to understand *why*.

Gia's eyes flashed with a pain and fury to match that raging in Caitlin's chest. "Because he lost the money." It was a whisper, but one that carried weight, dropping the words heavily between them.

"How?" It was a demand, not a request.

"I didn't know it at the time." Gia's jaw clenched and unclenched several times before she could continue. "All I knew was that my husband had given me a beautiful gift for our anniversary. One I passed on to a young woman, my daughter's best friend, who missed her father."

The locket. Caitlin felt the journals slip from numb fingers, hitting the floor by her feet with a thud.

"The diamond chip in the locket," Gia continued softly, "was embedded with the video of the robbery, as well as the bank codes and passwords where Grant had placed the money. There was no backup, no other recording of this information. Even with identification proving he was Grant VanMaar, the Swiss bank would not allow him access to the money without the codes or passwords."

Caitlin felt her knees weaken. "But Hudson and the other kidnapper…they didn't ask me for the locket."

Gia shook her head. "Grant didn't know I gave it to you. I remember him searching the house for something, but I had no idea it was for the necklace. He never asked me where it was, most likely fearing I would put the pieces together and link it with the kidnapping."

"But…Marci…"

"He never would have thought Hudson could kill a child," Rick said softly from beside her, and Caitlin jerked reflexively, not realizing he had stepped so close.

"I didn't put the pieces together myself until years later. Do you know what it's like?" Gia's voice was a trembling whisper, her eyes darkening with something Caitlin couldn't begin to fathom. "Do you know what it's like, watching videos of your daughter being hit…abused…*tortured*?"

Caitlin was filled with horror as the memory of hearing Marci scream through the thin walls plagued her mind. Silence fell, neither Caitlin nor Rick knowing what to say.

Gia finally straightened her shoulders, her chin lifting. She took a deep breath. "Grant never asked about the locket after Marci's death. It shattered him, and I finally figured out why."

"Guilt." Caitlin whispered the word. Gia didn't need to confirm it that time; they all knew it was true.

Caitlin looked up suddenly. "Did Dad figure it out? Grant killed my father…didn't he?"

"I assume so," Gia said simply, apologetically.

Forcing herself to take a deep breath, Caitlin held up her hands as if to ward off any more revelations. She needed a minute, she needed to process everything. The problem was – there wasn't time.

Shoving her emotions into a box and locking it away in her mind, Caitlin tilted her head and looked hard at Gia VanMaar. "So where does Ghetto 40 killing Britt factor into this story?"

Sighing, Gia clasped her hands behind her back. "I'm sorry, about Troy's wife I mean. That…that wasn't supposed to happen."

Fury that had been directed toward Grant now surged full force toward Gia. "Why *did* it happen?" Caitlin asked through teeth bared in rage. "Why did you need those flash drives so badly you felt it would justify the loss of a woman and her two children?" Again, she felt Rick's hand come down on her shoulder, and again Caitlin shook it off.

Gia must have sensed a dangerous shift in Caitlin, because suddenly her hands were out from behind her back, clutching a revolver that she pointed calmly at Rick and Caitlin. Caitlin could have kicked herself. Of course there was a gun in the safe. When did Gia get it? When she landed a stunning blow of information, no doubt, distracting Caitlin and Rick from her actions.

"Because it is evidence of the second kidnapper," Gia said, her tone casual and innocent.

Caitlin wanted to lunge across the space separating her from Gia and beat her with her own fists. She wanted to feel bones break, wanted to inflict even a fraction of the pain Gia VanMaar so indifferently caused Caitlin, Troy, and his girls. Caitlin had never hated someone so completely.

As she watched, Gia's eyes lost all warmth, becoming twin flints of ice. "I want that money, Caitlin. My baby died because of my husband's greed. Without that money, Marci died for nothing." Gia's head tilted to the side. "I can't have her death be in vain, Caitlin."

Her blood turning to ice in her veins, Caitlin stared at the woman across the room. Gia appeared so calm, so…nonchalant. For the first time, Caitlin began to understand that Gia was seriously unhinged.

"I'm going to leave now," Gia said quietly, keeping the gun trained on her two guests as she began circling the outer edge of the room.

Caitlin tensed, trying to think of a way to get to Gia before she reached the door. Nothing she came up with ended any differently than a bullet stopping her short. Frustrated, she couldn't do anything but watch Gia reach the sitting room door.

"Find me that locket, Caitlin. I'll be in touch."

As soon as Gia disappeared, Caitlin lunged forward, pulling her .45 from her shoulder holster. "Caitlin, wait!" She ignored Rick's yell, racing through the sitting room and skidding into the hall. Taking a hard left, Caitlin continued pursuit, nothing but capturing Gia VanMaar entering her mind.

A door slammed and Caitlin turned right, cutting through a short hallway and into the kitchen. The mudroom door flapped in the wind and rain. Caitlin headed for it without a second thought.

"Caitlin, you're going to get yourself killed!" Rick roared behind her. "Stop!"

That wasn't an option. Driving rain lashed at her face, instantly soaking her clothes as Caitlin ran into the darkness, gun up and ready. The garage was to her left, but Caitlin couldn't see any movement around the large structure. The doors were closed. There were no shadows in the streetlights down near the road; Gia had vanished.

Suddenly a shot rang out, and Caitlin ducked. The oxygen in her lungs left in a harsh exhale as Rick collided with her, tackling her to the driveway and covering her body with his own.

"Stay *down*," he hissed, and Caitlin stopped struggling.

"That was a warning, Caitlin." Gia's voice cut through the night, but with the pelting rain, Caitlin couldn't tell which direction it came from.

Several seconds passed, Rick still covering Caitlin with his body, gun clenched in his fist as he scanned the darkness around them. Finally, Caitlin had enough. Gia was getting away, and Caitlin wasn't going to lie there and let her.

She managed to get a fist out and angle it enough to deliver a punch to Rick's side. It wasn't her best shot ever, but it was enough to weaken Rick, and Caitlin pushed him away as his body relaxed from the shock. Rolling up onto her side, Caitlin stumbled to her feet, peering through the rain. Which way would Gia go?

Caitlin finally made a wild guess and ran full out for the road at the end of the long driveway. A Jaguar whizzed past, giving an angry blast of its horn as the startled owner caught sight of Caitlin at the edge of the road. She ignored the car, turning right, then left, searching for any sign of Gia. Nothing.

Gia VanMaar had disappeared.

Chapter 41

"It's not from VanMaar's boat."

"It has to be." Caitlin pulled her boots from the *Nightwatch* conference room table, letting them thud to the floor as she sat straight in her chair.

Troy shook his head and ran a hand through hair already standing on end. "Trust me, I'm more stunned than you, but it's not the same. There is no way the varnish on Fetterman's and Willard's boots came from the VanMaar's boat."

Caitlin exhaled hard and slumped back in her chair. "Now what?"

Troy and Rick looked at each other, then at Caitlin. James and Charlie were holed up in James' office, trying to verify Gia VanMaar's story – or find any holes. There was also the matter of trying to find out where she went. It was almost midnight, and Caitlin felt fatigue moving in swiftly. Her hair hung in limp strands around her face, and her clothes remained damp from the rain. She had insisted Rick bring her to *Nightwatch* after it became clear they wouldn't find Gia by roaming the rain-soaked streets of her neighborhood, but now she just wanted a hot shower.

Sighing, Caitlin rubbed her eyes, then leaned forward and rested her arms on the table. "Okay. A few things are bugging me."

Rick nodded. "Hit me with them."

"Was Grant VanMaar's death really a suicide? After listening to Gia, I'm starting to wonder. The woman is ruthless."

Troy shrugged. "I had Charlie hack the coroner's report and nothing indicated someone else fired the weapon that killed him. Grant had gunshot residue on his hand and clothes, and the angle of the entry wound was consistent with him firing the shot himself."

"Could he have been threatened or coerced?"

Rick placed his hands flat on the table and shrugged. "It doesn't matter, does it?" he asked quietly. "Bottom line, Grant VanMaar is dead. What we need to know is how deep his wife *really* was in all of this."

"She was willing to kill my wife for those flash drives." Troy's hands balled into fists. "She claimed it was because the second kidnapper's voice was on the recording?" Rick nodded and Troy's eyes narrowed. "That doesn't fly with me."

Caitlin and Rick stared at Troy. Rick's own gaze narrowed. "Okay, why not?"

"Why would she care?"

Caitlin felt the fatigue ebb away as her mind began clicking along Troy's train of thought. "She just wants the money."

Troy nodded. "So why does she care who the second kidnapper is, or that we have a recording of his voice?"

Rick shrugged. "At the sake of repeating myself, does it matter? We know who we're up against right now, and that's Gia. We can track down the second kidnapper later."

"But that's not the point." Caitlin was leaning forward now, excitement building. "The point is that she wants the evidence we have against the kidnappers. But why?"

"The only reason I can think of," Troy jumped back in, "is if she wants to hunt down the second kidnapper herself."

"To take him out?" Rick asked, his forehead creasing. "So there's no one else to lay claim to the money?"

"Or to protect him." Caitlin spoke the words quietly, absently, hardly aware they passed her lips.

Two heads snapped in her direction. "What?" Rick's voice was hard, disbelieving.

"What if they're working together?" Caitlin could see Troy's eyes become distant as she voiced the thought that popped into her head only seconds earlier.

Rick swore and ran his hands down his face. "Great. So we could be chasing a team; that makes it more complicated. Are we sure she's not just acting on her own? Why hasn't the other kidnapper stepped into the ring at this point?"

Caitlin shrugged. "If Gia's the ringleader and telling him to lay low, why would he? As long as he gets his cut in the end, he doesn't care."

The room fell silent for several minutes as each thought through various scenarios in their minds. Finally, Rick swiveled his chair to fully face the other two. "Okay, so Gia and the second kidnapper working together may be a possibility. The way I see it, that's in the background."

Troy looked confused. "Not sure what you mean."

"It all comes down to the locket." Rick spread his hands wide, arms muscles rippling.

She wasn't sure why, but Caitlin suddenly felt irritated. "I don't get why the issue of this locket is suddenly popping up after seventeen years. No one has mentioned it to me before the last week."

Rick's chair creaked as he leaned forward. "Ah, but after listening to Gia and thinking about it, they have."

He had their attention. Caitlin and Troy exchanged a look, waiting for Rick to continue.

"Think, Caitlin. Over the last several years, both Grant and Gia have indirectly asked about the locket. I think they were trying to jog your memory, see if you remembered wearing it, where it might have been lost." Rick stared intently across the table. "Think back over conversations with them, think hard."

Caitlin searched her mind, concentrating as hard as she could, but she couldn't remember any conversations where the locket had been mentioned. Now she also had a headache.

"I'm sorry, I don't remember."

Rick looked closely at her. "You can't recall *any* conversation that might have even alluded to the necklace?"

Caitlin rubbed her forehead and sighed. She tried again, thinking back over the conversations she had with both Grant and Gia. Finally, she straightened in her chair. "I visited Gia once, years ago. I remember now that she mentioned losing a locket Grant had given her. It went right by me; I had no idea she was talking about the necklace she gave me."

Troy's fingers drummed the table. "To use Rick's phrase, does it matter? If you can't remember where you lost it, Gia and Grant talking to you about it doesn't make a difference. We already know they wanted it; the question is, *where* is it?"

She was failing them all. Caitlin knotted her hands in her lap, despondency washing over her. She couldn't remember, she had holes in her memory, and she was failing them all by not knowing where that locket had been lost.

Caitlin could tell Rick was as frustrated as she; he abruptly pushed his chair back and stood to his feet. "Try to remember, Caitlin. Finding that necklace is what will draw Gia out. We need to know where it is." He walked out of the conference room.

Silence cloaked the room. Caitlin had never felt uncomfortable while alone in Troy's presence before, but not knowing how he felt about her was unbearable. Between that and the strain of trying to remember where the necklace was, Caitlin felt a crushing weight on her chest.

"It's not your fault."

"What?" Caitlin looked at Troy in surprise, not quite believing he had spoken.

Troy sighed. "It's not your fault, Aednat. The locket, the memory loss...Britt." His voice caught, and Troy cleared his throat. "None of it is your fault."

While relief rushed through her at Troy's words, Caitlin also knew they weren't true. "But-"

"No." Troy's hand slammed down on the table, making her jump. "You aren't doing this to yourself, Caitlin. What happened to you seventeen years ago, what's happening now – that's not on you."

Caitlin stared into Troy's eyes for several seconds. "It's not on you either," she finally said softly.

A muscle in Troy's jaw jumped, and he looked away. Finally, he spoke. "Try to get a few hours of shut-eye. I'll go see what James and Charlie have found." He got up from the table and walked toward the door.

Caitlin watched him go, feeling defeated. Knowing Troy didn't blame her was weight-lifting, but she could tell something had shifted between them. Panic threatened to move in as she wondered if their relationship would ever be able to get back to where it had been before. The thought was paralyzing, so she shoved it to a corner of her mind and slammed the door. Troy was right; she needed sleep.

Pushing away from the table, Caitlin dragged herself over to the leather couch along the far wall of the conference room. Collapsing onto it, she stretched out, boots and all, pulling the throw blanket off the back of the couch and over her body. Just a few minutes. She would sleep for just a few minutes and then find out for herself what James and Charlie had found…

Caitlin woke as her body slammed onto the wood boards beneath her. Her head pounded from the hit of her kidnapper's fist, and even though she was blindfolded, Caitlin squeezed her eyes closed against the pain.

It was cold, unbearably cold. Caitlin could barely feel her fingers, and she tried raising her bound wrists, hoping to blow some warm air on her hands. Muscles screamed in protest at the movement, and she felt a cramp begin in her right leg. How long had she been in this small prison? And where was Marci?

For the first time, Caitlin tuned in to the swaying motion of the cramped space. It became more and more obvious, and Caitlin felt confused. Was she in a moving vehicle? There was a low hum, like an engine. Suddenly, her body was jostled sharply, her body coming up and then landing on the boards below her once again. It was just a slight jarring motion, but it was enough.

A boat. I'm on a boat, Caitlin thought. The realization terrified her. Where were they taking her? How far from land were they? Not being able to see even a sliver of light was petrifying. How long had she been encased in darkness, never able to see what was around her – or what was coming at her? Caitlin had no answers, and that scared her as well. Everything scared her; she felt like she was in a permanent state of terror.

Suddenly, the low hum changed, as did the swaying motion. They were slowing down. Even though the fear of being on the boat was paralyzing, the thought of what lay in store once they reached the kidnappers' destination was worse. She strained her ears, trying to hear anything that would indicate what was coming next.

Boots thudded across wood, low male voices murmured somewhere above her. A slight bump – had they docked somewhere? Caitlin listened even more closely. Where was Marci? Why couldn't she hear her friend? Shouldn't she hear something….crying, screaming for help, banging on the walls holding her captive? Of course, Caitlin wasn't doing those things either, but that escaped the young girl as she continued straining for any sound.

More footsteps, more murmurs. They were coming closer. Instinctively, Caitlin shrank back, but there was nowhere to go. The voices were louder now, and Caitlin's ears prickled as one kidnapper spoke. She couldn't make out the words, but the voice…the cadence of speech…

The door to her prison swung open, and Caitlin screamed in surprise.

"You want to get knocked out again, girl? Shut up!"

Trembling, Caitlin clamped her teeth together as rough hands grabbed her aching arms and pulled her from the space. She could tell she was supposed to stand, but her legs hurt after being pulled up to her chest and immobile for so long. Caitlin stumbled, losing her balance and falling to the hard floor.

"You're more trouble than you're worth, you know that?" The hands grabbed her again, hauling her upright, and this time Caitlin managed to stay on her feet. She forced herself to; she didn't want him touching her. "I'm glad this is almost over."

Caitlin felt her stomach roll. "Almost over?" Her voice came out raspy, the cold and disuse combining to make a harsh sound. She shrank away as the man towering over her laughed.

"Yeah, though I wouldn't get too excited if I were you."

Confused, Caitlin stumbled forward, the man keeping one hand under her armpit. Her shoes hit something hard, and the kidnapper ordered her to pick her feet up and walk up the steps. Even colder air slapped her in the face as she reached the top, and Caitlin could feel the boat swaying under her feet. She also heard soft sobs. To hell with what her kidnappers thought.

"Marci?" Caitlin called, twisting one way, than the other, even though she couldn't see. "Marci! Where are you?"

"Over here," came the soft sob, and Caitlin turned to her right.

"Quiet! Move!"

Pulled across the deck, Caitlin could hear the second kidnapper doing the same to Marci. They directed the girls over the side of the boat and onto more wood. A dock. A hand at her back shoved Caitlin forward, and she stumbled, then managed to catch herself. A presence at her shoulder caused her to wilt slightly in relief.

"Marci?" she whispered.

"I'm here," the girl whispered, then sniffed back more tears.

"Move."

Caitlin hated that voice. The girls walked forward, staggering when their feet abruptly left the boards and met rutted dirt. The sudden change knocked Caitlin off balance, and she stumbled. With her hands tied, she couldn't catch her balance and she fell backward, landing in a sitting position in waist-deep water.

The kidnapper swore, and Caitlin heard him wade into the frigid water and once again grab her arm. He hauled her to shore, profanity filling the air near her ear. A hard rectangular object pressed against Caitlin's hip, and she suddenly remembered the recorder. Dismay filled her as she wondered if the recordings she took of the kidnappers would work after being submerged in water.

"We don't have all day, keep moving!"

Caitlin stumbled over the uneven ground and gasped, struggling to stay upright. Her wet clothes clung to her body, and Caitlin shivered with cold. Her shoulders ached. How long had her arms been tied? First behind her back, now in front…had it been hours? Days? Time was running together in the darkness. So much darkness…

Tears ran down her cheeks, escaping the blindfold defiantly. Marci whimpered from some place next to Caitlin, her own fumbling footsteps loud as she crunched through leaves and dry grass.

"It's okay," Caitlin whispered, wishing she could reach out to her friend. But she couldn't even see Marci, much less touch her. "It's okay," she repeated. Maybe if she said it enough she would believe it was true.

Deep down, she knew it would never be okay again...

———————

The scream ripped from her throat, and Caitlin flailed wildly as the impact from the bullet tore through her chest.

"Caitlin! *Caitlin!* It was a dream, just a dream!"

Hands pinned Caitlin to the couch, but that made it worse. She fought, bucking her body violently as she tried to get away from everything – the bullets, the kidnappers, the hands holding her down.

"Caitlin! It's Troy, it's *Troy!*"

Suddenly the arms weren't pinning her down, they were surrounding her, and Troy's lips whispered in her ear. "It's *me*, Aednat, it's me!"

Coming fully awake, Caitlin left the nightmare and collapsed against Troy's chest, sobbing. If only she *could* fully leave the nightmare behind. Unfortunately, her nightmare was also reality, and it would never leave her completely.

Troy kept his arms wound tightly around her for several minutes, and finally Caitlin felt the horror recede enough to lean back from Troy's embrace. Wrapping her own arms around her stomach, Caitlin rocked back and forth on the couch. Now that the terror of the nightmare wasn't forefront in her mind, her thoughts turned toward analyzing what the dream revealed.

Looking past where Troy knelt on the floor in front of her, Caitlin noticed James and Charlie at the conference room door, their faces lined with concern. They must have heard her scream and come running with Troy. That, however, was the last thing on her mind.

"I was on that boat," Caitlin said firmly, shivering as if she was still folded into that frigid prison. "I was on that boat, and I lost the locket there."

Troy looked hard at her, then glanced over his shoulder at James and Charlie. Finally, he turned back toward Caitlin. "Then let's get you on that boat."

Chapter 42

"I forgot to call Rick."

"Rick?" Troy looked over at Caitlin in the passenger seat.

Caitlin nodded, her hands clenched into tight fists in her lap. "I forgot to call Rick." She loosened her fingers, relaxing her hands, then tightened them into fists again. She hadn't been this nervous in a long time. Her stomach rolled as she wondered if she was finally going to be able to end this nightmare once and for all.

"I can have Charlie call him," James said from the backseat.

Caitlin didn't respond, her gaze blank as she stared out the windshield. The lights from the marina loomed in the distance, hundreds of boats lined up in perfect rows in the boat slips. The thought of stepping foot onto one was nauseating. One of those boats led Marci to her death.

One of those boats. The words ran in a loop in Caitlin's mind. What was niggling at the back of her head? It came to her abruptly, as Troy's headlights illuminated the marina entrance.

Caitlin had been transported to the forest by boat, but how could she be sure she was taken across the lake by the *VanMaar's* boat? Troy said the varnish from the thugs' boots didn't match the varnish from the VanMaar's boat, but that must be a mistake. They had linked Gia to Ghetto 40; she was heavily involved in all of this, even if they didn't understand all the *hows* and *whys* yet. It *had* to be the VanMaar's boat. The thought that it could be another, requiring the search of every vessel in the marina, was daunting and made Caitlin's chest tighten.

Yet, doubts persisted. How had the kidnappers gotten hold of the VanMaar's boat to take Caitlin and Marci across the lake? *Why* would they use Grant and Gia's boat? As poetic justice, because they liked the irony of using the boat to kill Grant's daughter?

Caitlin didn't have time to pursue the thoughts further. Troy pulled into a parking space and killed the engine. "There," he said, pointing to a large boat down the boardwalk. "Let's go."

They climbed out of the vehicle, each making sure they had flashlights in hand and guns secure. Caitlin paused, taking a deep breath to steady her nerves. James stopped beside her and laid a hand on her shoulder.

"You're not alone this time, Caitlin."

That was all he said, but it was enough. Caitlin felt her frayed nerves settle, and she briefly touched James' hand before he removed it from her shoulder. Turning, she met Troy's expressionless gaze. He looked away and began walking toward the boardwalk.

They were beside the boat much faster than Caitlin was ready for, but she forced her mind closed to her emotions. *It's just another job, just another lead on another investigation.* To her surprise, the mental pep talk worked, and Caitlin followed Troy up the wood planks leading from the boardwalk to the deck. James brought up the rear.

It was quiet, Caitlin noted. At four in the morning, there wasn't much happening at the marina. The soft slap of water against the hull of the boats was oddly soothing and chilling at the same time. Caitlin clicked on her flashlight as her boots hit the deck. The sway of the water under the boat immediately transported her back to her nightmare.

"It was a small space," she said, sweeping her flashlight around the deck. The beam landed on a door leading into the cabin. "Down steps. There were steps." She walked forward on autopilot, Troy and James following closely.

The door gave way beneath her hand, and Caitlin descended the stairs, the beam of her flashlight constantly moving. Reaching the bottom, she paused. The light danced and slid over sleek, polished wood, expensive cushions and pillows. Crystal glasses glinted and flashed in the beam of the flashlight. None of it registered. She was looking for a space. A cupboard, a closet…something that would fit a thirteen-year-old girl.

"If you quit blocking the stairs, we'll help you look," James said wryly.

Caitlin looked over her shoulder, then moved to the side. "Sorry," she muttered.

Troy and James joined her in the cabin. No words were spoken as they began searching. Every door was opened, items removed from cupboards to evaluate the space's true size. It wasn't long before they realized all compartments were too small, or the wrong shape. The place Caitlin had been kept was rectangular and narrow, situated on the floor.

"It has to be here," Caitlin snapped, her frustration and confusion causing the words to come out harshly.

"The seats," Troy said suddenly. He walked over to the bench seats along one wall, ripping off cushions and knocking on the wood. All were hollow. "These would be used for storage."

Caitlin and James joined him, quickly lifting up the front flaps of wood to reveal hollowed out compartments under the seats. Reaching inside, Caitlin pulled out life jackets, blankets, and decorative pillows. Running the beam of her flashlight over each space, Caitlin felt her shoulders roll forward in defeat.

"They aren't big enough." She sat back on her heels, utterly deflated.

Troy sighed. "Are you sure it was this boat, Caitlin? Remember, the varnish from the boots didn't match the varnish on this boat. Besides, how would the kidnappers get access to the VanMaar's boat anyway?"

Caitlin shook her head stubbornly as James' phone rang in his pocket. She refused to acknowledge, even to herself, that she had similar thoughts only moments ago. "No. I was on this boat. It's the only thing that makes sense."

"Guys, you need to hear this." James walked closer to them, holding his phone in the palm of his hand. "Charlie, you're on speaker. Go."

"I've been doing some more digging. Tested out some ideas and theories I've had running through my head."

The sound of crunching and chewing filled the cabin. Caitlin rolled her eyes and pressed her lips together impatiently. Didn't Charlie ever do anything without eating? For that matter, didn't she eat anything that didn't crunch loud enough to wake the dead?

"You're going to find this very interesting."

"Just tell us what it is, Charlie."

Both Caitlin and James glanced at Troy, surprised by his short tone and obvious irritation. Somewhere in the bowels of *Nightwatch*, Charlie huffed an annoyed breath.

"Fine. Let's just say the VanMaars weren't the only people involved in this mess who own a boat."

Chapter 43

This can't be happening, this isn't real, this *is the nightmare.*

Caitlin's mind ran wild. As much as she tried to reign in her rampant thoughts, they refused to be shuttered and compartmentalized. They turned on a dime, ranging from utter despair and betrayal to raging denial.

They're wrong, they have to be, there is no way he would do this…

"Did you know Rick had a boat?" James' words lacked any emotion, a direct contrast to Caitlin's wild mental ramblings. He was laser-focused as his boots thudded against the boardwalk; his large hand gripped the butt of his gun.

"Of course she knew he had a boat," Troy snapped, his own weapon in hand. His steps were long, matching James stride for stride. Caitlin had a hard time keeping up. "But we trusted him."

We trusted him, we trusted him…I trusted him. Caitlin felt lost, adrift in the waves buffeting the pylons and shore. *He's my* godfather.

Family. They were family. This was wrong. Rick wouldn't do this. How many times had he told her, "Family first." It was simply a coincidence; lots of people had boats. That didn't mean they were kidnappers and killers.

James held up a closed fist, and they all halted on the boardwalk. "This is it. Three vessels down, white with metallic blue striping."

I know what it looks like, Caitlin thought waspishly. *I've been on it often enough.* Until she was kidnapped and suddenly had a baffling fear of boats. A fear that remained mysterious and impenetrable until the last few days.

"Remember what Charlie told us on the way here," James said, eyes still on the gently swaying vessel. "He could already be on his boat."

"She didn't tell him to meet us here, did she?" Troy's words were sharp.

James shook his head, eyes continuing to scan the area. "She'd already begun to suspect him after some digging she'd done."

"Then why would he be here?" Caitlin asked, confused.

James' eyes found hers briefly. "The bugs."

It took Caitlin a second, but then her eyes slid closed in understanding. After Mara Dunn was neutralized, everything began moving so quickly that the bugs at *Nightwatch* were forgotten. They thought the threat was gone, and the small listening devices in each office and the conference room were summarily overlooked; they had never been removed.

Breathing deeply, Caitlin forced herself to remain calm; there wasn't anything they could do about it now. Guns heavy in hand, waves slapped at the wood beneath their boots.

"Aednat."

Caitlin turned to see Troy facing her, his expression one she hadn't seen in a long time. Stepping closer, Troy raised his hand and pressed his palm to her cheek. Caitlin felt rooted to the spot, his touch igniting something she couldn't name. It also grounded her, bringing her back from a land of stunned disbelief.

As they stared into each other's eyes, Caitlin and Troy both knew what this meant. If Rick was truly part of what happened seventeen years ago, then he was also responsible for the deaths of Marci, Donovan, and Britt. Caitlin and Troy found themselves inexorably linked seventeen years ago, but due to the circumstances of the last few weeks, that bond allowed them to truly understand each other. They could read each other's thoughts as clearly as if they were spoken aloud.

Both of them had lost more than was bearable, and if Rick was part of that loss...

He'd better run.

* * * * *

The sleek boat was dark. The trio didn't dare use their flashlights in case Charlie was right and Rick lay in wait. The water pulsing against the boat hid their footsteps, but they still cringed at each scuff and footfall.

Adrenaline spiked through Caitlin's blood, and she had never felt more alive. A dark part of her mind still couldn't believe Rick would have been involved in this conspiracy; the other part didn't care. If he was responsible for the deaths of the people she loved, she would take him down.

James once again took the lead, and Caitlin was happy to let him. The boat tipped slightly as an aggressive breeze slid across the water. Caitlin shivered as the damp cold sliced through her thin jacket. They inched across the deck, trying to avoid the upper cabin windows. Once near the stairs leading to the lower cabin, they paused. The darkness at the bottom of the steps was complete, and James gestured toward their flashlights. They didn't have a choice.

James descended the stairs smoothly and quietly, Caitlin and Troy following close behind. James stopped briefly at the bottom of the stairs, barring Caitlin and Troy from the cabin as his flashlight swept the immediate area in front of him. When he stepped to the side, Caitlin and Troy moved down the steps to stand on his left. Just as James moved to sweep his light to the right, Caitlin felt him stiffen and freeze. She glanced at him questioningly at the same time she heard the voice.

"Don't move."

The voice was cloaked by inky blackness, but Caitlin recognized it instantly, and her blood ran cold. A sharp click ricocheted off the walls of the cabin and light flooded the room. Caitlin could now see the gun held to James' temple, her godfather's face hard and lined with resolve on the other end of the weapon.

Rick's gaze slid past James and met Caitlin's eyes briefly. A sardonic grin lifted the corner of his mouth, though his eyes remained cold. "Hello, Caitlin. I've been expecting you."

Chapter 44

"Drop the guns and flashlights."

Caitlin felt fury coming off James in waves beside her, could feel the tension radiating off Troy on the other side. Keeping her gaze on the man she trusted her entire life, who she considered *family*, Caitlin hesitated, her grip tightening on both objects Rick demanded she give up. He wouldn't really hurt them…would he?

"Yes, I would," Rick said softly.

Caitlin jerked in surprise. Had she spoken out loud? No, she realized a heartbeat later. He simply read her thoughts.

"Your father chose not to listen to my advice, Caitlin," Rick chided from the other side of James. The lines of his face grew more pronounced. "Look where that got him."

Blinding rage tore through her, and Caitlin felt the gun in her hand begin to rise. Suddenly Troy's arm pressed hard against hers, a silent warning. Forcing herself to inhale deeply, Caitlin clenched her jaw and bent her knees, keeping her eyes on Rick as she set both her gun and the flashlight on the floor in front of her. James and Troy followed suit.

"That's my good Aednat," Rick said, voice dripping with condescension.

"You don't get to call me that anymore," Caitlin hissed through her clenched teeth. "Never. Again."

Rick shook his head in mock regret. "Such anger in that small body. I have often wondered how it hasn't consumed you over the years."

Slowly, Rick moved back a step before moving to place himself before the trio. Instead of continuing to stand, Rick lowered his body onto a couch directly facing the stairs. One leg crossed over the other, his right ankle resting on his left knee. Everything about his posture was casual, down to the easy smile now parting his lips. Everything, that is, except for the gun he continued to clench tightly, now resting on his crossed leg and pointed directly at the three newcomers to the cabin.

Caitlin stayed quiet, analyzing the man before her. She could tell by the stillness of the two men beside her that they were doing the same. Rick didn't seem to be in a hurry; in fact, he seemed to become quite settled and comfortable right before their eyes. Like he was waiting.

"Gia should be here soon," Rick confirmed, once again interpreting her silence correctly. "I let her know you were on your way. She is very interested in your progress in regard to finding the locket." His look turned questioning.

Caitlin ignored his coy request for information. Right now, she wanted answers; the locket didn't interest her. "So you are involved in all of this."

"As deep as it goes, sweetheart."

It was like she was looking at a different man. Caitlin remembered laughing when Rick tickled her as a little girl, riding on his shoulders and reaching for the clouds. He would bring her trinkets from the different countries he went to while working for Grant VanMaar's security company, he taught her how to ride a bike without training wheels, and was first in line for a hug at every graduation. Where was that man?

"What happened to 'family first'?" It was all she could get out past the tightness of her throat.

"Money," Rick said simply. His gaze was direct and unashamed. Rick shrugged. "And, you know me. It was fun to break the rules too."

Caitlin narrowed her eyes. "Until you got double-crossed, anyway."

Rick nodded in acquiesce. "That put a damper on things, yes."

"Everything Gia told them was a half-truth," Troy broke in, gesturing toward Caitlin and James. Caitlin could tell he tried to keep the anger out of his voice so Rick didn't get riled up. "You and Josiah Hudson stole the rubies together."

Rick sighed and shifted on the couch, settling deeper into the cushions. "This stall tactic is not going to work."

James shifted his feet and crossed his arms. He didn't appear intimidated by either the man on the couch, or the gun pointed in his direction. "You owe Caitlin answers, Bannan. This isn't stalling, this is due diligence."

Dark eyes regarded the retired soldier, then shifted back to Caitlin. "Fine. Yes, Grant and I came up with the idea of stealing the rubies together. I hand-picked Hudson; he was the best on the team."

"But when you got back and turned the jewels over to Grant, he stole the money right out from under your nose." Caitlin smirked. She'd be lying if she said it didn't feel good to know her godfather had been duped.

Rick's jaw tightened, then released with effort. "None of us knew he'd encrypted the diamond in that locket with the codes and passwords."

"Not even Gia?" Troy was digging as well. He had been forced deep into the whole mess as soon as he agreed to help search for two missing young girls seventeen years ago; he wanted answers as badly as Caitlin.

"No." Rick shook his head. "The kidnapping was all me and Josiah. We knew Grant would cave if his daughter was in danger. You," he continued, looking at Caitlin, "were right all along that you were simply collateral damage. The plan had nothing to do with you."

Her hands shook, and Caitlin formed them into fists to hide how deeply her fury and disgust was rooted within. "That's why I only heard Hudson speak. You knew I would recognize your voice." *Until that boat ride across the lake,* Caitlin realized suddenly. *When I heard them talking and something didn't seem right...*

Rick looked at her closely. "You seem to have the answers, so why the Q and A?"

She was wrong before; Caitlin thought she couldn't hate anyone as much as she despised Gia, but Rick was knocking it out of the ballpark. "Grant gave the locket to Gia as an anniversary present, but no one expected her to give the necklace to me."

"Right again. That part of her story was all true."

"Grant couldn't give you the money because he no longer had the locket, and he couldn't reveal anything about the locket without implicating himself in the theft of the rubies in Kenya."

Rick nodded, but stayed silent. The gun resting on his knee never wavered.

"So why kill Marci?" Caitlin whispered. "How *could* you?"

"Grant needed to learn a lesson about betraying those who trusted him."

"And *Marci* needed to carry that message?" Caitlin yelled. Troy placed a hand on her arm and squeezed. James shifted his stance so he could stop her if she rushed Rick. Caitlin didn't care. Her entire body shook, rage combining with the adrenaline flowing through her veins. "A thirteen-year-old girl had to carry the punishment of her *father?*"

"The option was on the table." Rick tilted his head, unbothered by her accusations and clear of remorse. "Then Marci managed to pull my hood off during one of our…conversations."

"Torture sessions," Caitlin spat. "Call it what it was, Rick."

Rick's gaze narrowed, and she could see her godfather trying to control his temper. He had never liked being talked down to.

"And me?" Caitlin had no intention of slowing down. "What about me? You had to kill your goddaughter as well?"

"We had no way of knowing how much you two had been able to communicate. As much as we tried to keep you apart, there were ways and times you could have slipped each other information."

"She never had a chance, you bastard."

Rick shrugged. "Better safe than sorry."

Troy's hand squeezed harder, and Caitlin knew it would leave a bruise. Troy was trying to keep himself in check as much as he was Caitlin. He had touched Marci's body only moments after her death; it had still held warmth. It was something he relived in his own nightmares.

"Who shot Marci?" Caitlin's voice was guttural, her emotions raw.

Sighing, Rick rolled his neck before answering. "Hudson."

"And me?" It was a whisper.

Rick blinked slowly. "Me."

Caitlin felt like he had punched her in the stomach. Even James emitted a low grunt of surprise at the admission. "What kind of person..." Caitlin had to stop and take a deep breath. "What kind of person...could *do* something like that?"

A muscle in Rick's jaw jumped, but he stayed silent. Several seconds passed, as Caitlin fought to regain some control over her thoughts and emotions. There were still many questions left unanswered.

"When you found out I survived, you joined Dad at *Nightwatch*, offering to help catch the men who did this to your daughter." Caitlin glared at the man across from her. "But you really did it to keep an eye on me, didn't you?"

Rick inclined his head in a short nod. "We were at a stalemate. Grant couldn't reveal who murdered his daughter without exposing his own part in the theft and becoming an accomplice to Marci's murder. We couldn't go after him, because he truly didn't have the money. It was years before the truth came out about the locket. We all tried asking you about it indirectly, but there were things you didn't remember – that was one of them."

Between her dreams and Rick's admission, it was definitely coming back now. Caitlin closed her eyes briefly as flashes of memory bombarded her. Yes, Gia and Grant asked about the necklace, but...so had Rick.

"When did Gia become aware of all this?" James asked.

"She's a smart lady. Gia overheard Grant talking with Caitlin about the locket during one of her visits, remembered his frantic searches of the house, and put two and two together. She confronted Grant, and he told her everything."

"Gia knew her husband, you, and Hudson were responsible for her daughter's death and she stood by and did *nothing*?" Troy asked in disbelief. "I'm sorry, but that doesn't jive."

Rick once again inclined his head in affirmation. "You're right. She hated all of us, but she hated Grant the most for instigating the whole process that ended up taking her daughter's life. She wanted to destroy him."

"So she joined forces with you, is that what you're saying?" James asked incredulously.

"Yes." Rick's voice remained calm. "We both had our axes to grind with Grant, and we both wanted the money. Me, for obvious reasons, and Gia to make her daughter's death seem less…meaningless."

Caitlin felt like her thoughts were scattered in a windstorm, leaving her to snatch at them frantically. Pieces were falling into place, but this was *nothing* like what she could have imagined.

"I did have to talk her out of killing Hudson," Rick continued without provocation. "She wanted the blood of the man who actually pulled the trigger on Marci. I managed to convince her that Josiah showing up dead would cause too many questions. In truth, his days were numbered anyway."

"That's why you shot Hudson instead of letting us interrogate him at his house," Caitlin said in astonishment. "You were afraid he would say too much and implicate you and Gia." A thought occurred to her, and she looked closely at Rick. "Did you threaten Grant? Is that why he shot himself?"

Rick shrugged and lifted his free hand in a *you got me* gesture. "Yes to both. Grant needed to go – he knew if he didn't end his life, I would do it for him. As you have probably figured out, that's also why I shot Mara in front of *Nightwatch* after it had been revealed she was the mole. We couldn't have her revealing too much." He sighed. "That was unfortunate; she proved quite useful in helping me keep an eye on you and your father. Mara didn't know the whole story, of course," Rick continued. "Just that there would be a big payday for her at the end of it all."

"What about my wife?" Troy spit out harshly. "How much of your reaction while looking at the dead body of my wife, in our *home*, was a sham?"

"All of it, my man," Rick said, actually managing to look regretful. "However, Britt's death held no satisfaction for me."

"And Dad?" Caitlin asked, her voice dangerously low.

"He got too close to the truth," Rick sighed. "Hudson and I took care of that one; Gia didn't want to get her hands dirty. We stole Donovan's journals, but there was nothing about the kidnapping in them. His computers disappeared before I could get my hands on them." Rick looked pointedly at the three in front of him.

Caitlin barely managed to keep her place. She shook her head in fury and disgust. "How many bodies need to pile up until the money isn't worth it anymore?"

The corner of Rick's mouth turned up. "At twenty million dollars, there is no limit."

That caught all three of them by surprise, and Caitlin, James, and Troy all made grunts of shock at that admission. *Twenty million dollars?* Caitlin had no idea that much money was in play.

"That being said, my dear, this has gone on long enough."

The tension mounted as Rick leaned forward. All three watched closely, looking for any slight inattentiveness or lowering of Rick's weapon, but the man's eyes were steady, and so was the gun.

"This *was* the boat you rode in to reach the woods across the lake," Rick said softly, his eyes intent on Caitlin's face. She fought not to reveal any emotion. "It goes without saying that I have searched it many times without finding the locket. But Gia will be here soon, and from your conversations in the *Nightwatch* conference room, I know you lost it here. I would like you to take a look." Rick used his free hand to gesture toward his left.

Caitlin, Troy, and James all turned as one to the right, for the first time noticing the long bench seat along the far wall. Rick had already removed the cushions and pulled up the front flap of the storage area. Life jackets, fishing waders, and tackle boxes were scattered on the floor nearby.

"As you can see, I have done the majority of the work for you." Rick stood up, the gun held loosely at waist height. "All you have to do is find it."

Caitlin remained at the bottom of the stairs. Staring at the small storage space, she knew instinctively she had been kept there seventeen years ago, cold and helpless, for hours. Sweat formed at her temples and on her upper lip at the thought of walking over to that spot again.

"I don't have all day, Caitlin. Let's find that little gift for Gia, shall we? Things will go better for you if you have it in hand when she arrives."

"Don't you mean things will go better for *you?*" Caitlin sneered.

"No," Rick said, his voice cold. "I meant what I said."

A shiver snaked its way down her spine, and Caitlin straightened her shoulders. She could feel the two men on either side of her silently offering their support. *"You're not alone this time,"* James had said. She took a deep breath and walked forward.

Chapter 45

She had to get on her hands and knees to peer into the storage compartment. It was very similar to the seat on the VanMaar's boat, and at first Caitlin thought Rick was lying – there was no way she could have fit in that storage area. Then she noticed the middle support section had been knocked out, joining the two sections and creating a space big enough for a young girl to curl up in.

Terror worked through her as she crawled closer to the opening. She could feel the sway of the boat beneath her, she could feel the draft coming from the open compartment, and instantly she was blindfolded and transported back seventeen years. A harsh sob escaped her throat.

"You bastard, let me do it," Troy snapped at Rick, already moving forward.

"No." Rick's voice was commanding and cold. Troy stopped moving.

Caitlin forced herself to breathe and shove her emotions down. "I'm fine, Troy," she said finally without looking back at him. Her words were steady, but her hands shook as Caitlin moved farther toward the cabinet. "I need a flashlight."

"No."

"Come on, Rick," Caitlin snapped, exasperated. "It's dark in here. I need light."

"No."

Swearing under her breath, Caitlin began moving her fingers over the boards, sweeping her palms over the wood, digging into every crevice she could find. Within seconds, her mind was solely on the task at hand, her police training taking over as she began looking at the storage compartment as carefully as she would a crime scene. After a few minutes, she sighed in frustration. This wasn't working.

"What are you doing?" James asked sharply as Caitlin shifted and began sliding her body into the small space.

She didn't bother to answer. Concentrating, Caitlin pulled her legs in, breath hissing between her teeth as her knees came up as high as her chin, her thighs pressing uncomfortably into her stomach. She was bigger now than she had been seventeen years ago.

Once she was settled in on her side, Caitlin closed her eyes. She couldn't believe she was actually welcoming a memory from her past, but she did. Working back in time, Caitlin brought her hands up to her neck, like she had in her dream. She imagined the sharp movement of the boat that jarred her hands, breaking the fragile chain.

Where could it go? Caitlin thought to herself. She kept her eyes closed, her fingers moving over the wood just as they had that night. *It would have fallen here…there was a small divot over there…wait.* Caitlin's eyes flew open as she remembered something her mind closed out long ago.

Struggling to move her head far enough back, Caitlin moved her hands up to the wall near the top of her head. There. At the base of the wall, where two boards met, was a thin separation. A separation just wide enough to fit a delicate locket…

Wincing as a sliver of wood sliced into her thumb, Caitlin felt her heart jump as her fingernail touched something cool. Prying at the wood with her fingertips, Caitlin frantically dug at the chain, finally managing to hook enough over her nail to tug. Excitement filled her as the chain pulled free, the locket following after.

"I got it!" she yelled.

"Bring it out," Rick ordered.

Sliding out of the compartment, Caitlin took the hand James offered and stood straight, her muscles protesting even the small amount of time they had been forced into the small space. The necklace was clasped tightly in her hand as she looked at Rick.

"Nice work." A grin stretched across Rick's lips. "Let's head up to the deck. Gia should be here any minute."

Caitlin held out the locket, not wanting any further part of the necklace and what it represented. Too many people she loved had died, simply because of what was hidden in the small center stone. She hated the locket that once meant so much to her – but Rick shook his head.

"Hold on to that," he said, waving the gun in the direction of the stairs leading to the deck. "After all this, I think Marci's best friend should be the one to give Gia what she's wanted for so long." A cell phone ping sounded in the small cabin, and Rick pulled it from his pocket, giving the device a cursory glance.

"All right, let's move. Don't think about running once you get to the top," he said, the grin turning sadistic. "Gia just informed me she has arrived and is waiting."

Caitlin, Troy, and James glanced at each other, but stayed silent. They were all thinking the same thing; they couldn't see a way out of this.

Taking the steps slowly, Caitlin quickly slid the necklace down the front of her shirt and into her bra, using minimal movements. She wasn't sure what caused her to hide the necklace, but she had learned to always follow her gut. Caitlin led the group up and into the colder air sweeping the deck. The wind had picked up even more, and strands of hair from her ponytail whipped at her neck. Caitlin scanned the deck as soon as she cleared the doorway, looking for options, but met the cold eyes of Gia VanMaar instead.

"So we meet again," Gia drawled, the moonlight glinting off her hard eyes matching the glint of the gun in her hand. "Hopefully with better results than last time."

Troy and James stepped onto the deck, followed by Rick. Gia kept her gun trained on Caitlin as she watched the men line up beside their boss. She glanced at Rick. "She found it?"

Rick nodded. "She found it."

"Good." With a decisive, quick movement, Gia moved the gun off Caitlin and onto Rick. Pulling the trigger, she shot him point-blank between the eyes.

Chapter 46

Caitlin couldn't move as Rick's body hit the polished wood deck. There hadn't been *time* to move or react. By the stillness of the men beside her, Caitlin could tell they were equally stunned.

"What the hell?" James breathed, the words barely audible even to Caitlin right beside him.

Staring at Rick's prone body was like having an out of body experience. Caitlin didn't feel horror that the man who helped raise her lay staring sightlessly into the heavens. She couldn't even muster satisfaction that the man who mercilessly shot her in the chest and left her for dead could no longer hurt anyone else. She was simply numb.

The hole between Rick Bannan's eyes was perfectly round, neat even, with only a small trickle of blood exiting the wound. The back of his head, however, had been blown apart, and blood pooled beneath his body, reaching out with uneven edges to touch the sole of Troy's boot. He didn't bother to pull it away.

Caitlin tore her eyes from the macabre sight and up to Troy's face. Did he feel gratification that the man who helped orchestrate his wife's death was now dead? Did he enjoy the thought that Rick's blood stained his shoe, is that why he didn't pull away?

Gia's laughter brought Caitlin back to the reality at hand. Marci's mother glanced at Rick's lifeless form, then winked at Caitlin,

Troy, and James while giggling like a schoolgirl. After a few seconds, she managed to regain control.

"You think I'm crass?" Gia asked softly, the fingers of her free hand trailing over the warm barrel of her gun in a caress. The gun never moved from the three standing before her, and now they knew she could use it well. "Do you think I shouldn't revel in the death of a man who killed my family?"

Caitlin breathed in deeply, trying to orient herself, trying to bring her rambling thoughts into focus. Gia VanMaar had gone crazy, she was mad, and there was no way they would get out of this if they couldn't keep a cool head.

"Don't tell me you don't feel some relief, Caitlin," Gia said suddenly, sneering at the woman standing powerless before her. "I *relish* the knowledge that the last person responsible for Marci's death is dead." Gia spat the words into the air between them with venom, and Caitlin had to fight not to shudder with revulsion.

"What about us?" James asked, his voice cool and unshaken. "What happens now?"

Gia paused, eyeing James and Troy, then finally settling on Caitlin. "I am sorry, dear. You were just as much a victim as Marci."

Caitlin glared at the older woman. Her family had been taken from her once, and now Caitlin was finding out that everyone around who helped raise her had also betrayed her.

"*But…*" Caitlin said acidly, her gaze fierce.

"I truly did toy with the idea of letting you live. The problem is, you know too much. Unfortunately, you three will need to die, and I will simply…" Gia waved the fingers of her free hand in the air "…disappear."

The pleasant look left Gia's face abruptly. "Now, I need you to hand over the locket, dear. That is the last step in this process." She extended a slender hand into the space dividing them.

Caitlin felt James tense beside her, the soldier looking for an opening. She had no doubt Troy was doing the same. Her mind spun. There was something…but it was a long shot. It would all depend on how she could sell it.

"Well, then we have a problem."

Gia's expression immediately became shuttered. "What problem would that be?"

Caitlin could tell the other woman was losing patience. *Here goes nothing,* she thought. "I don't have the locket."

James moved slightly beside her, and Troy's boot scraped across the deck, the only signs of their surprise. *Don't blow this, guys,* she mentally begged. *Just play along.*

Gia's eyes narrowed. "Rick said you found the necklace."

"*Found* it, yes. Semantics."

The fingers around Gia's gun tightened. "I don't have time for this, Caitlin. Give me the locket."

"Sorry, can't."

Gia walked forward and pressed the gun to Troy's forehead. "Can you now?" she asked sarcastically.

Caitlin felt her heart jump in her chest. She forced herself to appear calm, almost nonchalant. "What Rick didn't have time to tell you before you shot him," she said pointedly, "is that Troy, James, Charlie, and I had come to his boat earlier and found the locket. Charlie took it back to *Nightwatch.* This," Caitlin circled her index finger to indicate the boat they were standing on, "this was us coming back for Rick. And for you. You know, to take you in," she added, the words dripping with condescension.

Gia's chest heaved, her jaw locked tight. The hand holding the gun began to shake slightly.

"We told Rick all this down in the cabin, but – what with your itchy trigger finger and all – he didn't have a chance to tell you before you decided to increase the air flow through his head."

James gave a little jerk beside her. Was he trying not to *laugh?* Caitlin had to fight a smile. They could practically see the wheels turning in Gia's head. Caitlin thought about telling her to go easy on the hamster up there, but then figured it might be pushing their luck.

"You're lying," Gia hissed.

Caitlin forced a patronizing smile and spread her arms wide. "Feel free to search us."

There was no way Gia could safely do that, not flying solo and against a trained soldier and police officer. The older woman knew that, and Caitlin could see Gia floundering.

"Give me one good reason why I shouldn't shoot you three right here, then go to *Nightwatch* and get the locket."

Caitlin felt the first flare of hope. Gia was now trying to justify killing them, when before she showed no compunction about ending their lives. She was unsure of whether she still needed them or not.

"We could come with you. Help convince Charlie to hand over the necklace."

Gia's lip curled. "Three against one on the trip over there. I'm not that naïve, sweetie."

Feigning exasperation, Caitlin threw her hands up in the air. "Look, I just want this to end. I'll make you a deal. I'll call Charlie and tell her to give up the locket. If you promise to let us live and not hurt Charlie, then we'll let you go. Just take the necklace, the money, everything – and just *go*."

James glanced at her in surprise, and Caitlin could see Troy's jaw tighten. He winced as Gia pushed harder on the gun against his forehead as she pondered Caitlin's proposal.

"You're saying we all agree to step away from this. I get what I want, you get what you want, and we all leave each other alone."

"I don't want anyone else to die, Gia," Caitlin said quietly.

For several seconds, the only sound was the lapping of water against the hull of the boat. Finally, Gia took three steps back from Troy, and Caitlin felt jittery with relief.

"I'll take that deal," Gia said, her gaze moving between the three in front of her. "With one caveat."

Foreboding washed over Caitlin, and tension seeped back into her shoulders. "What would that be?" she asked, keeping the words level with effort.

Gia looked at the younger woman apologetically. "I have to make sure you won't follow me and renege on our deal."

Caitlin searched the eyes of the woman behind the gun, her heart pounding. Beside her, James felt like a coiled snake, tight with tension, ready to pounce. "Gia…"

"I'm sorry, Caitlin. I really am sorry."

Without the slightest hesitation, Gia pulled the trigger, and Troy fell heavily to the deck.

Chapter 47

There was blood everywhere, *Troy's* blood. It was pumping out of him faster than they could stop it.

Caitlin ripped off her jacket, shoving it into the hole in Troy's abdomen. At such close range, the bullet had gone straight through, exiting his back. James ripped off his jacket and rolled Troy onto his side, pressing the rough cloth to his back.

"Don't do this to me, Troy," Caitlin whispered, tears streaming down her face as the wind whipped strands from her ponytail. "You can't leave me, too. You're all I have left." Troy didn't answer, unconscious from the loss of blood.

Gia was long gone, and Caitlin barely noticed as James bolted for the cabin. All she could see was Troy's blood on her hands, soaking the knees of her jeans as she knelt, keeping pressure on the wound in his stomach.

"Here." James slid through the blood as he knelt beside her, a roll of duct tape in his hands. "Sit him up."

Even though she wasn't sure what James was planning, Caitlin obeyed instantly. Grabbing Troy's shirt in one hand and sliding her hand behind his neck with the other, she pulled hard, lifting his slack body as much as she could. The sound of ripping duct tape as it lifted from the roll was deadened by the wind.

Moving quickly, James attached one end of the duct tape to Troy's side, then across Caitlin's jacket and the wound. Continuing the strip around Troy's body, James taped the jacket he had placed there earlier to the back wound, then brought it to meet the other end of the tape. After three times around Troy's abdomen, he finally let Caitlin lay Troy back down.

"He's going to make it, right?" Caitlin knew better than to ask, but she couldn't help herself. She raised a hand to move Troy's hair back off his forehead, leaving a streak of blood across his skin.

James' silence unnerved her. Finally, he said, "He's tough."

That wasn't a yes, and they both knew it.

Ambulance sirens tore through the quiet morning. *They're almost here, Troy,* Caitlin thought as she looked into his still face. *Just hang on.*

"Keep pressure on it," James said, placing both her hands on the jacket and duct tape. "Lean into it, hard."

"Where are you going?" Caitlin asked, frantic as he stood and began walking away.

"I have to call Charlie. We won't make it to *Nightwatch* before Gia does."

* * * * *

Charlie paced the length of James' office, her fingers flexing in, then out. In, out. In, out. She didn't like not knowing what was happening on that boat. Circling back behind the desk, she glanced at the blip on the screen that indicated all three cell phones were still active and on Rick's boat. They hadn't moved in several minutes.

The pacing resumed, and Charlie tossed around ideas in her head. Hacking into the street cams near the marina hadn't worked; she couldn't see Rick Bannan's boat from any angle. The mental debate of whether she should drive to the marina picked up where she abandoned it earlier, but Charlie rejected it as fast as she had the first time. If they ended up needing tech support, she should stay put.

In, out. In, out. Charlie's fingers continued to flex; it was a nervous habit she had since she was a kid. Frustrated, Charlie stormed out of the office and toward the small kitchen. She needed thinking food.

A few minutes later, Charlie jerked open the fifth cupboard door and wondered if these people ever ate. *How do you* not *have food in a kitchen?* she thought. Charlie closed the cupboard and reached for the next one. *Ah, there you are!* Reaching inside the dim space, Charlie snagged the small bag of pretzels and headed back toward the hall.

Popping a pretzel in her mouth, Charlie entered James' office and glanced at the computer. Frowning, she set the bag down on the desk and leaned closer to the screen. Two blips moved in one direction, one moved in another. *What the-?*

Before she could investigate further, a soft click sounded from down the hall. At any other time, it would have gone unnoticed; at almost five in the morning, the sound echoed in an otherwise silent building. Charlie's head snapped toward the office door, her eyes narrowing. Slowing her breathing, the hacker waited, her body as still as a block of ice. Another click reverberated softly down the hall, and that was when Charlie began to move.

* * * * *

Caitlin managed to match James' long strides as he sprinted through the marina, but barely. The sound of approaching police sirens faded into the background as they ran. At least the ambulance had arrived before the cops; it allowed Caitlin and James to leave without being delayed by questions while the EMTs worked on Troy. Caitlin tried not to think about whether Troy would live or die, knowing that she needed to keep a clear head for what was coming.

Charlie wasn't answering her phone, and the odds of them reaching Charlie before Gia were impossible. They also knew the likelihood of Gia letting Charlie live ran the same level of odds.

The Challenger's doors unlocked with a *thunk* as James hit the key fob. Sliding into the car, Caitlin got a good look at James' face. She had never seen the soldier so pale, and Caitlin felt a shaft of pain. She was the reason Charlie was in danger, and whatever feelings James may have implied to Caitlin, the private investigator knew there was a connection between James and Charlie that the soldier hadn't confided to her yet. She could see it in the set of James' jaw as he spun the wheel, navigating the streets of Healey at a speed Caitlin didn't know the car was capable of.

Her thoughts disjointed and abstract, Caitlin stared at the hands lying limp in her lap, sticky with Troy's blood. She couldn't seem to think about anything but the fact that everyone she cared about was dying, and there wasn't anything she could do about it.

"Try her again." James' voice was tight, like he had to force the words past his lips.

Caitlin reached for the phone he had thrown on the console as he got into the car. She knew Charlie would answer faster if she saw James' name show up on her phone than if it was Caitlin's. It rang three times, then kicked over to voicemail.

"Nothing."

"Text her. Tell her Gia is on the way and wants the locket. She may not be able to answer the phone, but she might be able to read a text."

Caitlin began typing, her blood-stained hands shaking as she fought the sudden premonition that no one was getting out of this alive.

* * * * *

Swearing softly, Charlie ignored James' name as is flashed up on the screen of her phone and slapped the light switch, plunging the office into darkness. Moving quickly, she flipped down the top to her laptop, pulling flash drives and cables at the same time. Shoving the flash drives in her pocket, Charlie pushed the laptop into a drawer and closed it softly.

Crouching behind the desk, Charlie took a few seconds to evaluate her options. Her phone vibrated in her hand, and the hacker looked down as James' name filled the screen once again, this time with a text.

Gia on her way to Nightwatch. Thinks you have the locket.

Charlie swore. Great. She'd bet everything she owned that the sounds she had been hearing at the back of the firm were Gia VanMaar.

Now what? She didn't carry a gun, and if James had an extra in his office, she didn't know where it would be. *Mama Lewis.* She kept a .45 in her desk drawer up front. Charlie closed her eyes briefly. The desk was at the front of the firm. Suddenly that seemed miles away.

Whining isn't going to save your hide, Charlotte Janine. Charlie peered around the desk, then moved in a crouch toward the open door. All of the offices were dark, but the hallway and lobby were lit as bright as a sunshiny day. She would be exposed the entire trek to the front of the building.

Thinking quickly, Charlie moved back toward the desk and grabbed the brass letter opener from the pencil caddy. It wouldn't do much good against a gun if Gia had one, but it was the best she could do. Back at the doorway, Charlie listened hard. Nothing. Taking a deep breath, she gripped the letter opener, stood to her full height, spun out into the hall, and began sprinting toward the lobby.

Five steps later, a blast of sound and the bullet thudding into the wall next to her brought Charlie up short. Chest heaving, she turned around and toward the back of the firm, hands up in surrender, letter opener still clasped tightly in her right hand. Gia VanMaar walked slowly toward her, gun held ready to fire again.

"I don't like being shot at. It pisses me off."

Gia looked startled at Charlie's blunt statement. After a beat, her eyes hardened. "Then give me what I want, and I'll let you go."

Charlie laughed. "Yeah, right."

Shrugging, Gia took another step closer. "It's true. I made a deal, and I'll keep it." Her eyes narrowed. "Providing, of course that you don't put up a fight. I'm tired, and I'd really like to be on my way. Give me the locket."

"Why don't you come and get it."

Before Gia could react, Charlie threw her body to the left, diving into the closest office. She heard the shot and felt the air from the bullet as Gia fired, but Charlie ignored both, scrambling through the darkness until she reached the desk. Ducking behind it, she clutched the letter opener and waited.

"I'll admit, I am disappointed." Gia's shadow blocked the light from the hall. "This could have ended so much differently."

Charlie remained mute, listening as the other woman's footsteps moved across the carpet.

"You think you'll win against a gun," Gia continued, still moving.

Charlie felt her heart pound, adrenaline flowing rapidly through her veins.

"Tell you what," Gia said, moving farther into the office. "I'll give you one more chance." Her feet stopped at the desk. "Come out, give me the locket, and you can go."

Charlie shot to her feet behind the desk. "I'll pass, but thanks." Lunging toward the startled woman, Charlie swung the letter opener as hard as she could.

Gia managed to twist at the last second, and the blade plunged into her shoulder. Screaming with pain, Gia aimed wildly and pulled the trigger. Charlie ducked, then threw her body forward, catching Gia around the knees in a full tackle. They both went down, and Charlie heard the gun thud onto the carpet. In the darkness, she couldn't see it, and she swore.

Gia managed to land a punch at Charlie's temple, stunning the hacker. Grunting with effort and pain, Gia rolled up and onto her knees, pulling the letter opener from her shoulder.

Charlie blinked rapidly, trying to shake off the punch to her head. She had to get out of there, but her body didn't want to listen. Gia stood, looming over Charlie. The letter opener in her hand noiselessly dripped blood onto the carpet. The light from the hall illuminated the side of Gia's face just enough for Charlie to make out a wild glint in Gia's eyes. Charlie felt her skin crawl as Gia barked a short, hysterical laugh.

"Now I'm going to make this hurt," Gia promised.

"Me first," Charlie grunted, and lashed out with her foot, catching Gia in the knee. The blow threw the other woman off balance, and Gia crashed into the desk, moaning in pain.

Charlie scrambled to her feet, stumbling as she ran out of the office and into the hall. Damn it, she was seeing stars, and her legs wouldn't work right. Her shoulder hit the wall, and Charlie pushed away, trying to make her body move faster. A burst of triumph rushed through her as she made the lobby, but Gia was already racing down the hall toward her, her face twisted with rage.

Stumbling toward Loretta's desk, Charlie reached out a hand to pull open the drawer that held the .45. Gia's weight crashed into her from behind, and both women slammed painfully into the desk, then fell to the floor. Stunned, Charlie couldn't react as Gia suddenly threw her leg over the hacker, straddling the younger woman.

"You have no idea how much I'm going to enjoy this," Gia said, a manic smile curving her lips. She lifted the letter opener and swiftly thrust it down toward Charlie's face.

Chapter 48

James slowly opened the back door of *Nightwatch* and spun into the hallway, gun extended. He immediately moved to his right, allowing Caitlin entrance behind him. In the next second he was gesturing down the hallway where a bullet hole marked the wall halfway down. James stepped into the first office on the right, using a small pocket flashlight to sweep the room.

Caitlin was about to do the same with the office on the left when something made her pause. Her gaze slid past the damaged wall and locked on the portion of the lobby visible through the entrance arch. Her ears pricked at a sound – was that a grunt? A hiss of breath?

Without exactly knowing why, Caitlin began moving down the hall, gun held ready. Two steps later, she began running as clear sounds of a struggle rent the air. Caitlin heard James swearing behind her as he came out of the office and took off after her.

While still three feet from the lobby archway, Caitlin saw Charlie sprawled on her back several feet from the front desk, Gia straddling the younger woman. Charlie clung desperately to Gia's wrists, a letter opener blade hovering mere centimeters from her left eye. Caitlin's brain kicked into overdrive as she calculated the angle of the shot she could take to neutralize Gia. In the next instant Gia gained ground, and the point of the letter opener was brought so close to

Charlie's eye that Caitlin thought for sure she was too late. There wasn't time to stop and aim carefully enough to take an accurate shot.

Still moving at full speed, Caitlin launched herself into the air, hitting Gia from the side. The momentum carried both women several feet farther into the lobby. At impact with the floor, Caitlin lost her grip on Gia – and also on her gun.

Pain ripped through her shoulder as it rammed into the floor, but Caitlin blocked it out as she rolled and came back to her feet in a crouch. Gia was also getting to her feet; she had lost the letter opener, but had found Caitlin's gun. The private investigator was staring down the barrel of her own weapon.

Movement near the hall caught both women's attention, and they turned to see James aiming his gun at Gia, his glare void of mercy. Everything suddenly seemed to move in slow motion as Gia spun to place James at the other end of the barrel.

Caitlin knew James wouldn't hesitate to pull the trigger, and Gia seemed to have come to the same conclusion. At the same moment, Charlie staggered to her feet, looking dazed and drained from the wrestling match on the floor only seconds earlier. She never turned her head to see James framed in the lobby entryway, and had yet to look in Gia and Caitlin's direction.

James and Caitlin both screamed Charlie's name at the same moment fire exploded from the weapon in Gia's hand as she fired two shots in rapid succession. James' training allowed him to jerk his finger off the trigger as Charlie blocked his view of his target. Gia, however, didn't have that training – and she didn't care whose body the bullets found.

Both shots slammed into Charlie's body as she unknowingly straightened to her full height directly in the path of the bullets. The hacker's body jerked violently, her eyes widening in confusion and pain.

As Charlie's body crumpled to the floor, Caitlin felt rooted to carpet, unable to move. It didn't matter how much training James had, the sight of Charlotte Vance being shot right in front of him had stunned the soldier to the point of immobility. The haunted look on his face as he watched Charlie fall to the floor was one Caitlin didn't think she would ever forget.

Gia didn't seem fazed in the least, and as James dropped to his knees beside Charlie, Caitlin's gaze swung to the older woman in time to see her finger tightening on the trigger once again, James in her sites. Rage consumed Caitlin like a wave flooding her soul, and she lunged forward, catching Gia around the waist with one arm while the other hand reached for the gun. The weapon discharged, and Caitlin felt the recoil pass from Gia's body through her own. She could only hope the shot had missed James.

The two women once again hit the floor in tandem, but this time Caitlin forced her hand closed around Gia's wrist like a vise, unwilling to lose her chance at gaining the gun. Grunting with effort, both women fought for possession of the weapon.

Gia's elbow slammed into Caitlin's side, and the younger woman felt her grip on Gia's wrist weaken as the breath was driven from her lungs. Using those seconds to her full advantage, Gia ripped her arm from Caitlin's grasp, bringing it up and then snapping it back down in a sharp movement. The butt of the pistol slammed into the bridge of Caitlin's nose.

The agony was instant as Caitlin felt the bone snap and warm blood cascaded down her face. She lay, panting for breath beneath the suffocating pain, as the room began to darken. *If you pass out, you're dead!* Caitlin's mind screamed. Suddenly she felt the barrel of the gun pressed to her forehead.

"I am sorry it's come to this, Caitlin," Gia said, her gaze anything but apologetic as she leaned over the woman who had been her daughter's best friend. "You should have just left it alone."

Unable to shake the pain paralyzing her body, Caitlin could only watch as Gia's finger tightened on the trigger. A thunderous *boom* caused Caitlin to gasp, and it took her several heartbeats to realize she was still alive. Gia, on the other hand, was suspended above Caitlin, her face twisted in a look of shock and disbelief before her eyes slowly lost all expression and went blank with death. Gia fell to the floor, the gun sliding away from Caitlin's forehead and landing beside her head on the carpet.

Her chest heaving, Caitlin stared up at the sight of Mama Lewis, the .45 still extended in front of her ample frame. Exhausted by the fight, agony ripping through her face, and struggling to comprehend she was actually alive, Caitlin said the first thing that popped into her head.

"What are you doing here?"

Loretta smiled briefly as she lowered her weapon. "It's five o'clock in the mornin', sugar. Don't you know the early bird always gets the worm?"

Before Caitlin could respond, the smile vanished from Loretta's face. "See what you can do to help, sugar," she said, jerking her head in the direction of where James cradled Charlie's head on his knees. "I'll get the ambulance comin'."

Doubting her legs would hold her, Caitlin crawled over to where James cradled Charlie's head with one arm, his other hand pressed over one of the wounds to slow the bleeding. She had been hit high in the shoulder and just right of center in the chest. Caitlin's heart sank as she heard the wheezing sound passing through Charlie's lips as the hacker struggled to breathe. Moving quickly, Caitlin forgot her own pain as she stripped off her jacket and pressed it to the wound in Charlie's shoulder. James didn't look up; he only had eyes for the woman cradled to his chest.

"Help is coming," James said, his gaze intent on Charlie's pale face. "You'll make it, Charlie, you just have to fight."

Charlie's hand fisted in the front of James' shirt, her face contorted with pain. "Damn it…Jimmy…hurts worse…than…thought it would," she wheezed.

Blood covered Charlie's teeth and the inside of her lips, and Caitlin felt hope ebb as she realized Charlie wouldn't make it if that ambulance didn't get there *soon*. Despair and fury clashed in Caitlin's chest as she realized yet another person may die because of her.

Charlie's breath thinned, whistling through her lips now as she kept her gaze on James' face. The soldier moved his hand from her chest to grip her jaw lightly in his hand. "Don't you do it, Charlotte Jean," he ordered gruffly. "This isn't your time."

Caitlin felt tears run hot down her face, mixing with her own blood as she pressed her hand to the wound James had released.

"Jimmy…"

Charlie's hand fell from James' shirt as sirens wailed in the distance.

Chapter 49

"Go home, Caitlin. Take a shower, get a change of clothes. I'll sit with him."

Caitlin looked up at James from where she was curled up in the hospital chair, then back at Troy's prone form on the hospital bed. After hours of surgery, the doctors were optimistic, but cautious. Caitlin wouldn't feel better until Troy regained consciousness.

She always looked to Troy for strength, always viewed him as the stronger of them both. Now, with a breathing tube shoved down his throat and needles and IV cords everywhere…it felt to Caitlin like her strength had been sucked out along with his. She couldn't go until she saw his eyes, until she knew Troy would be okay.

"Caitlin."

She didn't move. Her eyes stayed on his face. *Just wake up, Troy. Please.*

"Caitlin, you still have his blood on your clothes."

Looking down, Caitlin saw James was right. She wasn't dismayed by it; she couldn't seem to work up much emotion at all.

Suddenly, James' hands gently lifted her from the chair. "You need a shower and some rest."

Caitlin opened her mouth to argue, but James shook his head. "Tut needs food. It's been hours. You don't have to be gone long."

He was right. She knew he was right. That didn't make it any easier to walk away.

Caitlin turned away, then turned back again. "How is Charlie doing?"

The haggard lines marring James' face lessened slightly. "Better. Critical, but the doc is hopeful."

Relief moved through her slowly, and it felt good to feel something again. After one more look at Troy, Caitlin turned toward the door.

The shower did feel good, as did the clean clothes. Caitlin got King Tut's food ready, then sat cross-legged on the floor and watched as he ate. There was something calming about the slow, precise movements of the turtle, and Caitlin could feel some of the tension leave her body. When Tut was done eating, she gave him a few scratches under his chin and then left to head back to the hospital.

Sunlight glinted off the lake as it stretched along the road to her right. Caitlin felt her foot come off the accelerator as she neared the public access entrance. Without any particular plan, she turned the wheel of her car and parked. There were two other cars in the lot, but Caitlin didn't see anyone else.

Seconds later, she was at the edge of the water, hands shoved deep in her pockets. Caitlin stared at the water, watched the small waves as they approached the shore. It was calming, and she let her mind go blank. For just a few minutes, she didn't want to think, didn't want to worry.

Turning to the right, Caitlin began walking. Several yards down the shore, she noticed an abandoned dock. She followed the weathered boards as they stretched out over the shallow water, then stopped at the end. Looking down, Caitlin could see the dock ended at a steep drop off.

She finally pulled her hands from her pockets, and the locket with the diamond in the center dangled from the fingers of her right hand. Caitlin watched it spin, the sun flashing off the shiny gold and the clear diamond. So many people had died because of that necklace, because of a greed that superseded the bonds and love of family.

This is for you, Marci and Dad. For you, Britt.

Caitlin gathered the necklace in her palm and drew her arm back. As it spun through the air, the diamond flashed one last time before hitting the water and disappearing under the surface.

Caitlin stood at the end of the dock for several more minutes, then turned and walked back to shore.

Chapter 50

Caitlin stood at the window, hands wrapped around the warm mug of coffee. She smiled as Rebekah got a running start, then jumped on the sled and rode it to the bottom of the hill. Ranae squealed as their new Rottweiler puppy, Tank, ran into her from behind, knocking her into the snow.

"Do you need a refill?"

Turning from the window, Caitlin smiled as Troy held the coffee pot in her direction. "No, I'm good. Thanks."

Troy replaced the pot and carried his own mug over to stand beside her. "They're doing better. Not so many nightmares."

"Good." Caitlin continued to watch the girls and the romping puppy. "This is a nice house," she said after several minutes of comfortable silence.

"It hit everything on the girls' wish lists, if you can believe it." Troy sipped his coffee. "It came on the market at just the right time."

Caitlin glanced at him. "You seem like you've gotten back into the swing of things at *Nightwatch* pretty well."

Troy nodded, smiling down at her. "Yeah. It's good to be back."

Returning the smile, Caitlin turned back toward the window.

"How did you ever manage to keep James and Charlie on at the firm? I wouldn't think either one of them would be the type to settle down and work for a single entity."

Caitlin felt her smile turn wry. "I had to agree to let Charlie freelance from time to time."

"Ah. And James?"

Troy's gaze was steady on her face. Caitlin turned away, feeling a blush warm her cheeks. She shrugged, hoping he wouldn't push the subject. Her mind went back to the conversation that took place several weeks ago.

"I'd really like you to stay."

James looked at her, his gaze hot as he moved a step closer. "For personal reasons, or business reasons?"

Caitlin felt her body heat as her pulse quickened. In the back of her mind, she knew this would come up eventually; she just didn't think he'd push it so soon.

"I – I can't answer that."

"Can't, or won't?"

Caitlin stared at him, remaining stubbornly silent.

James took another step toward her, and Caitlin felt his warm breath caress her cheek. "Are you ready to define your feelings for Troy?"

"No." The answer was quick and sharp.

"Ah." James grinned knowingly.

Tit for tat. "Are you ready to tell me about your relationship with Charlie, Jimmy?"

It had the effect she was looking for. James' eyes narrowed. "No," he snapped. Stepping back, James turned to walk out of her office.

"Well?" Caitlin spread her hands in exasperation. "Are you staying, or not?"

James stopped at the door and looked over his shoulder, his expression relaxing. "I'll stay. I'm not giving up, either." He winked and was gone.

"Um, he didn't directly say why he would stay on at Nightwatch." Caitlin brought her mug to her lips and prayed Troy would drop the subject.

"How are your nightmares?"

It was an abrupt change of subject, and Caitlin tried to wrap her mind around the question.

"Still there."

A pause. "It will get better. Eventually."

Caitlin nodded, acting as if she believed him. "Eventually."

Another squeal caught their attention, and they laughed as Tank hopped on the moving sled with Rebekah. She shrieked, and halfway down the hill they both tumbled out into the snow.

"We've lost a lot, Aednat."

Startled, Caitlin shot a quick look at Troy, but he kept his gaze on his girls. She nodded, but chose not to say anything. Troy's arm settled warm and snug over her shoulder.

"But we still have each other. We still have this." His eyes continued to watch the scene out the window.

Caitlin closed her eyes, breathing in the scent that was pure Troy. Bringing her mug up to her lips, she opened her eyes and smiled before taking a sip.

"Yes. We still have each other. We still have this."

Author's Note

There are many special people in my life who are a large part of my writing career, and deserve the utmost thanks.

A hug thank you to Troy Ernst and his immense help in making sure the forensic science portions of this novel were accurate and true-to-life, which incidentally helped with characterization. My utmost gratitude to my friend (and Troy's wife) Kim, who allowed me free reign with her character with nary a complaint.

A shout-out to Nick Busse for making sure the weapons and explosives were accurate, and the deaths would be…well, possible in real life.

As always, a big thank you to Tom and his honest evaluation of my work. This book would not be where it is today if not for my editors: Matt, Karl, Marge, Rae, and Kim. Thank you to Eric and Matthew for your help in making every part of this book look great. I appreciate your work behind the scenes!

D. A. Reed lives in West Michigan with her family. Her thriller novels are the result of an overactive imagination that alternately entertains and scares the people who know her.

Written works by D. A. Reed include three other novels of the thriller genre: *Web of Deceit,* (a full-length novel), as well as *Toxic Love* and *Truth or Die* (novellas). D. A. Reed has also penned three YA novels: *Daisies in the Rain, Dancing with Shadows,* and *The Rejects of Room 5.* All of her books are ready for purchase on Amazon and www.lulu.com. Find out more about D. A. Reed at:

www.facebook.com/Author/Deborah.